TRIALS
OF
MAGIC

BOOK ONE
OF
THE HUNDRED HALLS

THOMAS K. CARPENTER

Trials of Magic

Book One of The Hundred Halls
by Thomas K. Carpenter

Published by Black Moon Books

Cover design by Ravven
www.ravven.com

Discover other titles by this author on:
www.thomaskcarpenter.com

ISBN-13: 978-1539067962
ISBN-10: 1539067963

Also by Thomas K. Carpenter

ALEXANDRIAN SAGA
Fires of Alexandria
Heirs of Alexandria
Legacy of Alexandria
Warmachines of Alexandria
Empire of Alexandria
Voyage of Alexandria
Goddess of Alexandria

THE DASHKOVA MEMOIRS
Revolutionary Magic
A Cauldron of Secrets
Birds of Prophecy
The Franklin Deception
Nightfell Games
The Queen of Dreams
Dragons of Siberia
Shadows of an Empire

THE DIGITAL SEA TRILOGY
The Digital Sea
The Godhead Machine
Neochrome Aurora

GAMERS TRILOGY
GAMERS
FRAGS
CODERS

THE HUNDRED HALLS
Trials of Magic
Web of Lies
Alchemy of Souls
Gathering of Shadows
City of Sorcery

For Rachel
who made this
book shine

TRIALS
OF
MAGIC

1

No one had died today. In fact, no one had died in the last seven days. It was the longest stretch since Aurie had joined the fourth-floor team as an orderly, which made it a joyous event, and simultaneously a superstitious one.

Aurie dodged around the Jell-O cart, skidding to a stop outside room 438. A sign in big red letters read "WARNING. No perfumes, magical ointments, or any alchemy reagents within thirty feet."

She gave her aquamarine scrubs a voracious sniff. While she'd washed her scrubs by hand that morning, using a plain soap bar in the shower, and used talcum powder for deodorant, Aurie was worried she'd picked up hitchhiking scents on the crowded train ride.

The only smell she detected was her mild body odor mixed with the talcum, so she went in.

An emaciated girl on the bed lit up. "Awesome Aurie!"

As she stretched her arms out, the dozens of wires connected to her limbs from scaffolding around the bed quivered.

"Elegant Emily," said Aurie, leaning over to give a hug,

careful not to break a wire.

Aurie hid a grimace as she realized how thin Emily had gotten.

"How's it going, kiddo?" Aurie asked.

Emily put up a brave face. Suddenly, the car noises in the street outside quieted. Aurie could feel her heart press against her chest.

"I heard the doctor tell the nurse that she's out of spells," she said, staring at her bone-thin hands.

"I'm sure that's not true. There are always more spells. The doctor probably meant that *she's* out of spells, and needs to learn a few more to treat you," she explained.

Aurie reached in her pocket and pulled out a painted miniature about two inches high. The figure wielded twin scimitars in a fighting pose with the suggestion of winds swirling around her.

"It's you. A wind dancer," said Aurie while she tucked a strand of errant blonde hair behind Emily's ear.

"There's no such thing as a wind dancer," said Emily.

"You can be the first then, and have your own hall," said Aurie.

Emily offered a bittersweet smile as she cradled the miniature as if it were a puppy. The poor girl had been cursed by a vengeful air elemental to be near weightless. The wires kept her from floating to the ceiling. Without gravity acting on her body, she was wasting away like an astronaut in space for too long, and the airiness of her body made her susceptible to allergens.

"She looks like you," said Emily.

Aurie squinted to bring the details into focus. She'd had a friend paint it for her, but hadn't had a chance to study it.

"Yeah, I guess she has my olive skin and dark hair. I don't see any freckles, though," said Aurie.

"Or those dark circles," said Emily, touching Aurie's cheek below the eye.

"Sleep's overrated," said Aurie reflexively. She'd worked the night shift at a convenience store on the outskirts of Invictus. "Hey! Maybe this means I'll be your first student at the Hundred Halls."

Emily shook her head with faux indignation. "That's silly. You have your Merlins tomorrow." Then her eyes went wide as if she'd said something wrong. "I...I need the nurse," she said suddenly, jamming the call button.

"What's wrong? Are you okay?" asked Aurie, examining Emily for signs of danger.

The hard soles of running nurses echoed in the hallway. Aurie spun around expecting an emergency team only to find the doorway full of smiling people: doctors, nurses, orderlies, the rest of the patients—the kids.

"Surprise!" they yelled.

Aurie nearly tripped over her own feet, trying to figure out why they were surprising her, or even if it was supposed to be for her.

"I don't understand," she said.

Dr. Fairlight stepped forward as the spokesman for the group. She handed Aurie a small wrapped present about the size of a fist.

"With your Merlins tomorrow, we won't be seeing you much after that—"

Aurie interrupted with hurried breath. "I'm still going to work here. I have a job, right?"

Dr. Fairlight squeezed Aurie on the shoulder. "As long as I'm head of this floor you have a job here. Especially since this was where your dad did his residency."

"I miss him," she said.

Dr. Fairlight gave a comforting nod and continued, "But

we know you won't have as much time. Especially when you get into Arcanium."

Guilt welled up inside Aurie. "The Aura Healers are my second choice. It's just..."

Everyone laughed. "You don't have to justify anything to us," said Dr. Fairlight. "You'll be great whatever hall picks you, though it'll be the Aura Healers' gain if Arcanium is too stupid to take the brightest student in decades."

Everyone always seemed to think that Aurie wouldn't have any problem passing her Merlins and getting into the Hundred Halls, but even some of the best students had to take them more than once. It wasn't usually an issue, but this was her one and only chance. She turned twenty in a month, which meant she'd no longer be able to take the Merlins. It was first time, or nothing.

"Open it," said Dr. Fairlight as the rest of the floor leaned forward. The kids crowded around her, eyes bright with the anticipation of her present.

Aurie patted a few heads before making a production of the opening. Some of these kids wouldn't be alive at their next birthday to experience presents again.

She tore the paper excruciatingly slow while the kids laughed and giggled and cheered her on. "Open it! Open it!"

"Hurry up!" said Emily from behind her, poking her with a bone-thin finger.

Finally, after a dramatic finish, Aurie crumpled the paper and threw it into the waste basket.

The kids practically climbed into her lap in trying to get the first glimpse of the gift. The open box revealed a pair of shiny earrings, eliciting an "ohhhh" from the crowd. Bright little rubies stared back at Aurie from the setting.

"You didn't have to do this," said Aurie, shaking her head at Dr. Fairlight, who'd crossed her arms and had a smirk on her face.

"Nonsense. We know it's been a rough go, what with you and your sister on your own. We wanted to get you something you could remember us by," said Dr. Fairlight. "Press the ruby and say 'lux.'"

When the words left her lips, a ruby-red glow filled the space around Aurie.

"They're perfect for late night studying when you don't want to disturb your roommate. They also help you see in the dark beyond the glow," said Dr. Fairlight.

"I don't know what to say," said Aurie, dumbfounded.

"Say thank you," said Dr. Fairlight.

"Thank you all!" said Aurie, then she gave out hugs, taking care not to aggravate the young patients' ailments. The "Children's Floor for the Irrevocably Cursed, Magically Ailing, and Supernatural Virology" housed kids afflicted with all sorts of strange ailments. Emily's weightless curse wasn't the worst by any stretch.

After everyone left, Dr. Fairlight winked and said, "Now get to work."

Aurie saluted. "Yes, ma'am!"

The rest of the shift went like a dream. There were no brown messes to clean up, lunch was cheese noodles, which was her favorite, and all the kids were in a good mood. It would have been the best day ever at the Golden Willow Clinic for the Sick and Infirm if some VIPs hadn't arrived right before her shift ended.

A nervous whisper traveled through the floor as Dr. Fairlight notified everyone that one of the directors was giving a tour to a potential high-end donor. Tension squeezed lips flat, and even the kids seemed to catch the spreading quiet.

From a side hallway, Aurie spied the VIPs. She'd heard from the station nurse that the potential donor owned the

Herald of the Halls, the local newspaper that covered the halls and the city of Invictus.

The older woman, Camille Cardwell, wore a gold lamé jacket that made her look like she'd walked out of a fashion magazine from twenty years ago. The daughter, Violet, followed behind her mother while staring at her phone, obviously not paying a bit of attention to the tour.

To Aurie, Violet looked like the caricature of every rich girl she'd ever watched on TV or in a movie: blonde, rich, and vain. Granted, she'd never actually encountered a girl like that in the many high schools she'd attended over the years. The high schools Aurie went to were always on the seedier side of whatever town they were in, rather than the private schools that this girl had so clearly been a member of.

Aurie felt a little guilty for assuming that Violet wasn't a nice person. People had always made up stories about her and Pi whenever they'd been the new students, which had been too often. It wasn't fair that she did the same.

So Aurie went back to mopping the hallway, which took her the other direction, daydreaming about being able to enchant mops to clean the floor automatically. By the time she'd finished, the shift was nearly over. She pushed the bucket towards the closet near the main area.

A whiff of perfume caught Aurie's nose. She was so used to the antiseptic smell of mop water that the sudden infusion of musky plum snapped her head around. Violet walked alone, busily typing on her cell phone while nodding to the music she was listening to on her headphones.

The girl was oblivious to her location, let alone paying attention to the bold red sign outside of Emily's open door. Normally the nurses on duty warned people away if they weren't paying attention, but the station was completely empty.

Aurie dropped the mop and started running. "Hey! Stop!

You can't go there! Stop! Stop!"

Oblivious to her surroundings, Violet kept walking. She was only a few feet from Emily's door. The last time someone had mistakenly worn perfume on the floor, Emily had gotten a severe case of hives, and that had been when she was heavier and healthier. A dose this close could be fatal.

Without thinking, Aurie lowered her shoulder and drove it into Violet. The girl looked up at the last second, surprise overtaking her bored expression. Together they went flying backwards, sliding a good ways on the recently mopped linoleum. It was a miracle that Violet didn't hit her head.

"What the hell is going on?" said Violet, pushing at Aurie to get off.

"It's Emily, I had to protect Emily," said Aurie, climbing off the girl.

She ran back to the doorway, preparing to call the nurses or hit the emergency button, only to find Emily's bed missing. Aurie panicked for a moment, thinking the worst, until she noticed the scaffolding was gone too. Then she remembered they were all going to watch a movie down the hall in the special theater.

"Oh, shit," said Aurie under her breath. She turned and held out her hands. "I'm so sorry."

At that moment, the director, Dr. Fairlight, and Camille Cardwell came strolling around the corner.

Violet wasted no time, pointing her finger directly at Aurie and saying in a controlled rage, "This, this girl just attacked me. She knocked me clear down the hallway, landing on top of me." Violet marched over to her fallen phone, picked it up, and presented the broken glass to them. "See."

Camille turned towards the director. "Randall. What kind of operation are you running here?" She had a light New York accent. She moved to her daughter's side with grace and not a hint of concern and began examining Violet as if she were a prize show dog at a competition. Violet looked a little shaken as she rubbed the back of her head.

The director, a man in a suit who looked more like a banker than a hospital director, said, "Is this true?"

"Wait. You don't understand," said Aurie. "She's wearing perfume. You can't go near Emily's room."

The director wrinkled his bald forehead in confusion before shaking off her words as if they were a bad sign. He repeated his question, this time more emphatically. "Is this true?"

"Well, yes, but you have to understand," said Aurie.

"Then get out. You're fired," said the director.

Dr. Fairlight put her hand on the director's shoulder. "Randall, you can't do that. And she's right. Look at the sign."

"The hell I can't. This girl just attacked the daughter of an important donor. Do you want our kids to get better, or do you want a mop girl?" asked the director in a gruff tone.

Aurie couldn't even move. It was like she'd been encased in ice.

"Randall," said Dr. Fairlight in the voice she used in emergencies, "that girl put one of our patients' lives at risk through her inattention. Aurie was just doing what I would expect any nurse to do."

A lump seemed to catch in Randall's throat. He glanced back and forth.

Camille finished her examination and put her hands on her slender hips. "She's got bruises up and down her backside. And look where she's at. Not anywhere near that girl's room, which I might add is empty."

The director turned to Dr. Fairlight. "I'm sorry. She has to go."

"What does she think?" asked Aurie, stepping forward

and pointing to Violet. "I'm sorry I tackled her, but the girl who's normally in this room is very sick. I was afraid for her. The perfume you're wearing could kill her, and you were about to walk in front of her room."

Violet's nostrils flared as everyone stared at her. She glanced at her mother, eyes red with a mixture of tears and anger.

"Go ahead, Violet," said her mother. "I'll respect your wishes, whatever you say. Is that fine with everyone?"

After a round of nods, Aurie's stomach climbed into her throat. She needed this job. The Hundred Halls was expensive. She barely had enough for her and Pi for the down payment. Keeping up the payments to stay in school was going to be challenging enough even *with* this job. And the kids needed her, and she found in that moment that she needed them.

Violet glanced towards Emily's open door. Then she pointed to a location behind her, about where they'd ended up after the slide.

"I was nowhere near that door. You had no reason to tackle me, except that you're just a jealous mop rat. She doesn't deserve to work here," said Violet.

Dr. Fairlight burst into argument, but Aurie knew it was over. She looked back down the hall.

"Can I say goodbye?" she asked the director.

He jammed a thumb behind him. "Get out. Now."

Dr. Fairlight was crying as Aurie walked by. She gave a brief hug, but Aurie didn't want to linger and cause any more problems. Violet wouldn't make eye contact with her, while the mother stared with sour distaste.

The worst part about leaving was that she didn't get to say goodbye to the kids. Somehow that seemed worse than losing her job. She felt like she'd let them down.

2

The bouncer took a long look at Pi's ID card. He looked like a rhinoceros without the horn. The reflection off a passing car made him blink.

"What kind of name is Pythia?" he grumbled.

"The kind that doesn't like questions," said Pi.

"You don't look like you're twenty-six," he said.

"And you don't look like you're smart enough to work the door at the Glass Cabaret, but Radoslav's still employing you, so that counts for something," she said.

The bouncer twitched. Pi knew what he saw. She had the body of a twelve-year-old boy, short dark hair, cutting blue eyes, and she was wearing tight black jeans, a white crop top, and glitter across the warm olive tones of her exposed shoulders. She didn't even look seventeen, which was her age, let alone twenty-six. Which either meant she was lying or had enchanted herself to look younger.

Pi met his gaze until he looked away and unhooked the velvet rope so she could pass.

"That's what I thought," she said, doing her best to strut into the bar, which felt a little ridiculous.

The inside reminded Pi of a noir film. A faint mist, neither vapor nor smoke, hung in the air. A small stage in the back was currently empty. Some French sounding mood music was piped in. Glasses clinked amid the occasional bass notes.

Radoslav was standing behind the bar, cleaning cherry guts off a cleaver with a rag. He was everything she expected him to be: tall, thin, chalky-gray skin, hair so dark it absorbed light, and an expression so sour it would curdle milk at a hundred paces. He was attractive, but in a way that made it hurt to look at him.

Pi summoned her courage and approached the bar, trying to maintain the arrogance that had gotten her past the bouncer. It took one flickering glance of his gray eyes to dispel her ruse.

"I don't deal with students," he said in a melodic voice.

The urge to sprint out the door nearly overwhelmed her. Beneath the edge of the bar, she pinched her side.

"I'm not a student," she said.

He met her gaze. She felt suffocated by it, as if she'd been dumped into a pit of asphalt fumes.

"That's what I thought," he said, mimicking her tone with the bouncer. He'd known she didn't belong even before she'd entered the bar.

"Hurry along now," he said. "Wouldn't want mommy and daddy to worry."

Mention of her parents, long deceased, put steel into her spine.

She couldn't meet his gaze, but she said with fervor, "I need a summoning focal."

A sharp laugh exited his lips. He stared at her with amusement, revealing gleaming white teeth.

"What would a whelpling like yourself need with that?" he asked, suddenly devoting his every attention to her, which made her skin crawl.

"That's my business," said Pi, staring at the meticulously clean bar top. Not one errant drop of liquid marred its surface.

"If you want a focal, then it's my business too. I'd prefer not to have my bar shut down because some irresponsible youngling summoned something she couldn't handle and put people's lives at risk," he said.

Pi bit her lower lip. "I need to summon a faez demon. Nothing major. But it has to be something above an imp."

Radoslav took another long look, as if he'd underestimated her yet again. Wry amusement was perched on his lips like a carrion bird.

"You have no patron, which means you're either a fool to expose yourself to faez madness, or"—he tapped his chin with a manicured fingernail—"you aspire to the Cabal...probably the Coterie of Mages."

Pi didn't bother acknowledging the correct answer. It would only annoy Radoslav further.

"Assuming you can meet my price, can you perform the deed? What's your barrier material?" he asked.

"Sea salt with a touch of silver dust," she said.

"Silver dust? Oh, yes, no patron. How savvy," he said. "What about your mechanics?"

Pi produced two quarters from her pockets, flipping them both into the air to catch them on the back of her knuckles. Then she started rolling them back and forth, making them dance across her fingers as if they were marionettes. When she was finished, she threw them into the air and deftly let them fall into her back pockets.

Radoslav clapped softly. A modicum of pride welled up in her chest. Then like a snake strike, he grabbed her arms. He put his face up close and dug his fingernails into her wrists.

Pi couldn't look away from his gaze. She felt him probing

her mind briefly before he broke away.

"More than sufficient power," he said, licking his lips. "What's your Merlin score?"

"Never been tested," she said.

"Tell me then," said Radoslav. "Why Coterie? Why not another hall? You don't strike me as the power-mad type."

The first thing that flashed into her mind was her parents' faces, followed by the years of various orphanages and foster families. Pi rubbed the ropelike scar along her forearm.

"It's the only way to be safe," she said.

Radoslav drummed his fingers on the bar. "I guess the only question now is can you meet my price."

"I assume that a favor from a future member of the Coterie won't suffice?" Pi asked hopefully.

"Despite your promising abilities, you have a long way to go. Many a Coterie mage has disappeared due to hubris," said Radoslav. "So I'd prefer my payment in something more immediate and binding."

The way he looked at her put a twist in her gut. She felt like an antelope being sized up by a lion.

"I want your soul," he said.

"What? You must be kidding," said Pi.

"You know what I am?" he asked.

"Yes," she said. "A maetrie. City fae."

Radoslav winked. "Then you know I'm not kidding. But don't worry. I don't want your soul forever. Just a three-year lease."

"That's a lot to ask for a summoning focus," she said.

"A bargain if it helps you get into the hall of your desire. Besides, you've no other way to attain such a valuable magical device; otherwise, you wouldn't have come to me," he said.

A three-year lease on her soul. It would mean he could make her do just about anything, and she couldn't refuse.

"What will I have to do for you?" asked Pi.

"Errands, little jobs, things like that. Don't worry. It'll be fun," he said, his lip curling at one corner.

Three years. It was a long time. But she needed to summon the faez demon to impress a Coterie mage enough to be her sponsor. Without the focal her preparations were useless. But to purchase one outright was so prohibitive it was laughable.

"I don't need to own the focal, only borrow it. One-year lease on my soul," said Pi.

"Own? That was never my intention. The three-year lease was to borrow it," said Radoslav.

Pi wished she had more time to think, but she knew that the deal would only get worse if she didn't take it now. She thought briefly about what Aurie would think, but that answer was swift like an axe strike. Her older sister barely approved of her interest in the Coterie, thinking it was a passing fancy rather than a life-long intention.

"Deal," said Pi, holding out her hand. "A three-year lease on my soul in exchange for borrowing the summoning focal."

Radoslav laughed at her gesture. "That's not how we complete our agreement."

"Then how?" asked Pi.

Radoslav flashed a grin so wide the Cheshire Cat would have been proud.

3

The streets of Invictus were abnormally busy on that Sunday afternoon. Aurie made her way across the city, using the Red and Blue Lines, cringing every time she had to purchase a ticket. She would have hoofed it, but she needed to catch Pi before her shift at Freeport Games ended.

With her face pressed against the train window, Aurie watched gondolas float through the sky on invisible wires. The airy modes of transport were reserved for professors and upperclassmen at the Hundred Halls. Someday she hoped to ride in one.

The Blue Line brought her past a building shaped like a giant stone flower unfolding to the sun. It was the Acoustic Architectural Institute of Design, but everyone called them the Stone Singers.

Seeing it only made her long to bear witness to Arcanium Hall. The hall of her dreams was built like a medieval castle. Aurie always imagined brown-robed monks moving through the halls carrying candles on their way to vast libraries when she looked at the ancient building. Arcanium had been one of the founding halls of Invictus.

Not only did she have to pass her Merlins, but the Hall had to choose her as well. But Aurie couldn't imagine herself anywhere other than Arcanium.

The brick building that housed the Freeport Games had once been a meat-packing house back in the 1800s, a tavern in the early 1900s, and even had a stint as an insane asylum. Or at least that's the story that Hemistad, the owner, liked to tell the kids that frequented his store.

Inside, the steady hum of people gaming made her grin. A Magic tournament was going on in one section, while a couple of groups were playing various role-playing games on the other side. Adjacent rooms that could have been old holding cells were filled with terrain tables for miniature warfare.

Aurie made her way to the back, where collectable sales were conducted. She hadn't seen Pi yet, but assumed she was lurking somewhere in back, sorting cards or organizing inventory.

Hannah, one of Pi's friends, waved from her table. She was running a role-playing game for a bunch of younger kids. Hannah normally looked like she could have played football with the boys, but in this case, she had a robe on and was making silly voices for her giggling players.

Coming to the store was always bittersweet for Aurie because she knew that in another life, one in which her parents hadn't died, she might have been one of the kids who lived at the store, sucking down energy drinks and trading collectable cards with her friends.

Behind a glass counter filled with every color of dice imaginable stood the owner of the store, Hemistad. Most of the younger kids just thought he was Swedish, but the regulars knew he wasn't human. Pi had a theory that he was an old werewolf because of the gray hair he had growing above his collar and on his ears, but Aurie thought he was something more ancient, more dangerous.

"Aurelia," said Hemistad, his wrinkly face cracking a grin. "You never visit. I thought you loved my store."

"I do, Mr. Hemistad," said Aurie. "It's just I'm rather busy these days."

"Nonsense," he said, tutting. "You're a young woman. You should make more time for a little fun. And stop calling me Mister. I've told you before, it's just Hemistad."

"Yes, Mi—Hemistad. Is my sister in back? I need to talk to her," said Aurie.

His bushy caterpillar-like eyebrows wagged. "Pythia? She's not working today. She asked for the day off to prepare for the tests tomorrow."

Aurie choked back an expletive. Pi knew they needed the money. How like her to take the day off.

"Is something wrong?" asked Hemistad, faced creased with worry.

"I...it's just...never mind," said Aurie. "I just need to find her, that's all."

Aurie turned away, but Hemistad asked if there was anything he could help with.

"Actually, yes," she said, "though I feel this is rather forward of me."

"Go ahead."

She chewed on part of her lip. "Could I have a job?"

"Why of course," he said. "You're always welcome to work here. I'm not sure why you think that was so forward."

She rubbed the cold edge of the glass case while she summoned her courage.

"Do you think I could have a loan against my future wages?" she asked.

When Hemistad's wrinkled face went through contortions, Aurie thought he was going to refuse.

"You and your sister work harder than anyone I know. How do you not have the money for your Merlins?" he asked.

"Pi got sick last year and had to spend a week in the hospital, which wiped out most of our savings, and two years before that our so-called foster parents stole our money," said Aurie.

A flash of anger passed across Hemistad's face. The brief transformation from a docile old man to a maniacal killer left Aurie shaken, but after it was gone, she wasn't sure she'd really seen it.

"People can be monsters," he said, in a way that made her question what he meant.

"Yes, they can," she replied.

Hemistad ambled to his cash register and pulled out the drawer. "How much do you need?"

When she told him the number, his lips soured, but he pulled out a stack of bills and handed them over.

"I promise I'll work all the hours you need to pay you back," said Aurie.

His bushy eyebrows wagged again, all traces of the previous anger absent. "Once you're in the Hundred Halls, you won't have time to do mundane work. I have more important, higher paying jobs that need to be done."

"Like...?" she asked.

Hemistad reached out and patted the back of her hand, still clutching the stack of bills.

"It's nothing that you would expect. But I want to leave it as a surprise. Humor an old man," he said.

Aurie thanked him and left the store, wondering not only what she'd agreed to do for Hemistad, but exactly what she'd seen for that brief terrible moment in his eyes.

4

Pi avoided the drug dealers at the front of her apartment by going through the laundry room at the back of the building. She stepped over a guy passed out by the dented washing machine. He smelled like old alcohol and urine.

A three-year lease on her soul for a chance to get out of this hole seemed like a good deal. Pi touched the heavy object in her pocket: the summoning focal.

She'd been nervous when Radoslav said they had to complete the agreement his way. She'd expected him to say that she had to kiss him. Not that he wasn't attractive, but he seemed like the type that would taste like an ashtray.

Instead, he'd poured shots from an ancient dusty bottle that he kept on the top shelf, along with a single drop of blood from their index fingers. The shot tasted metallic and had made her teeth hurt.

Afterwards, he'd given her the summoning focal and a smooth stone with some runes etched in it. The runestone was a marker that indicated her employment with Radoslav.

Pi slipped into the apartment and, after locking the door, pulled out the focal. It was a golden scroll that fit on her palm.

It wasn't real gold, but painted metal. Radoslav said it'd come from the base of Invictus' tower. She didn't question its power, because she could feel it thrumming in the palm of her hand.

She threw the focal on her desk. The object was swallowed by the mess of crumpled papers. Then she started collecting the gear she was going to need for the summoning.

A box beneath the bed had the video equipment she'd borrowed from her friend Adam. The only problem was going to be shielding it from the summoning, since electronics and magic didn't always mix.

There were a few other things she needed, but those were easy to find since they were on Aurie's side of the one-room apartment. Her sister's folders were neatly organized in a color-coded system matching cross-reference tabs in her books. The whole setup looked like it'd been organized by someone with a My Little Pony fetish.

Pi ran her fingers along the row of books as she thought about her sister.

"I'd wish you good luck, but I don't think you'll need it. I don't think anyone's been more prepared for a test in the history of the halls," said Pi.

She finished her preparations, putting everything she needed into a cardboard box with carrying handles. Then she grabbed some mints she had on her desk and shoved them into a back pocket. Then she put a warm Diet Coke she wanted for the caffeine into the box. She went through the list in her head, almost forgetting the golden scroll she'd thrown onto the desk.

Pi rescued the summoning focal and placed it in the box with the other items. She slipped on a black T-shirt with the words Don't Blink over her white crop top and threw a grease-stained towel over the top of the box to discourage curiosity.

With the box in hand, Pi left the apartment. She left

through the front since the drug dealers seemed to be distracted by something further up the street. They'd surrounded an older woman in a gaudy hand-knit sweater carrying bags of groceries.

The relief that she didn't have to deal with the drug dealers faded as she heard them taunt the woman.

"If you don't like it, then get the fuck out of our neighborhood," said one of the drug dealers to a chorus of laughter.

"Not my problem. Not my problem," muttered Pi as she started hurrying away.

A heavy crash startled Pi. They'd ripped one of the bags. Spaghetti sauce in canning jars shattered. The woman's legs were splattered in red marinara.

Pi stopped and sighed.

"It's not my problem," she said, before marching back to the front of the apartment and shoving the cardboard box beneath the half-dead bushes in front. She grabbed the Diet Coke to have something to do with her hands.

As she approached the drug dealers, she tried to form a plan, but nothing came. There were five of them standing around the woman, laughing. She was holding onto the second bag as if it were her children.

Pi contemplated using magic, but that would be stupid. Besides her need to conserve in preparation for tonight's summoning, any magic use without a patron risked faez madness. She didn't want to be one of those crazy bums that lurked in the alleyways making trash cans dance for their amusement.

"Hey fellas," she said from twenty feet away. "Why don't you leave the lady alone. Don't you guys have some puppies to torture?"

They turned and looked at her.

"What the? You're one nutty bitch to think you can tell us what to do," said the tallest drug dealer. He had a red bandana around his neck. He started walking towards her with his hands clenched into fists at his sides.

Pi flashed an inviting grin, full of confidence.

"Hey, isn't that one of those sisters studying to be mages in the Hall?" asked one of the other dealers.

The red bandana dealer slowed to a stop. "Nah, man. And even if she is, she can't do nothin' yet if she ain't in one. That's how it works."

"Actually, that's not how it works. Anyone who has ability can use magic. It just gets a little messy without a patron, that's all. So rather than just knock you down with a spell, I might accidentally tear your head off or transport you into the faez realm. Oops. No big deal, right?" said Pi, with a sarcastic shrug.

Doubt crept into their eyes, especially the ones in back. But the guy in front shook his head, as if he couldn't be bothered.

"No. No way. I ain't listenin' to your *bull*shit," he said, marching towards her, preparing himself for violence.

"Crap," Pi muttered under her breath. She thought about running, but that would only make things worse. "Luck favors the bold."

Remembering an internet video Aurie showed her once, Pi pulled the mints from her back pocket. Then she tore the wrapper off the side, opened her Diet Coke, and started chanting: "E pluribus Unum. Annuit coeptis! Turn this soda into acid!"

Red Bandana was only a few steps away when she palmed the candies inside the soda. The reaction was immediate. Brown foamy liquid jettisoned from the plastic bottle. As soon as Red Bandana saw it, his face dropped, and he turned and ran.

Pi pointed the bottle at the other drug dealers and moved towards them, chanting the same words over and over. They broke and ran. Pi threw the bottle after them.

"Thank you," said the woman. She had threads of gray in her hair and soft lines around her eyes. "I'd made enough sauce for the year."

"I'm sorry," said Pi. "They're a bunch of jerks."

The old woman shook with rage. "They're a bunch of fucking good-for-nothing hooligans is what they are. I hope they eat a bag of dicks."

"Wow," said Pi, shocked at the profanity from the old woman. "Are you sure you're okay?"

The old woman calmed, her brow smoothing apologetically.

"Forgive my mouth, it gets the best of me. Thank you for your quick thinking, young lady," she said.

"Yeah, no problem. Sorry I wasn't quicker. I might have saved the first bag. But if you're good, then I've got to go. Things to do and all," said Pi, walking backwards, waving.

"Good luck with whatever it is you have to do," said the old woman.

Pi jogged back to the bushes and retrieved her cardboard box before heading to the subway to take the Blue Line to the twelfth ward.

Luck favors the bold. She hoped she hadn't used it all up helping that woman, because she was going to need some tonight. Pi hadn't been completely honest with Radoslav when she'd told him what she planned on summoning. If she had been, he would have never given her the focal.

To get in the Coterie, she needed a sponsor. The one she wanted had told her he wouldn't even consider her unless she could successfully summon a Faez Lord. Which was probably about as dangerous as one could get.

The good news was that if she failed, she wouldn't have to worry about getting into the Coterie. Either there'd be nothing left of her body or the Faez Lord would enslave her and take her back to his realm.

She wondered how that would work with Radoslav's lease on her soul. Would the demon have to wait for the lease to be up to claim her, or would they have to take their disagreement to some sort of faerie court?

"Let's not find out, Pythia," she told herself as she descended the subway entrance. It'd be a terrible blow to Aurie, right on the heels of getting into the Arcanium. Better to think about them both succeeding. Maybe they could pool their loose change and take each other out for an artisan cupcake in celebration of them both getting into the Hundred Halls.

5

On the way back to their apartment to find Pi, Aurie made a brief detour to the Enochian District. She'd already stopped by the bank to deposit the money, and as long as it was daylight she was safe, but she kept a wary eye just the same. The buildings on the cobblestone street had bars in the windows and graffiti across the bricks with phrases like "Go home sub-humans" or "Kneel before the Cabal."

It was one of the older parts of the city. When her parents had been students at the Hundred Halls, it'd been a bustling historical area. Since the death of the city's founder and head patron, Invictus, thirteen years ago, the street, along with the rest of the city, had fallen into disrepair.

Aurie reached the old copper fountain in the shape of a dragon at the center of the square. No water had flowed for years, and a pale green patina had formed on the surface of the fountain. She flicked her black nail against the edge, eliciting a dull thunk, and regretted the noise as soon as it echoed into the square.

Out of the corner of her eye, she saw shapes move in the windows. She knew it'd be foolish to look. Best to do what she'd come to do, and get out.

Nestled amid the cobblestones was a marble plate etched with a poem titled *Invictus*. These plates were found in many locations around the city, but this one was special for Aurie and her sister.

After giving the street one last glance, Aurie placed her hand on the plate. The stone was warm from the sunlight. After a few seconds, a glistening gossamer light formed around the edges of the words.

Aurie stood back and listened as first a male voice began singing, and then a female one joined in. The song was a cheesy '80s' ballad by Cindi Lauper called "Time After Time."

She listened in complete silence, concentrating on the voices and their earnestness. The voices were her parents'. They'd enchanted their voices into the stone sometime during their years at the Halls. They probably weren't much older than she was when they made the recording.

After the song was over, she said, "*Dooset daram.* I miss you, Mom and Dad."

Aurie wished Pi was at her side. When they were feeling down, they would come to the fountain together and hold hands while they listened to the song. It put an ache in her breastbone that she was alone.

A bit of rustling echoed from one of the nearby alleyways, but Aurie ignored it. She didn't care about anything else at that moment.

"We're finally going to do it," she told the stone. "We have our Merlins tomorrow. I wish you were here. I know you would be cheering us on." Aurie took a quivering breath. "It's been a tough few years. When Pi got sick, I didn't know what to do. But we made it, we made it through. Now, we're going to get into the Halls, I know it. I just wish...you know...I'm..."

Aurie collected herself, pushing her fingernails into her

palms to keep from crying. The shadows were getting entirely too long. She needed to leave soon, but she hadn't said what she wanted to say yet.

She ignored the itchy feeling between her shoulder blades that told her she was being watched and continued speaking. "I just want to say, I need to say...I'm sorry. Pi and I were just letting a little of our faez magic out. Every kid did it, and I'm not saying that makes it okay, but I don't know how it got away from me. I know Pi says that it wasn't me. She still claims it was some guy who she saw in the neighborhood, but I know she's just trying to protect me. I'd do the same for her. But I know it was me. The magic got away from me, it always does. But I'm going to fix that now. Arcanium's the best place for me. They can teach me how to control it so something like that never happens again. I swear it. And I'll make sure Pi is okay. I always have. I know you would have wanted it that way, that we stayed together and looked out for each other. I'll keep her safe. For you. For her. I miss you, Mom and Dad. I miss you a lot. But we'll get through this. I'm going to do my best. My very best. I—"

The crash of toppled cans startled Aurie out of her speech. The sun was almost below the tops of the nearby apartment buildings. Aurie felt pressure on her skin, like she was a bubble being pushed out of liquid.

She kissed her fingertips and brushed them against the singing stone, then hurried out of the square. She barely made it onto the train before the sun set.

As she rode towards home, she thought about her sister. Something in her gut told her she needed to find her. It wasn't like Pi to lie about work unless she was planning something that she knew Aurie wouldn't approve of.

Aurie had a feeling that whatever Pi was doing had to do with Coterie. The elite Hall required sponsorship from one of their alumni. The whispers of tasks attempted by potential students made Aurie's skin crawl. Coterie believed in power for power's sake, and there was no telling what Pi might have to do.

As the train rode up an elevation, heading over Tinker Town, Aurie caught flashes of lightning in the west. She couldn't see the line of clouds rolling towards the city, but a storm was coming.

6

The abandoned warehouse was the perfect place for a summoning. Pi had found it a few months back. The locks and wards on the doors were still intact, but she'd found a way in through the basement, bypassing them completely.

Over time she'd cleared the concrete floor of dust and rat droppings, until she had a nice, clean area for a circle of protection. In fact, she had everything she needed, including a cloudless night, which had been her biggest worry. Most demons could feed off nature's energies, which would make it harder to control if there was a storm.

One of the reasons she needed a big space for the summoning was to safely record the event for proof. Magic and electronics didn't play nice together, so the cameras had to be a good distance away from the circle.

Sea salt with a pinch of silver went in a wide circle around the summoning focal. She was careful not to complete it until she was ready. Then she made a triangle outside of but touching the circle, placing a different symbol in each of the smaller triangles that were created. Candles she'd liberated from nearby churches were placed at precise locations, including anywhere lines intersected.

Pi placed a handful of graveyard dirt, a drop of her blood, and a chunk of fulgurite on top of the focal. Once she was safely outside, she closed the circle with the last of her salt. It was important that she not have any salt remaining.

Standing on the west side, which was closest to the nearest leyline, Pi began chanting in Latin and manipulated her fingers into complex forms. As she worked, Pi let out small amounts of faez to give power to the movements.

The faez funneled into the summoning circle, giving the lines a faint glow. Pi kept this up for a while, being careful to enunciate each word correctly and shape her fingers precisely. The author of the spell claimed it was the equivalent of playing one of Mozart's piano concertos flawlessly.

She was almost done with the summoning when the rumble of thunder crashed against the warehouse windows, rattling them. Pi nearly lost her concentration. Faez surged from her, the glow burning too bright.

Shit, she thought while maintaining the ritual, *bad timing*.

It was too late to stop. She had to forge ahead even as the incoming storm brought gooseflesh across her arms and made the little hairs on the back of her neck rise.

When at last she got to the end of the spell, she called out the demon's name three times in a loud voice:

"*Pazuzu! Pazuzu! Pazuzu!*"

Lightning split the sky directly above the warehouse.

A shape appeared inside the circle. He had the body of a man, with wings and a scorpion's tail. The demon lashed against the walls of the circle with his tail, bringing sparks.

Pi held her breath while the demon of storms, Pazuzu, spun around testing his cage. If she'd made any mistake in her preparations, he would break free of the circle. Death would be the most favorable outcome if it came to that.

"Pazuzu, Prince of Storms," she yelled above the rising winds, "hear my question and answer me."

The demon spat against the cage, speaking in an unintelligible tongue. Or at least Pi couldn't understand it. Learning the Infernal tongue would have taken too long, so she'd set up the cameras so her sponsor could understand the answer.

A torrent of rain splattered against the windows. Pazuzu grinned at the flashes of lightning and held up a wicked talon. The demon jabbed it against the barrier repeatedly, like a miner digging through stone. Through the link of her faez, Pi felt the barrier weakening.

"Pazuzu, Prince of Storms. Hear my question and answer me!" she shouted, pouring faez into the pain symbols in the three triangles around the circle. "Where is the Rod of Dominion?"

The demon lord thrashed around the circle as the symbols assaulted it. Pi repeated her question, followed by another dose of faez into the pain symbols.

A crash of thunder rattled the windows. The center of the storm was almost over the warehouse; Pi could feel it. As she prepared to ask the question a third time, lightning hit a tree right outside, sending sparks into a fountain and breaking a huge branch free to swing through the upper windows.

The opening released the storm's fury into the warehouse, blowing out half the candles. The salt circle seemed to vibrate from the wind.

"Pazuzu, Prince of Storms. Hear my question and answer me! Where is the Rod of Dominion?" she shouted.

This time she didn't hold back. Using too much faez was a danger, but it would be much worse if the demon got loose. She had to get the answer and send it back to the faez realm before that happened.

The demon whipped its scorpion tail against the barrier. The blow translated through her magic, feeling like a kick in the gut. She poured everything she had into the symbols.

Finally, it seemed to affect the demon. He bent backwards, screaming in rage. Then he answered in his rough, garbled tongue.

She didn't even care if it wasn't the answer. Pi started chanting again while the wind blew drops of rain into her face. The banishing was much shorter, but her heart threatened to jump out of her chest. She focused on the ritual, shaping her fingers exactly as required—no more, no less.

Unhampered by pain, Pazuzu attacked the barrier with fervor. Pi was reminded of an enraged xenomorph in a glass barrel.

She only had a few more lines before the demon would be banished. Then the rest of the branch came through the window, sending shards of glass in all directions. It was a miracle that she didn't get hit, but Pi would have preferred it to the damage done to her summoning circle.

A gust of wind blew a hole into the salt, releasing the demon from its barrier. Pi fell to her knees as the magic gave way. Pazuzu, the demon Prince of Storms, was free.

7

Aurie had gone to the apartment, fully expecting not to find her younger sister. A quick cataloging of their belongings revealed a few key items missing: a bag of tea lights, a salt funnel, a ritual knife, and a hunk of fulgurite.

Also absent was the box of recording gear. Pi had claimed she was going to make a YouTube video about Freeport Games to help Hemistad get more business. Now, she knew that was a lie.

It took about thirty seconds outside the apartment to figure out where Pi was located. The storm had rolled over the city, and an abnormal amount of lightning activity was happening over the twelfth ward. That part of the city had many abandoned warehouses from when the city of Invictus had a thriving magical trade industry.

The whole train ride, Aurie reviewed the possibilities of what her sister was trying to do, but only one answer was clear: Pi was trying to summon a demon. Aurie had no idea where her sister could have gotten a summoning focus—that was a problem for a different time—but the power of the storm worried her. Even an imp could be troublesome with this much natural energy in the air.

The rain started around the time she left the station, along with gusts of wind that made Aurie squint. The air was alive with electricity. Even soaking wet, she could feel the energy crackle across her skin.

A purple bolt of lightning slammed into a huge tree on the next block, sending sparks up in an arc. The brief flash revealed a black funnel hanging beneath the clouds, rotating in a slow churn.

Aurie had no doubt where Pi was located, and broke into a sprint towards the center of the storm. Coaxed by the violent energies in the air, Aurie's faez rushed to the surface. It was like running with a full bucket of water, trying not to spill a drop.

When she got to the warehouse, she could hear Pi's chanting. She banged on the metal door, but the magical wards seemed to absorb her blows.

Aurie searched her pockets for magical reagents that might help her bypass the door, but she'd run out of the apartment without even a sprig of mistletoe. She would have circled the warehouse looking for where Pi might have gotten in, but she knew her sister wouldn't leave an obvious entrance to the location of a summoning. It would be foolish to allow some drifter to wander into the middle of a dangerous magical event.

An inhuman roar echoed from within, sending Aurie into a panic. She cupped her hands around her mouth and screamed Pi's name, but the storm swallowed her words.

Aurie threw herself to the ground when a bolt of lightning slammed into another tree, followed by the crash of glass.

"A window," she muttered as she ran towards the metal fire escape near the massive oak tree.

The winds waved the tree limbs around, making them

creak and crack. Aurie kept expecting another branch to come off, whistling at her head. The entrance to the fire escape was directly under the tree. The stairs rattled as she climbed.

Inside, Pi was shouting commands, and Aurie began to make a mental image of the scene inside, but that didn't prepare her for what she saw when she reached the broken window with the tree branch sticking through it. Aurie was simultaneously angered and proud of her younger sister when she saw the demon Pi had summoned.

The demon screamed in Infernal as its tail slapped against the invisible barrier, eliciting sparks. The skillfully drawn circle contained the demon. A quick glance told her that Pi had taken every precaution necessary, but she hadn't factored the surprise storm.

As if coaxed by her thoughts, a gust of wind pushed Aurie against the wall. She put her hand out against the broken glass, daring the shards, rather than upset the precariously balanced tree branch. But the wind had pushed the angled limb as well, tipping it forward, shattering the window and blowing everything into the warehouse.

Moments later, the demon wailed in Infernal. Aurie knew snatches of the language, but no translation was needed for that victorious noise.

Pi was thrown to her knees by the breaking of the circle. Aurie didn't hesitate and leapt into the warehouse, using the huge tree branch as a makeshift slide.

The scorpion-tailed demon advanced on her sister with talons extended. It was going for a quick kill.

Aurie didn't have time for fancy tricks. She picked up one of the camera tripods that had fallen over and threw it at the demon.

"Get away from her, you fugly bastard!"

The demon recoiled for a moment, before he realized it

was only another young girl. The demon looked between the two sisters, deciding which one he would kill first.

"Aurie, no! Get out of here!" yelled Pi, climbing to her feet.

The demon started to turn back to Pi, so Aurie let an unhealthy amount of faez collect into her fist until it glowed. The demon whipped its head around, quickly reevaluating Aurie as the larger threat.

With faez dripping from her fist like a handful of golden honey, Aurie backed away from the demon, being careful not to knock the salt lines or step on any candles as she stepped into the center of the circle. The demon came after, his tail slapping against the concrete, avoiding the salt lines. The impact sprayed bits of venom in a wide arc. If the demon hit her with his tail, the end would not be pleasant.

Pi threw a few rocks at the demon, but it ignored her. "Aurie, what are you doing?"

"Once it's inside, close the circle behind me," she shouted over the storm.

"What? No!"

Aurie ducked under a swipe of the demon's tail. "Just do it!"

Focused on her, the demon didn't see Pi running up behind. But Aurie barely noticed as she dodged the demon's lazy attacks. He clearly sensed danger, by his slow advance. It was the only thing saving Aurie from being impaled at this point.

"Come on, you bastard, step forward," she said under her breath, being careful not to kick the salt lines behind her.

The scorpion-tailed demon paused before putting his second leg into the circle. He started to turn his head, which would give him a good view of Pi, right behind him.

Aurie threw faez at him, which was ineffectual at best. The unformed magic splattered against the demon's bony leg before slumping to the floor and dissipating. But it had the intended effect.

The demon stepped forward, and when his second foot crossed the barrier, Pi slid next to the salt lines and repaired the circle. At the same time, because she didn't want to get trapped, Aurie kicked a hole into the side nearest her. She stepped through and quickly reformed the barrier.

At this point, the magic was paper-thin. The demon threw himself against it. Aurie poured faez into the protection circle. A moment later, Pi joined the effort. Together, they were able to make the barrier strong enough to keep the demon from breaking through.

"Hold the barrier," Aurie yelled at Pi.

Pi opened her mouth to object, but Aurie had already stepped away, chanting a simple banishing spell. It wasn't the ideal way to get rid of a demon, but without a good look at the ritual Pi had used, it was the fastest way.

After a good thirty seconds, Aurie finished the spell and the demon howled as he returned back to his realm.

The moment after the demon was gone, the storm broke. Winds died down, and the rain stopped hammering the warehouse, turning to a light sprinkle.

"What the hell were you thinking?" asked Aurie, the adrenaline from the encounter hammering at her heart until her hands shook. "That was a fucking demon prince."

Pi scowled and went running over to the tripod that Aurie had thrown. The camera was busted into black plastic and circuit boards.

"Shit. Everything's fucked. Why'd you have to throw that? You're always trying to save me, and ruining things instead," she said, digging her fingers into her short black hair.

"Is this for Coterie?" Aurie asked.

Pi looked away, the scowl still affixed to her face. "He

said he would sponsor me if I got an answer to his question. Without that, I can't get into Coterie."

"Then you can be in Arcanium with me," said Aurie.

"I don't want to be in Arcanium," said Pi, then when she saw the hurt on Aurie's face added, "I'm sorry, Aurie. I really want Coterie badly. Arcanium's my second, but it's not for me. You know that. I don't ever want anyone to be able to take my family away from me again."

Aurie didn't want to get into their old arguments after the battle, especially with their blood hot, so she bit her lip instead.

"You really want to be in Coterie?" Aurie asked quietly because it hurt to even ask the question.

"Come on. You know that. Not that it matters without the video," she said.

Aurie let a sigh out through her clenched teeth. "What if I told you I know a little Infernal."

"You do?" asked Pi, nose wrinkled with confusion.

Aurie threw her hands up. "It might be useful for the Merlins. You never know what they're going to throw at us."

Pi ran over and hugged her sister. Aurie was taller by a head. She wrapped her arms around Pi.

"Thanks, sis," said Pi, then added, "*Dooset daram.*"

Hearing the words let the air out of her rage. Aurie responded in kind, "*Dooset daram.*"

Pi pulled away. "So the translation?"

"Don't get too excited. I'm not completely sure what I heard. And what is that Rod anyway?" asked Aurie.

"The key to me getting into Coterie," said her sister with a forced grin.

"Fine. This is what the demon said," said Aurie, then she repeated the Infernal phrase, which made her throat hurt. Speaking Infernal was like gargling salt water and hot sauce.

"And that translates to?"

"Something about 'beneath city of lights in the halls of the dead,'" said Aurie, then added in a slow drawl, "but I could have a word or two wrong."

"That could mean the catacombs of Paris?" asked Pi.

"Well, there you go. A plausible answer. Your sponsor should be happy," said Aurie, holding back her concern.

Pi pushed her hair back, head rotating as she surveyed the destruction. "What a mess."

"Let's get this cleaned up and get back to the apartment," said Aurie. "We're gonna need our rest. The Merlins are going to be harder than this."

8

After Aurie fell asleep on her side of the tiny apartment, Pi grabbed the broken camera and quietly went out the door. The drug dealers she'd tangled with earlier in the day were in the lobby having a party. Their whoops and hollering echoed up the stairwell. Pi went out the back hallway window and used the metal fire escape to get down to street level.

The bottom part of the stairs had been ripped off, probably for scrap metal, which was a violation of building code, but no one cared about anything in the thirteenth ward. The alleyway smelled like stale beer and urine.

Using the Green Line, Pi headed to the fourth ward's city library. The old building had enchanted stone lions outside that watched your approach. She patted their heads before going in.

Pi used the library's computers to check if anything was left on the camera's drive. After bending back the little brass nubs in the connector, she was able to get a garbled version of the events to come up on the computer screen.

Half the summoning was distorted, including the part where the demon gave his answer, but there was enough to use as proof that she wasn't just making something up. Pi recorded a video screen capture, leaving out the parts with Aurie, and made two copies.

Pi headed to the first ward using the Red Line. The whole way across the city, her knees bounced as her mind went through all sorts of scenarios. What if he isn't home? What if he forgot what he'd tasked me with? What if he thinks the video was a fake? What if he won't sponsor me?

These thoughts chased themselves around her head until the Red Line train ascended above the buildings, giving her a clear view of the city, distracting her. Lighted gondolas looked like slow-moving fireflies floating above the buildings. Some of the city's famous halls were visible: the Society for the Study of Animals' ark-like structure, the Order of Honorable Alchemists' eight-sided dome, and the Coterie of Mages' imposing obsidian tower, which was commonly called the Obelisk.

Seeing the Obelisk made Pi flush with excitement. It wasn't the tallest or biggest tower—that prize went to the Spire, which was in the center of the city and housed the administration of the Hundred Halls—but the Obelisk had a weight that conferred to Pi that it would always be there for her.

The city disappeared from view as the Red Line train neared her stop. Leaving the station, she received many a withering glance as the men and women in their business attire quickly identified that she didn't belong in her black hoodie and ratty jeans.

The first district was alive with magically steered Rolls Royces and ornate carriages being pulled by unseen beasties. Pi lost count of the expensive sports cars whose brands she'd never heard of after the first two dozen. The blight that had affected the rest of the city went unnoticed in this ward.

She found the home of her sponsor after a couple of double

backs avoiding roaming security guards. It annoyed her that she didn't know her sponsor's name. He had a masking enchantment on it. But she knew where his home was, which was good enough.

Pi didn't dare circumvent the ornate cast-iron fence that circled the three-story shotgun-style home. She knew the sort of protections he employed were well beyond her skill level.

A security guard stood in the shadows outside the gate. Pi caught the whiff of metal, which warned her that the guard was a supernatural.

She'd barely taken one step towards the gate when a silky voice came out of the shadows.

"You don't belong here. Go away," said the female voice.

The words wrapped themselves around Pi's feet, and she found herself back on the sidewalk before she realized it. She had the urge to keep going towards the train station, but willed herself to stay put.

Pi hadn't anticipated a succubus guardian. It both frightened and excited her. A sponsor with this level of power was worth the effort.

Steeling herself against the voice, Pi marched back up the drive.

"I said, go away," said the succubus with a tinge more threat.

While fighting the urge to obey the command, Pi held out the copy of the summoning. "Your master is expecting me. Give this to him."

A hiss came out of the darkness. When the succubus moved forward, Pi averted her gaze.

"You're not on my list, and if you're not on my list, you're not welcome. *He*," —which didn't come out as the male pronoun, as the name was obfuscated by his enchantment— "told me I can have anyone who's not welcome."

Panic set in, but Pi held her ground, holding the disc out and shaking it. "He won't be happy if you turn me away."

The succubus moved close. Pi's boot inched backwards. Doubt consumed her. A sharp fingernail poked into Pi's chest.

"Go away, sweetling," said the succubus. "You're just a whelp, and there's nothing on this disc that my master wants to see. Go away, before I indulge my hunger."

Pi clamped her eyes closed as the demon moved within inches. Every fiber of her being ached to obey. She dug into her pocket and pulled out the runestone that Radoslav had given her. She shoved it into the succubus' face.

A noise of surprise left the demon's lips. "Where did you get this?"

"I work for Radoslav," she said, which was the truth, but she didn't think he'd intended for her to use his name like this. She hoped it wouldn't get back to him.

"What would Radoslav want with a whelp like you?" hissed the succubus.

Pi shook the disc emphatically.

"Fine," said the demon, snatching it from Pi's grip. The demon vanished through the gate without opening it. Pi wondered what kind of magic it employed.

But more so, she wondered if her sponsor would remember her. Now that she'd handed over the disc, she had her doubts. Pi had gotten an audience with him by confronting him in the men's bathroom at the Luminaire, a high-end restaurant. She'd gotten a job there as a dishwasher and waited until he was in the stall to make her request.

When the succubus came back, Pi almost forgot to avert her eyes. The demon moved close and growled, before saying, "Come with me."

Pi moved towards the gate, and after a few steps, she found herself inside the house. Looking out the window by the doorway revealed a different lawn than she'd expected, which told Pi that the mansion on display from the street was different than the one she was standing in.

The entryway was an immaculate display of marble and gold. The statue of an imposing mage with a knifelike nose and piercing eyes was nestled into an alcove.

The succubus tugged on Pi's arm. In the light, she caught a glimpse of the supernatural creature's uniform, which consisted of copious amounts of black leather across her milky white skin.

The guard left Pi in a study that was larger than her whole apartment by a wide margin. Pi suspected even the bathrooms would be bigger.

Pi didn't have long to investigate the room before she heard a voice from behind her. "I assume you're not here to waste my time."

Her sponsor was cloaked in a shimmering shield that looked like heat waves from a summer highway, but she remembered the voice. It had an aristocratic tilt that dripped with disdain.

"I have the answer, if that's what you mean," said Pi, and then she repeated the Infernal phrase.

While her sponsor chewed on the answer, she massaged her throat.

Suddenly, he was upon her. He grabbed her, digging his fingers into her wrist.

"How did you get this information?" he asked, the threat as plain as a knife to her chest.

"I...the demon, Pazuzu. You saw it," said Pi.

He released her arm and stalked away. His shield reflected his mood, shifting around, distorting his features even more severely. Then just as suddenly as he had become angered, a calming wind overtook him.

"It's quite impressive, Miss Pythia. A considerable feat for a mage not even in the Hall," he said. "Not unprecedented, but impressive, nonetheless."

Pi caught the undertone to his message: he hadn't expected her to actually succeed. A wave of embarrassment flushed her skin, but she kept a stoic face. He'd given her the task to get rid of her.

"The storm played a big part, in both your success and near downfall, but something else was at work," he said, sounding like he was speaking to himself. "But no matter. The important thing is that you succeeded in your task. And I am not one to renege on my promises."

The sudden reversal was a little disorienting. Somehow she knew that things could have gone quite differently, badly even. She resisted the urge to blurt out her thanks. She knew a man like him didn't care about the little niceties. He respected power, and nothing else. Pi didn't want to go so far as employing demons for protection, but she surely wanted the security that his kind of power enjoyed.

"I will send a note to the Coterie and let them know that you have a sponsor. But know that if you don't pass your Merlins, my offer is retracted," he said.

Pi opened her mouth to reassure him of her impending success, but before the words left her lips, she found herself back on the sidewalk, momentarily wondering if it had happened at all, until she heard a low chuckle from the succubus guard in the shadows.

9

The morning of the Merlins, Aurie woke well before sunrise and reviewed her binders of notes on spells, rituals, and other magical studies. After Pi groaned awake, they shared a couple of granola bars for breakfast. Aurie was still hungry afterwards, but too nervous to eat anything else. Pi shoved the remaining bars from the box into her hoodie to eat later. It was the last of their food.

Pi left the apartment early so she could take the broken equipment back to her friend Adam with a promise of getting it fixed later. Aurie assumed her sister was also taking the summoning focal back to whomever she'd gotten it from. Aurie would have asked about it, but being test day, she didn't want to distract her sister.

It took a few tries to find the right outfit for the trials, not because she was trying to look fashionable—that was Pi's thing—but because she kept imagining the different types of exams they might throw at her and what clothing would work best. In the end, she decided on a pair of comfortable fitting jeans, the stained running shoes she'd gotten at the thrift store, and a gray tank top. Her dark hair was in that weird place that was too long to style and too short to put in a ponytail.

Aurie poked the puffy dark bag beneath her blue eyes. She just needed to get used to them. It wasn't like she was going to get any more sleep if she got in Arcanium—when she got in Arcanium, she reminded herself.

The weather mirrored her mood: flashes of exuberant sunlight followed by thick gray clouds. Aurie tried not to think about the Merlins on her way to the Spire, but it was so hard. It wasn't like anyone knew anything about them. The only thing the administrators would tell her was to "be ready for anything."

There were prep classes to take, and tutors to hire—not that they could have afforded them. The Internet had thousands of videos about what might be in the trials. A whole industry had sprung up around preparing for the Merlins. But in the end, no one knew anything. And that scared Aurie the most.

Her whole life teetered on this one day. It made her sick with worry. She had no idea what she would do if she didn't get in. It'd never been a part of her mental vocabulary.

When she neared the city center, Aurie headed for the gondola station designated for potential students. It was one of the few times non-Hall members could ride in one. She'd left with plenty of time to reach the Spire, deciding it was better to wait nervously at the test place than to risk being late.

As she turned the corner into the waiting area, Aurie smelled musky plum. Violet Cardwell and her mother, Camille, waited at the head of the line for the gondola. Camille wore a flamingo pink dress with a pillbox hat and an Alchemist guild pin next to the flower on her lapel. Violet had on a sensible, but fashionable light blue workout outfit. She looked ready to run a marathon with her blonde hair high in a ponytail.

Surprisingly, Violet was not face-down in her phone. Her

lips soured as she saw Aurie. Then Violet got her mother's attention and nodded towards Aurie.

"Shit," said Aurie, getting in line, wishing she'd worn a hoodie like her sister so she could hide her face from the Cardwells.

To keep from getting freaked out, Aurie studied the other people in line. At least half of them were potential students. She could tell by the way their eyes shifted around, never resting on one place, mind clearly on the upcoming Merlins. The other half were either parents of the nervous, or administration types.

A relief-filled exhalation of laughter traveled through the line when the gondola was sighted sliding through the air towards the station. A quick count confirmed that she would ride up on the first trip. She'd have to share a car with the Cardwells, and Violet's awful perfume, but it was better than waiting.

Aurie might not have caught the spell except she was staring straight at the gondola attendant when Camille moved forward to enter. She leaned closer, as if she had something to say, and her hand squeezed something on her chest, the flower perhaps. A mist spritzed the attendant's face, and he jerked slightly.

Aurie looked around to see if anyone else had seen it, but they were talking amongst themselves. She was the only one. Then her stomach dropped as Camille pointed back into the crowd, directly at Aurie. Based on Violet's smug expression, Aurie knew this wasn't going to be good. She hoped that Camille had just made the request that Aurie not ride in the same gondola as her daughter. It would be disappointing not to be in the first car up, but she'd still be fine riding in the second. She didn't allow herself any other thoughts, for fear of them coming true.

As Aurie moved up towards the open door, she tried to keep her head down. But when the attendant noticed, he pointed directly at her. His eyes had a hazy fog to them, as if he was under some sort of enchantment.

"This gondola is closed to you for safety reasons," he said in a monotone voice.

"I can go up in the next car then?" asked Aurie.

The attendant blinked and repeated, "This gondola is closed to you for safety reasons."

The other people in line and in the car began to notice that something was wrong. Aurie felt the gaze of many eyes upon her.

"I'm here for the Merlins. You're supposed to take me up," said Aurie, trying to project a confident pose.

The attendant appeared to fight the enchantment for a moment, but the magic took over. "This gondola is closed to you for safety reasons."

"What safety reasons?" Aurie demanded. "I saw her spray something in your face. She's put a spell on you because her daughter doesn't like me."

Murmurs rumbled up from the silence behind her. People were either asking for the line to move or what the safety reasons were. It wasn't the first time people had made assumptions about her due to her looks, but it'd never come at such a delicate time.

The attendant opened and closed his mouth like a fish drowning in air.

"See?" Aurie said to the crowd. "He's fighting it. He knows it's bullshit too."

A few people looked away, and she thought she might be winning the argument, until someone shouted from the back: "I'm not getting on the gondola with her if it's not safe."

The spark lit the crowd as if it were tinder. Suddenly,

people were shouting, making demands about their safety, and pushing her away from the open door. The parents were the main offenders, claiming they hadn't paid this much money to risk their kids. Aurie tried to claw her way towards the gondola, but there were too many against her. In no time, she was standing at the back of the line, with dozens of eyes glaring at her.

Someone shouted, "Go somewhere else! You're not wanted here."

The laughter that followed was a cold knife to her heart. She stumbled out of the station. It was too far to another designated gondola and at least four miles to the Spire, not including hundreds and hundreds of stairs.

A burst of sunlight hit the windows on the upper portion of the Spire like a starting signal. The massive building was at least the size of four skyscrapers bonded together. The upper portion swirled into the sky and on cloudy days would disappear into it. Aurie took off at a run, thankful that she hadn't worn her boots.

Not long after the first mile, Aurie regretted not having a larger breakfast. The whole time her legs burned, but each time she thought about slowing down, she imagined not getting into the Hundred Halls, and pushed harder.

As she neared the Spire, the landscape changed. She had to climb stairs to move upward. She wasn't familiar with the streets, so when she came to a decision point, she was afraid the wrong path would lead to her being late.

The whole time she ran, a clock ticked in her head. She might have cried during the run, but it was hard to tell since she was soaked with sweat.

But as she neared, a kernel of hope formed. The last gondola had passed her a few minutes ago, but she knew there was a little more time.

Then she ran into a construction roadblock at the head of a long archway. A group of Stone Singers were modifying a bridge that connected the road to the inner Spire platform. The chorus of voices rose and fell in a somber dirge that made Aurie's ears itch.

The road ahead was curling back towards the singers, drawn by the magic in their voices. The concrete bent as if it were merely rubber that would spring back into shape.

The head of the construction unit yelled at her to stop, but Aurie kept running. She climbed up the curl, trying to make it to the top before it tipped over. She pulled herself up and was confronted with a gap. The inner platform was about ten feet away, and maybe fifteen feet below her. She hesitated for a moment when she realized that if she missed, she'd fall another forty feet to the lower street.

Aurie leapt before the gap grew too large. She hit the concrete hard, rolling onto her side and slamming her shoulder. With a grimace, she climbed to her feet and soldiered on.

The last flights of stairs into the Spire were the cruelest. Each step was a fire in her gut, in her thighs. She was dizzy from hunger, but forged on.

Finally, she reached the proper floor. The registration hall was empty except for a few parents milling about near the elevators. A few attendants were starting to break down the tables and put the computers in rolling boxes.

Aurie ran up to the nearest one that was still connected. "I'm here. I'm here."

The attendant, an older woman with a streak of gray in her brown hair, glanced towards the hallway at the other side of the room.

"You're late," she said, with brow furrowed.

"There was...it doesn't matter. I need to sign in. I preregistered," said Aurie frantically, feeling as if the world was collapsing around her.

"Name?"

"Aurelia Maximus Silverthorne."

The woman shrugged, leaned down, and typed into the computer, shaking her head the whole time as if she thought it was a waste of time.

"Yep, all registered," she said, handing her a pin to attach to her shirt.

Aurie started to run, but the woman stopped her, pointing to an impressive tome. A feather quill in an ink pot sat next to the book.

"Sign your name, and list the halls you want," she said.

With a shaking hand, Aurie scribbled her name. She'd barely written Arcanium on the section beneath her name when the woman said, "Run now. They're closing the door. You're not going to make it."

Aurie dropped the feather and took off at a sprint.

The woman shouted, "Run! Run!"

Aurie had never run so hard or so fast in her life. The hallway seemed to stretch on forever, but she churned her legs, pushing past the burning, past the pain, past the fear. At the end of the hallway were massive rune-marked double doors.

The doors were closing. They were almost closed. She didn't even have time to yell.

Aurie slipped through at the last moment, the edge of the door brushing her bruised shoulder. She'd made it. She was inside. She could join the trials of magic.

10

Pi lingered at the Hall registration with the quill perched on her fingertips for a good minute. On the first line of the form, she'd written "Coterie of Mages" in a messy scrawl. Despite what she'd said to Aurie, Pi had no intention of listing a safety school. At the time she'd thought she'd rather wait another year if she didn't get into Coterie. But her sponsor had warned that if she didn't get in this year, his offer was retracted.

Eventually, she scribbled down Arcanium. Not because she wanted to. Mostly she did it because that's what she'd told Aurie.

When she passed the runed doors and entered the welcome hall, Pi searched around, expecting to find Aurie waiting for her. When she didn't see her sister within the area right inside the room, Pi began to worry. It wasn't like Aurie to not be stupidly early.

The welcome hall was a huge area that could hold a couple thousand people at least. A platform sat at the center of the circular chamber. At locations around the outside wall, interspaced between the huge windows, large blank tapestries hung. It gave her a moment of dislocation when she realized that the windows revealed the city in a round, yet she'd run down a long hall to reach the room, which meant the doors had teleported her to another level in the Spire.

Pi decided that Aurie had gone to the bathroom or seen someone they knew from Freeport Games and had gone exploring. So Pi wandered around, checking out the other potential students. Blue-robed attendants circulated through the room, answering questions from the other initiates.

The nervous energy was palpable. She could almost taste the fear in the room. Most of the others were talking in small groups, barely making eye contact with each other.

Few looked as confident as she felt. A handsome dark-skinned guy wearing a martial arts outfit stood alone with his hands resting on the knot of his black belt. He winked when they made eye contact.

A pair of twins, tall, nearly albino, and probably Scandinavian, practiced their finger exercises, doing mock battles with each other, playing Five Elements. Pi thought they might almost be as good as she and her sister were when they played.

Near the runed doors, Pi spied a blonde girl in a light blue running outfit that didn't look intimidated by the situation. She thought about going up and talking to her, since she looked like the kind of girl that would be in Coterie, but a beautiful and heavy woman with long honey-brown hair, wielding a twisted oaken staff, announced that things would be starting soon and that everyone needed to pay attention.

Pi looked around frantically. Why hadn't she seen Aurie yet? Was something wrong?

When Aurie slid through the doors right before they closed, Pi almost let out a cheer. Her sister was drenched in sweat, all the way through her jeans and tank top. The students nearest wrinkled their noses in her direction and stepped away.

Pi wanted to go check on her and find out what happened, but the instructor on the platform banged her staff against the hard wood, silencing the chattering.

"Attention please. I am Professor Delight," said the instructor, eliciting a few whistles from the crowd. "Yes, please. Do that again and you'll find your balls shriveled to the size of pine nuts for the next year."

At a few locations in the crowd, there was pushing and shoving as students tried to get away from those that had made the catcalls. Pi hoped that Professor Delight was a member of Coterie, but didn't expect it since there were so many halls.

"Congratulations, potential initiates!" said Professor Delight. "You made it here today. Know that only one in a hundred are invited to attempt the Merlins."

She paused, and the space erupted into raucous applause. Pi looked over to share a smile with her sister, but Aurie looked like she was still recovering from whatever had kept her.

"One in a hundred. Which, I might add, is not why we call it the Hundred Halls," said Professor Delight. The crowd chuckled at her comment. She was a skilled presenter. Pi thought she could listen to her all day.

"You made it. You're here. That's the good news. The bad news is that not all of you get to stay. But you knew that coming here. Well, I hate to say it, but the bad news gets worse. The Merlins are not only a chance for you to prove that you can make it in the Halls, but the hall of your dreams has to want you in return. Unfortunately, the number of spots available is the lowest it's been in fifty years. There will be far fewer getting into the Hundred Halls than in the past. I can make it simple for you. Look to the person closest to you on your left. Look to the person closest to you on your right. Only one of you can get in," said Professor Delight, then she paused for effect.

Concerned murmuring rose from the crowd. The professor slammed her staff twice, silencing everyone.

"That's right. Only one in three will get in, maybe less if the halls don't find candidates that fit their requirements. So I hope you cocky ladies and gentlemen didn't put just one hall on your list. I've seen it happen before, where an initiate who scored very high on their Merlins wasn't matched with a hall because they'd only written one name. If that's you, good luck, but I'll probably be seeing you back next year.

"As for the Merlins, know that the number of the trials shall be three, and three shall be the number of the trials. No more, no less," she said, an amused smile on her generous lips.

The scattered laughter around the room told Pi who her fellow nerds were. She was pleased to see the dark-skinned guy in the martial arts uniform chuckling. Blonde ponytail was definitely not amused, and seemed to be glaring at the others around her.

"The trial will test not only your skills, but how you solve the problems given," she said, raising her voice for emphasis.

Professor Delight turned in a slow circle, letting the assembly chew on the information.

"You might wonder why you didn't know this before. Mostly because we're cruel and capricious—that means fickle for you C students—but mostly because we want to know the true you, and that can only happen in times of crisis. What kind of student are you? How do you choose to wield your magic? And have you actually bothered to prepare? You also didn't know this because every student who's ever taken the Merlins has been enchanted not to spill the beans, and because we change them every year."

Professor Delight put a hand on her hip while the other

one held the staff confidently. Pi glanced over to her sister, hoping to get eye contact and share a bit of excitement, but Aurie was busy staring at the blonde girl in the light blue track suit with supreme animosity. When the brief staring match was over, Pi made a gesture with her hands, asking about the girl, but then the professor started up again.

"Some of you have been wondering how you can wield your magic in the Merlins without risking faez madness. For today only, you will link to one of the patrons of the Hundred Halls. With great pleasure"—and she said the word as if it truly gave her pleasure—"I introduce the patron of Arcanium, Semyon Gray."

The polite applause that followed was cut short when what looked like a miniature supernova exploded above Professor Delight's head. Everyone ducked in unison.

When Pi looked back to the center, an attractive dark-skinned older man with short hair and a lightly graying goatee was standing next to Professor Delight. He wore dark robes over his gray suit, and surveyed the room with the sort of intense stare reserved for picking out weapons before a duel.

Patron Gray spoke in a light British accent that had probably been blunted by long years in the States. "Welcome, potential students. You are, without a doubt, nervous but thrilled to be here. You're looking forward to passing your Merlins and joining the ranks of the Halls. I'm sure Professor Delight has filled you with the expectations of success, but I'm here to give you the reality. Magic is dangerous. Not just dangerous, but deadly. The Merlins are not designed for safety. They are designed to test you to the very edge of your ability. Potential students can and have died during the Merlins."

A smattering of people made shocked noises, but Pi wasn't one of them. She and Aurie had talked about it at length. The language was pretty clear in the preregistration about the

Hundred Halls not being responsible for any liability, in any situation, period. There was a lot of legal analysis online that explained the patrons, or anyone associated with the Hundred Halls, could practically murder you and get away with it.

"Those that are having second thoughts about the trials may leave at any time by going to the runed doors, placing both hands on them, and saying 'I am defeated' three times. You will not be missed," he said.

The nervous laughter that had been present during Professor Delight's portion was long gone. Everyone around Pi looked like they'd just found out their dog had died. Pi was actually refreshed by his honesty. Of course, she'd summoned a major demon and pledged her soul to a city faerie in the last twenty-four hours, so maybe she was a little more prepared to hear it.

Once Semyon realized that no one was going to move, he continued, "Now, if no one is going to be brave, I will be your patron for the day. So open yourself to your magic, let it collect into your fist, and hold it up high. When you feel the tingling in your arm, pull the faez back inside of you. Do not let go. It will feel uncomfortable for a little while. Once the link is there, and you will know when it is, you may put your hand down. If I have to perform the link a second time, I will be unhappy. Ready, begin."

Hundreds of fists were immediately thrust into the air, followed by even more. Pi joined them, letting the faez collect until her hand looked coated with glowing honey. Patron Semyon rotated slowly. As he faced her, a tingle formed in her arm. She retracted the raw magic back into herself, and the tingle turned to needles. It felt like she'd fallen asleep on her whole body. But she didn't let go and after about twenty seconds, a wave of pleasure rolled through her, and she let a gasp out.

Pi laughed a little and let her arm fall. The others around her were doing the same. Everyone had the same wide-eyed elation.

"I could do that again," she said to no one in particular.

After Semyon finished a single rotation, there were about fifty fists remaining in the air.

"Those of you who failed to follow directions, please come forward and group right here," he said.

Once they had gathered, he made a few elaborate finger gestures—so fast that Pi couldn't determine the nature of spell—and suddenly a list of names appeared on blank tapestries around the walls. After each name was the same number: -200.

"You see the names on the wall. These are the names of the simpletons before me. For their inattention, or inability to follow directions, they have been docked two hundred points. Every year we get a few, but this might be the most I've ever had, which does not bode well for the rest of you. As you compete in the trials, you will be scored. Your scores will be recorded on the tapestries. If you do not meet the minimum cutoff at the end of each round, you will be released. If your score is too low to reach the upper third, you will be released. And last, the lower your score, the less of a chance you will be selected by your desired hall, or even at all. For example, I regret to inform those of you that wish to join the Arcanium that we only have twenty slots this year. So good luck, and report to the red door on the other side when your name flashes on the tapestry."

As Semyon turned to finish linking to the group of unhappy initiates, Pi ran to her sister and gave her a hug. She ignored her sister's sweaty shirt.

"Are you okay? Are you sick or something? I freaked out when you weren't in here before me," said Pi.

Aurie pressed her palms to her eyes. "I'll explain later. I just need a little—"

But the whole place quieted as a name flashed up on the tapestry nearest the door. Anton Smith. Then the name moved to the next one over, and a new name appeared. Cinder Appleton. As new names appeared, they moved around the room. Then as the novelty began to wear off, Aurie's name appeared.

"Don't worry," said Pi, giving her sister a second hug. "You're going to do great."

Aurie's jaw tightened, her blue eyes flickering with concern.

"I know what you're thinking," began Pi. "You want in Arcanium. Just as bad as I want Coterie. But if you don't get in, you can still be in Aura Healers like Dad."

Her words didn't have the desired effect on her older sister.

"I'll be fine," she said.

But Pi knew Aurie, and she didn't sound it. Pi watched her sister march towards the red door as if it were an execution.

In the quietest voice, she said, "*Dooset daram.*"

11

Twenty slots. There would only be twenty slots out of thousands. The words sounded like doom to her ears.

"Don't worry, Aurie," she told herself on the walk over to the red door. "Mom and Dad always said the important things in life were difficult."

She just hadn't expected this many odds stacked against her. Before this day, Aurie had prepared herself to score the highest amongst all other students. She just hadn't expected to actually need to do that well.

When Aurie reached the red door, she was ushered into a round room. Professor Delight was waiting for her. She was even more beautiful up close, with long lashes over her green eyes. Light perfume tickled Aurie's nose pleasantly. She was appreciative that the professor made no faces at her appearance.

Aurie quickly reviewed the room. A table sat against the wall, with a wand, a tome, and a vial filled with pink liquid on it. On the opposite side of the red door was a stone archway that led into billowing darkness.

"Greetings, Aurelia Silverthorne," said the professor,

giving a perfunctory bow. "Before you is a proving grounds filled with many dangers. You must reach the other side to pass the trial, using the three items on the table. You must use each item once, and only once. The wand fires a force bolt, the spell will repel a ghost, and the potion will allow you to fly for five seconds. You will be judged by the speed of your passage and the method of your success. Gather your items and good luck."

"May I use other magic?" asked Aurie.

The professor quirked a smile. "If you can manage it."

Aurie quickly memorized the spell, took a cleansing breath, and plunged into the proving grounds.

It wasn't as dark past the archway as she expected, but she could only see the area directly before her because a light fog blocked her vision further out. A faint golden light hung in the distance.

Near her, huge stone blocks stood like silent sentinels. They appeared in broken lines. The way forward looked like a maze that had half the walls removed.

She held the wand before her like a sword as she moved forward, stepping carefully and checking around every corner, deciding that caution was better until she understood the trial's dangers.

But after fifty feet or so, she got anxious, wondering when the first challenge would arrive. Aurie moved faster, staying aware of her surroundings, but keeping a steady pace.

A lone howl erupted from somewhere in the maze ahead. The exhaustion she'd felt outside disappeared as her heart doubled its pace. Aurie kept the wand out, ready to blast whatever creature was hunting her.

She moved at an angle, away from the source of the howl, while trying to keep forward. She was so focused on potential attackers, she didn't realize she'd stepped on a trap until she heard the click. A pit opened up beneath her. She fell, a scream ripped out of her lungs.

The impact through her heels scrambled her bones and put a knife into her back. Aurie collapsed to her knees as spasms seized up her muscles.

"Shit," she said. "Barely the first trial and I've already screwed up."

Limping around the bottom of the pit, she took stock of her situation. Getting out was at least twenty feet up, and the walls were impossibly smooth.

Aurie pulled out the flying potion and thought about drinking it. It would be the easy way out. She uncorked it and put it to her lips. Then put the cork back in.

"No. There's got to be a different way out. Stupid pit's probably here to get initiates like me to use up their magic," she said.

Aurie went around the bottom of the pit, probing every inch with her fingers. Nothing.

"Think, Aurie. Think," she said, using her fists against her forehead, hoping to drum out some ideas.

The more powerful magics required focus items or reagents, of which she had none. Aurie took a quick inventory of her clothes, her shoes, even the lint in her pockets and the cork on the vial. Eventually, she settled on her shoes.

There were a lot of magics one could do using the properties of materials in existence. The trick was called transference. A bit of engine oil could make a gun impossible to hold, or a dead leaf could convince a freshly cooked meal to instantly rot. It was one of the few magics that could be performed ad hoc, without serious preparation.

Since she didn't have a knife, Aurie was forced to chew on the edge of her shoe rubber. She tried not to think of all the things she'd ever stepped in. It tasted like petroleum and dirt.

It took her a minute, but she was able to gnaw off a few pieces of rubber.

After putting her shoes back on, Aurie placed the rubber into her hands and blew some faez into them. The trick was to transfer the grabbiness of the rubber without getting one of the other properties like bounciness. She imagined the rubber melting, forming rubbery gloves over her hands.

The rubber chunks crystallized, then broke into dust that clung to her hands. A tingle went through her fingers and palms.

Aurie positioned herself in the corner and placed her hands on the wall. She was able to grip it as if it were one of those climbing walls at the gym.

It took a few false starts, but eventually she was able to make her way up the wall and out of the pit.

Feeling behind, Aurie got moving right away, pulling out her wand again. This time, she kept an eye on the floor, looking for telltale cracks that might indicate a pit.

Something moved at the corner of her vision. It was moving low and quick. Aurie spun and almost fired a force bolt. She pulled back at the last moment when she realized it was only a house cat.

"What are you doing here?" she asked, crouching down to pet the approaching orange tabby.

Mrrrwwwooeerr, said the cat with its tail waving lazily behind it.

Suddenly suspicious, Aurie jumped back. "Wait. What the hell is a cat doing in here? Stay back."

The cat stopped as if it understood English.

"Shoo," said Aurie, waving at the cat. "As far as I know you're a shapeshifter who's going to attack me when I'm not paying attention."

The cat stretched its lips in a very human smile before

scampering off in the direction that it'd come.

Aurie looked at her wand. "Damn thing almost got me to use this."

As she said the words, she realized that intent. They wanted to see how potential initiates would react. An unimaginative one would have fired their bolt, or had to use the flying potion to get out of the pit.

The line of thought made her realize that the items didn't have to be used as advertised. To keep from accidentally firing the wand, she shoved it into her back pocket.

Aurie resumed her journey through the maze, using the faint golden light in the distance as her destination. When she stopped encountering stone blocks, Aurie grew more alert, expecting a new challenge.

Two paths led up a rise. Aurie took the left one. It only went a short ways before descending into a hollow filled with movement. At first she thought it was more mist, but the mist had distinct edges and wore clothing. They were spectral beings—ghosts—and they floated in and out of the trees.

On the other side of the hollow was a red door. Aurie took a few steps into the hollow. The ghosts turned their incorporeal heads towards her and started howling. Aurie scrambled back up the hill so fast she fell once.

"Fine," she muttered and checked the right-hand path, finding a separate hollow ringed by a U-shaped pond. On the piece of land at the center of the still waters was a pair of menacing hounds with crimson eyes. Like the left-hand path, a red door waited on the other side.

She crept down to the edge. "Hey, little doggies. What would it take for you to let me pass?"

Neither of them growled, which she took as a good sign. Aurie took one step forward, then another. She was ten feet away from the nearest when it opened its furnace-like mouth and belched flame in her direction.

The fire caught the frayed edges of her jeans on fire. Aurie ran back around the pond and shoved her shoe into the water. Hundreds of fish with big mouths full of teeth sped towards her invading shoe. Aurie fell back onto the edge before the piranha could reach her.

"Great. Ghosts on one side. Hellhounds and piranha on the other," she said.

After climbing back to the top of the hill, Aurie put three fingers out and talked herself through the problem, tapping on each finger as she reviewed the magical items she'd been given.

"The potion might get me across, but five seconds seems too short. The spell could repel one ghost, maybe two, but it's not powerful enough to defeat a group of them, while the force bolt could only take out one hellhound, not two," she said.

She stared at the hounds until the mental clock in her head spurred her to action.

"What else do I have to work with?" she asked aloud. "On this path there's a pond. On the other one there are trees. What am I going to do? Poke one with a pointy stick or throw some water on it?"

One of the hounds bayed, and the sound went right through her midsection.

"Hellhounds are guardians of graveyards," she muttered, shaking her head. "Ghosts, well those ghosts could be anything."

She paced back and forth while the hounds, who were aware of her, matched her movements.

She snapped her fingers. "That's it." And ran down to the edge of the pond on the safe side.

The water was perfectly smooth. Inside the Proving Grounds there was no wind or vibration. A hellhound stared at her from across the narrow pond. She could feel its hot breath on her face.

"You know if you'd just drink some water, you might cool off that heat in your belly," she told it.

The hellhound growled.

"Fine, have it your way," she said, then focused on the water.

The surface was mirror smooth. Her reflection looked back up at her from the water. Aurie focused her faez to give power to the words she was about to utter. Catoptromancy, the magic of mirrors, only worked if you had sufficient magic to lend to the spirit to come over.

"Bloody Mary."

A ripple formed on the water. The hellhound growled again, low and dangerous.

"Bloody Mary."

Above her, a shape began to take form, like reddish mist being sucked into a vent.

"Bloody Mary."

The shape turned into a veiled woman in a white dress, blood splattered across her. A bloody dagger was held in her fist. Aurie rolled backwards as the apparition dove down to attack.

Bloody Mary's dagger passed by Aurie's shoulder. The ghost reoriented herself when she realized she'd missed. Before the ghost could close the distance, Aurie cast the spell she'd memorized at the entrance.

The words made Bloody Mary recoil as if acid had been thrown on her. Then the apparition turned and fled across the water, right into the hellhound. The murderous ghost set upon the grim beast, stabbing it with her dagger.

The battle drew the attention of the second hellhound, who spat flame upon the ghost. The first hound cried out with pitiful whines.

Aurie ran around the water's edge. She hesitated at the exit because the battle between Bloody Mary and the two hellhounds was only ten feet away. If any one of them noticed her, they could catch her and tear her apart before she could reach the door.

She hugged the other edge, staying as far away as possible. Once she'd crossed some invisible line, her feet refused to move slowly. Aurie fled towards the red door, feeling like a hellhound was going to bite her ankle from behind the whole time.

After passing through, she slammed the door shut and leaned against it until the shaking in her limbs stopped. The next area was pitch-black.

Aurie pressed her earrings, bringing warm light into existence. She stood in a wide hallway. The walls looked like a hole had been cut from an enormous tree and polished until they were smooth. Aurie rubbed her fingers across the wood as she walked, detecting a bit of warmth emanating from it.

Further down, she heard faint hissing, like the exhalation of a great beast. The air was damp. She kept expecting the hallway to open up into a vast swamp in which a great dragon slept, nestled in the jungle.

What she found instead confused her. The hissing came from one corner of a large room. A brass pipe spat steam into the air. At the opposite corner was a hunk of granite shaped like an egg. In the other corners were a hooded chicken in a cage and a bicycle frame without the tires, seat, or handlebars.

The only thing she clearly understood was the plate at the center of the room and the red door on the far side. An ancient version of eldritch runes encircled the five-foot-diameter plate, explaining that the door would open when one ton of material was placed on it.

The untold hours spent memorizing obscure written languages finally had paid off, making her smile. But her elation quickly evaporated when she remembered that Pi had never gotten around to it. Her sister preferred the flashier and riskier magics, thinking there was always a shortcut to get what she wanted. Aurie didn't want to be proven right, but she worried that Pi was going to be stymied by this task.

Of course, she reminded herself, reading the runes and solving the puzzle were two entirely different things. Aurie pulled the wand out of her pocket. The force bolt might create one ton of pressure, but the runes seemed to indicate that the door would only stay open if the material remained on the plate.

Once again, Aurie was left pacing and worrying that she was going too slow. She examined each corner more closely. The chicken seemed exactly as expected. She tapped on the cage to get a reaction, but it was asleep from the hood.

Aurie picked up the granite egg. Clearly it didn't weigh enough to depress the plate. The bicycle frame offered no clues to how it could be used. The outside was painted bright red, but the inside of the tubes flaked with rust.

Lastly, she examined the steam tube. Unlike the other corners, she had an immediate reaction to her investigation. When she cautiously placed her hand over the exhaling steam, the room shrunk around her. Within seconds, her back was against the ceiling.

Aurie backed out of the corner, bumping her head in the process.

"Owww," she said, rubbing it.

Suddenly much larger, and heavier, than she was before, Aurie headed towards the plate, one ponderous step at a time. She felt like a giant in a child's room. The plate groaned beneath her weight, but did not open the red door.

She realized that even if it had opened the door, it wouldn't have helped her. The moment she stepped off, the door would close again. She needed a way to hold it down. The granite egg came to mind, but the sudden increase in weight would keep her from moving it to the plate.

After a minute, she returned to her original size. The sudden shrinking gave her vertigo, which she ignored as best she could as she threw herself into the problem.

With a potential solution in mind, Aurie started experimenting. She tried using the bicycle frame to blow the steam over to the granite egg, which she'd left on the plate, but when the frame was exposed to the magical steam, it became too heavy to hold and fell over, and the steam came nowhere near the egg. It seemed the enlarging steam had to directly interact with an item to change it.

When she exposed the chicken to the steam, she spent a horror-filled minute avoiding the clawed talons of the massive creature as it stumbled around the room with the hood still on its head. It was possible the chicken could weigh one ton, but she didn't know how to get it onto the plate and keep it there.

Aurie was convinced the best method was to leave the egg on the plate and somehow get the steam over to it, but she didn't know how to accomplish the task.

Then an answer hit her smack in the face. Aurie pulled out the flying potion and uncorked the vial. It was something she should have remembered from her time in the hospital with Emily. Magical flight changed one's molecular structure to make them lighter than air, filling them with tiny helium bubbles.

The downside was that those bubbles made them vulnerable to particulates like dust or perfume. For Emily, it was dangerous over time, but for a few seconds, Aurie decided it wouldn't be too terrible.

With the granite egg sitting on the plate, Aurie chugged the potion. It tasted like that pink bubble gum that made your jaw hurt. Then as she felt herself lift off her feet, she shoved her hand into the steam. The effect was immediate. Aurie ballooned against the ceiling, but she kept her arm in the steam.

With the flying potion turning her body to one big sponge, Aurie absorbed the steam for the five seconds. Once it was finished, she fell against the floor, which shocked her knees. Before the steam could start escaping, she ran over to the granite egg and collapsed around it, hugging it to her chest.

The steam leaving her body was painful. It felt like she had constipation in every limb.

But as the steam hit the granite egg, it grew to an enormous size. Aurie slid off it before it crushed her against the ceiling. The red door opened as soon as her feet touched the ground.

Aurie had to wait until she shrunk to go through the door, but once she did, she breathed a sigh of relief that she'd successfully navigated the puzzle.

Her running shoes crunched on the snow. It was a field of white heading down to a frozen pond. A door stood on the other side. Aurie didn't have long to wonder about the challenge before the surface of the ice broke and cracked. A massive head formed, then shoulders and arms and legs. After a few moments, a giant made of ice was kneeling on the frozen lake. When it climbed to its feet, it was at least thirty feet tall. The ice beneath the giant reformed to perfect smoothness.

Standing about twenty feet from the edge of the frozen pond, Aurie pulled out the wand and said, "I'm going to guess that this isn't even going to scratch you, big fella."

The ice giant roared in response, sending a flurry of snow from its cavernous mouth.

Aurie spied some objects at the edge of the pond. Sitting

in the snow were a sword and shield. She picked them up and made a few tentative swings with the sword. She wasn't sure she could break an icicle, let alone an ice giant, while moving on a slippery surface, but after a few minutes, she didn't have any better ideas.

With sword and shield in either hand, Aurie took mincing steps towards the ice giant. The creature waited until she was about halfway across before charging her. The ice giant was at least three times her size.

It tried to smash her on the first pass. Aurie threw herself to the side, narrowly avoiding being crushed. She got up just in time to block the second blow with the shield. The impact threw her back across the ice and slammed her into the icy ledge that went around the pond.

Aurie spit out a little blood. Her lip was cut. She moved back up the hill before the ice giant could close the distance. She'd dropped the sword when it hit her. The giant picked it up like a toothpick and launched it into the woods behind the door.

Then it went back to its original position, and seemed to dare her to try again.

After a few minutes she came up with a plan. A stupid plan, but a plan nonetheless.

As soon as she stepped back onto the ice, the giant moved to attack. She set the shield on the frozen pond, facedown, and sat inside the concave surface. She held the wand before her, watching the ice giant as it picked up speed. The ice shook with each step.

"If this doesn't work, they're going to be scraping me off the ice with a Zamboni," she said.

Aurie waited until the ice giant was almost upon her. It raised its massive hands into the air. When it brought its arms down to smash her, she rotated herself to face the short rock ledge that ringed the pond, stiffened her arms, and fired the force bolt.

The reaction threw her backwards, beneath the giant's arms as it smashed the ice where she'd been only moments before. She flew across the frozen pond on her shield. The confused ice giant searched around its feet, trying to figure out where she'd gone.

After impacting the snow on the other side, Aurie climbed to her feet and went through the third door, which led back into the entrance room.

A triumphant gong signaled completion of the trial. Aurie nearly collapsed from exhaustion, but managed to gather enough energy to go back.

Cautiously, she went through the door back into the main area. It was as before: the central space was filled with hundreds of initiates, and the tapestries announced the names of those summoned to the Proving Grounds. But as Aurie entered, her name flashed up on the tapestry with a score in the thousands. Then the scoreboard appeared and her name went at the very top, above the students who'd received the penalty. She was the first to finish.

12

While Aurie went in search of her sister, the other initiates came up and congratulated her on the score. Aurie was confused about how they knew it was her, until she realized they were casting a simple identification spell on the H-shaped pin that she'd been given at registration.

It was another twenty minutes before the next competitor came out of the red door. A short stocky kid stumbled out looking like he'd survived a piranha attack. His score was within hundreds of her score, and his name went second beneath hers.

As time went on, more names appeared. Sometimes scores went on the tapestry without an initiate coming out of the door. Usually the score was much lower, in the hundreds, indicating they hadn't finished the Proving Grounds.

A few hours after Aurie had finished, Pi strode out confidently, despite being in her bra and panties. Aurie cheered when she saw her sister's score at third place, then ran over to greet her.

"I was so worried you were going to have trouble at the second challenge due to the eldritch runes," said Aurie, hugging her younger sister, partially because she was glad to see her, and to cover her up from the nearby stares.

A few halfhearted catcalls echoed in the vast hall—as the originators probably remembered Professor Delight's warning from earlier.

Pi pinched Aurie before returning the squeeze. "You never trust me to figure things out myself. I used a divining spell from materials I collected along the way."

Aurie led her sister to the dormitorium while they waited for the first day of competition to finish. Tapestries hung on the dorm walls, so they could see if anyone bested them.

As Aurie had been one of the first to arrive, she'd grabbed a corner bunk bed. The beds were enchanted for quiet, so they didn't have to bother with whispering. After Pi grabbed a shower, and her clothes were returned to her, they shared stories of their trial.

Pi had circumvented the stone maze by flying onto the blocks, then moving across the top of them, avoiding the traps and distractions. Then she'd walked through the ghosts, because all but one were benign, and used the spell on the only apparition that could harm her. In the steam room, after divining what the runes said, she enlarged the chicken with the steam, then killed it with the force bolt when it crossed the plate. The last challenge took the longest since she was out of items. Eventually she tricked the ice giant by creating a girl out of snow and clothing it in her outfit. The ice giant hadn't been enchanted with enough brains to determine the difference between them, and she snuck by while it was pulverizing the snow-girl.

By the end of the first day, Aurie remained at the top of the scoreboard and Pi had fallen down to fifth place. It was higher than either of them had dreamed. A third of the initiates hadn't met the minimum score and were dismissed. There were even a dozen or so that dismissed themselves, looking shaken by the trials. The only negative mark to the first day was that Violet Cardwell's name sat at number six.

That night, Aurie slept like the dead, feeling confident about her chances.

The next morning they assembled in the main room, and Professor Delight spoke to the group.

"Congratulations on making it to the second day. The first day was a test of your individual skills. Many of you passed with flying colors. Others struggled even to survive."

Unlike the previous day, Professor Delight had a serious cast to her expression, making Aurie wonder if someone had died the first day. Aurie reached out and squeezed her sister's hand.

"In our complex world, it's not enough to be a great mage. There's only so much you can accomplish on your own. Our founder, Invictus, created the one hundred halls because there are one hundred ways to solve a problem, and some problems need the talents of more than one hall.

"In this next challenge you will be paired with another initiate. Together, you will battle a third-year Hall member in a head-to-head match. You and your partner will receive items that will mimic at least two of the skills you will learn in the Hall you placed at the top of your list. The object of the match is to disable your opponent before they disable you. You will be judged by the way you use your chosen magics, but most importantly, the quality of your teamwork. Do not disappoint.

"You will find your partner by your pin. Know that some great friendships and even marriages have begun because of this trial. Once I give the signal, a beam of light extending from the pin will point you in the right direction."

Professor Delight paused, giving everyone a chance to absorb the information.

Pi whispered under her breath, "Didn't Mom and Dad say they met in the trials? Do you think it was like this?"

"I wouldn't be surprised," said Aurie.

The heavyset professor raised her hand. After a brief gesture, a wave of light traveled outward, sparking the pins to life.

The beam of light shooting from Aurie's chest went across the auditorium.

"Bummer, sis. I was hoping we'd be partners," said Pi, then she set off in a different direction.

The crowd of initiates were laughing as they dodged around each other. Aurie was buoyed by the general mood. It felt like a treasure hunt. She hoped she got a good partner.

Suddenly the crowd parted, and her beam of light hit the guy in the martial arts uniform right in the chest. She blushed, feeling heat rise all the way to the top of her head. His beam matched hers, hitting her right in the chest.

He cocked a smile in her direction, raising an eyebrow as he rested his hands on his black belt. The grin was as much a dare as it was an invitation.

Aurie was about to give him her best sassy look, the one she reserved for the cute, but cocky guys she always seemed to meet in every new school, when the beam of light veered off his chest.

It only took one look at the blonde head of hair coming around him for her chest to turn to ice. When Violet Cardwell's gaze followed the beam of light to its destination, her lips squeezed white.

The martial arts guy gave a what-do-you-do shrug and then moved off to find his partner. He winked as he left, but Aurie was too busy staring down Violet to notice. Neither girl moved.

Eventually, Aurie realized that her desire to pass the trials was more important than petty revenge.

She blew out a steadying breath and approached Violet, who had crossed her arms in a standoffish way.

"You probably made this happen on purpose," said Violet, her tone so sharp she could cut glass.

"Look. Neither of us is happy about this partnership, but if we want to pass the trials, we're going to have to work together," said Aurie.

"You tried to kill me at the hospital," said Violet.

Mention of killing and the hospital brought back a surge of anger at the thought of Emily's safety. Aurie put her hands behind her back and dug her fingernails into her palm so she wouldn't hit the blonde twit.

"Let's just call it a misunderstanding," said Aurie. "And you got your revenge when you kept me off the gondola. I came this close to not making the trials, and it's my twentieth birthday in a week."

The realization of what that prank had nearly caused seemed to soften Violet's expression. Not completely, but enough that Aurie thought they might be able to work together.

"What's your chosen hall?" asked Aurie, hoping to get them thinking about strategy and tactics rather than animosity.

"The Order of Honorable Alchemists," said Violet without a trace of irony about the honorable part.

Aurie declined to point it out, and said, "Arcanium."

"Arcanium?" asked Violet in disgust. "You're nothing but a bunch of book nerds."

Aurie feigned a sneeze and looked around at the other pairs. Everyone seemed to be getting along quite well. She forced a smile to her lips.

"I'm sure—"

But her words ended when the tapestries flashed, and pairs of names started appearing, then circled around the room. On the first day, Aurie had wanted a later trial so she could rest. Today, she wanted the earliest match possible so she wouldn't have to make small talk with Violet while they waited.

When new names stopped appearing, Aurie did her best to hide her disappointment behind a polite smile. Violet declined that grace, instead letting out a jet of disgusted air and rolling her eyes.

"We can use the time to talk strategy," said Aurie.

"There's nothing to talk about until we get our hall items and find out our opponent," she said.

Aurie opened her mouth to refute that idea, but Violet had already pulled out her smartphone and was talking within seconds of it reaching her ear. She put her back to Aurie and started complaining about the pairing immediately.

Aurie stuck her tongue out at Violet's back, before glancing around to see who her sister had for a partner. Pi stood next to a lanky guy with a shock of red hair. Neither of them knew what to do with their hands while they were talking to each other. Other pairs were busily discussing their strengths and weaknesses, even going so far as to draw invisible maps on the floor with their fingers.

The afternoon crawled to a near stop while Aurie waited for the second trial. Pairs of initiates went through the red door, and higher scores filled the tapestries, knocking both Aurie and Violet off the leaderboard. Unlike the first day, no one came back out. When Pi went in, Aurie gave her a parting cheer. Ten minutes later, her name went to the top of the tapestry.

It wasn't until the end of the day that they were called. The auditorium was mostly empty, with a few dozen pairs milling about the space, talk of strategy long since overtaken by boredom. Pi's name had fallen to fifth place, but it put her sister into a good position to claim the hall of her choice at the end of the trials.

Violet put the phone away right as they reached the red door. A blue-robed attendant handed them their hall items. Violet was given two vials containing fizzy silver and green liquids, respectively.

When the attendant handed Aurie a quill, and nothing else, she was confused.

"Shouldn't I get a second item?" asked Aurie.

The attendant looked around nervously. "That's all there was," he said. "Read the tag to find out what they do."

Violet read hers out loud: "Super speed and dragon skin. Awesome. What's yours? A red pen for marking up grammar?"

"Truth," said Aurie, flipping the tag back and forth to find additional information, but only the one word was written on the tag. Violet's tags had a line or two of description, despite the names making it obvious what they did.

"What does that do?" asked Violet, looking over Aurie's shoulder.

"I...I know what Truth does. It's one of the most powerful magics if you know how to use it, but I don't understand how this quill is supposed to work." Aurie glanced up to see the confusion on Violet's face. "Truth is kind of like making things stronger. Imagine walking across a beam four inches above the floor. Easy, right? Now imagine walking across that beam four hundred feet above the floor."

"That makes no sense. You sound like one of those self-improvement videos," said Violet.

The conversation was cut short when the attendant ushered them into the next room. The battle arena was a hundred-by-hundred-meter room with dozens of obstacles spread about the floor. The obstacles looked like a giant box of kid's blocks had been dumped into the room. Before the attendant left he explained that their opponent was from the Protector's Hall.

A deep voice from somewhere in the arena called out, "Come and get me, girls."

The urge to head into the center of the arena made Aurie take a step forward. She shook off the enchantment. Violet looked like she was recovering as well.

"Why couldn't we have been paired against a different hall?" said Violet. "Like those theater freaks. You know what the Protectors can do, right?"

"Voice of Command," said Aurie. "He can freeze you in place, but it only works from up close. So we'd better keep our distance."

Violet's forehead knotted with thought, prompting Aurie to wonder if she knew anything about the other halls. Just in case, Aurie added, "That voice thing works better on crowds. As long as we stay apart, it won't be effective. Otherwise, protectors are just bullies. Good with their fists and hell on intimidation."

"I knew that," said Violet. "And I know *just* the plan. Since you're completely useless, I'll drink my potions, we'll move on him together, and I'll take him out in hand-to-hand combat. The dragon skin will keep him from hurting me."

"Didn't you hear me? We can't take him up close. That's where they get their power. They're trained to take down bad guys, or pacify large crowds. We have to split up, and stay away, and look for a way to take him down," said Aurie.

"And what does your quill have to offer?" asked Violet.

"I don't know," said Aurie, a little too forcefully. "The damn tag was missing. But I'll figure something out."

"Well, I heard your plan, but I disagree. You should come with me. Protect my back. At the very least, he won't know who to defend against. A few hits with super speed and he'll be laid out," she said.

Before Aurie could argue, Violet chugged her potions, one after the other. The thick green potion turned her skin to dark green scales. Aurie thought she looked like a human lizard and expected a split tongue to snake out of her mouth. The second potion seemed to make her vibrate like a struck tuning fork.

Violet motioned at triple speed. "Follow me."

"Wait," said Aurie, not wanting to get caught by the Protector's mez or get up close.

Violet sped away, quickly disappearing behind a large block with an arch cut out the middle.

"Shit," said Aurie, and loped off after her.

A few seconds later, Violet screamed. The deep voice of the third-year Protector saying "Don't move" quickly followed.

"Double shit," said Aurie, and stared at her quill. "What the hell am I supposed to do with you?"

His voice carried over the blocks. "Come out, come out, wherever you are. I got your friend over here. If you give yourself up quickly, I won't bruise your face too bad."

Aurie knew better than to answer. He was trying to figure out where she was located.

Aurie snuck through the blocks, keeping a roving eye. Eventually, she came to a center area. She could see Violet on her knees, face wracked with effort, trying to break through the enchantment, but not the protector.

When she didn't see him, Aurie decided that he'd gone looking for her. She ran into the center to free Violet. Aurie started probing her with faez, trying to understand the magical compulsion, when Violet's eyes shifted to the right.

It was enough warning. Aurie dove out of the way just as a fist flew past her head. She broke into a sprint, dodging around the blocks until she reached the outer edge of the arena.

Breath heaving in her chest, Aurie looked around. Her opponent hadn't followed her because he needed to stay near to keep the enchantment. She felt like an idiot for not remembering that before, especially after mentally admonishing Violet for the same thing.

Aurie pulled out the quill. The obvious thing was to draw or write something. But what? Truth magic, or verumancy, used the energy of what was already there.

She wrote the word FRAGILE on the rectangular block next to her, focusing her faez as she wrote the word. Then she kicked the block. A crack went up the center, splitting the block in two. The larger half nearly crashed on top of her. Aurie dove out of the way just in time.

A voice came from the center of the arena. "Quit screwing around and come fight me."

Aurie ignored him and placed the tip of the quill against the inside of her forearm. The ink was cold. She wrote the word STRONG in big, bold letters while she let her faez flow into the quill. When she lifted the quill, the ink glistened like an oil slick.

After a few experimental flexes, she pushed the arched block next to her. To her surprise, it jumped an inch.

"That's promising," she said. "Sort of."

She didn't think she'd be able to make herself invisible or take flight, since those were things she couldn't naturally do. The truth had to be something plausible.

Aurie held out the quill and focused her faez. This time she wrote the word LIGHT on the block next to her. Using her strong arm, she pushed the block a good five feet so it pressed against another block.

The protector called out from the center of the arena. "You know they'll fail you if you just hide. No pain, no gain."

But you know, I've been doing this all day. I'm ready for a bar and a burner." He paused. "Though I am enjoying having little miss blondie on her knees here."

A quiet rage filled Aurie. She might have made an enemy of Violet, but she wasn't going to let him treat her like that. Aurie moved towards the center.

Looking through the gaps between the blocks, Aurie was able to find him. He had cut off sleeves and a thick neck.

Violet was on her knees next to him, clearly fighting the enchantment from his voice. Though she was covered in green scales, the ones under her right eye were purple with bruises.

He'd picked a good spot. Defensible. Clear sight lines. There was no way she could sneak up on him, and he was her superior in close combat.

Aurie wrote LIGHT on the nearest block, and shoved it towards the center. Then she moved to the next one and did the same.

"Stop moving the stupid blocks and come out and fight me. Are you afraid, little girl?" he called out.

Under her breath, she whispered, "No. Are you, Johnny?"

She didn't know if that was his name, but if asshole's had a name and a type, they'd be called Johnny.

She circled the arena, slowly closing him in. A few times Johnny looked like he wanted to move out and engage her, but each time he realized that doing so would free Violet.

When she was finished, she'd created a wall of blocks around him, except for three openings. He was forced to keep circling, fearing her attack from one of the other two.

Johnny grabbed Violet's hair, eliciting a scream. "You'd better hurry up, or I'm going to do a number on her face."

Aurie crept near an opening. It took her a moment to rotate the word in her head, but eventually she wrote FAR on her throat.

Imagining her voice on the other side, Aurie said in a singsong voice, "Warriors, come out and plaaayyyy."

As Johnny moved to defend the location her voice had come from, Aurie ran out and, using her magically strong arm, punched him in the head. He started to fall to his knees, but stopped himself halfway. She hadn't hit hard enough. He side-kicked her in the gut, throwing her backwards.

She landed on her back, knocking the air from her lungs. The quill had broken in half. She felt the magical strength fade.

Johnny stood over her, blood running from his bottom lip, which hung open awkwardly as if he were in a lot of pain. His face was bright red. His hands were fists at his side.

"I think you broke my jaw," he said, muffled. "I'm going to do a lot worse to you."

Johnny raised his fist, then crumpled forward, collapsing to his knees. Violet had been behind him. She'd kicked him right between the legs. A triumphant gong signaled their victory as Johnny moaned from the fetal position.

"Oh, thank you," Aurie said, holding her hand out so Violet could help her up.

"You let him do that to me," said Violet, and she stalked away.

Sighing, Aurie followed her out and returned to the dormitories to find her score was nowhere near the top. Pi found her, hugged her, and asked, "What happened? Did you lose the match?"

"No," said Aurie, bewildered. "Our strategy, or lack thereof, was a disaster, but we won. I don't understand why my score was so low."

A blue-robed attendant was walking by and overheard her. "You get scored on teamwork just as much as how you played the match."

"But what if my partner didn't want to work with me?" asked Aurie.

"Then you should have done a better job following her lead," said the attendant, before walking off.

"Great," said Aurie, staring at her score in the middle of the pack. "If I don't score near the top on the last day, I might not get in Arcanium."

13

The next morning in the auditorium, Aurie marveled at how few initiates there were compared to the first day. It appeared more had left during the night. And of those that had stayed, nearly all had visible injuries. The healers on staff had been busy making rounds in the dorms during the night.

The other initiates seemed to notice as well. There was a lot of glancing around and remarking at the emptiness of the room. It flushed Aurie with both pride and concern.

Professor Delight took the center stage once again. She wore a skintight blue bodysuit with the Hundred Halls "double H" emblem on the front that accentuated her generous frame. A businesslike braid hung over her shoulder. Many of the guys, and a few of the girls, leaned forward.

Professor Delight spoke in her melodic voice, amplified by magic. "You've made it to the third and final day. Congratulations."

Muted applause followed. Everyone had a concerned expression—except for Violet, which bothered Aurie. The blonde initiate looked entirely too pleased, as if she already knew she'd passed.

"The third trial is sometimes considered the hardest. It can also be the most dangerous because the interaction of so many students is hard to plan for," said the professor.

Violet was nodding along like she already knew this part. Aurie's stomach started aching.

"So this is your warning. If you thought the first two trials were difficult, or dangerous, this one will be much worse. Wielding magic is not for the faint of heart. Sometimes when things go wrong, the best option you can hope for is a quick death. So if you're not willing to expose yourself to grave danger, then leave now, because once you pass through the red door, you won't have another chance to leave."

The professor paused, holding her hands in front of her and glancing around the crowd. A gasp went up as a beefy-looking guy with a buzz cut went over to the entrance doors, placed his hands against them, and after a furtive glance at the crowd watching him, said, "I am defeated. I am defeated. I am defeated."

After he left, another three initiates followed him out. When no one else moved, Professor Delight started again.

"Only four. Good." She offered a grim nod to the assembled initiates. "The third trial is a group trial. Which means all of you will be competing at the same time. After I'm finished explaining, everyone will file through the red door. You will be given a pair of bracelets that you will place on your wrists, and a wand. The bracelets will allow you the power of flight in the arena. Just to warn you, the bracelets, and all the other items, are linked to the Spire and will not function outside of the trial areas. Unfortunately, that's a lesson that goes unheeded, year after year, by a select, and stupid, few.

"The trial will be a free-for-all. Everyone for themselves. There are no points adjusted by the observing judges. Your score is based on how many kills you make and how long you last in the arena. The wand fires a bolt that will feel like you've been stung by a giant wasp. If you're hit three times, you're out of the game. But I must warn you that the other initiates aren't the only dangers in the game. Good luck, and you may proceed to the red door."

As soon as they started moving, Aurie caught Violet's I've-got-you-now glance. A group of initiates formed around Violet, who gave them each a knowing nod as they arrived. Other initiates were quickly forming alliances as they walked.

Aurie spoke to her sister. "Violet must have known what the final contest was going to be. She's going to take me out first. You should group up with others, Pi. I don't want you to get knocked out because of me."

"No way," said Pi, punching her sister in the arm. "I'm not leaving you to that hyena. Let's find some allies."

Aurie tried to make eye contact with the girl next to her. She wore glasses and had her hair in a ponytail. She looked like the kind of girl that shared Aurie's love of books. As soon as the girl noticed Aurie, her eyes went wide and she quickly moved away.

Behind her, Pi was speaking to the red-haired guy she'd partnered with in the second trial. He was shaking his head.

When she came back, Pi said, "Your friend was busy last night. She warned everyone else that if they joined up with us, they'd be taken out next. And she promised those that joined her team would have a glowing article written about them in the *Herald of the Halls*."

"I'm sorry, Pi."

"Don't worry about me. I can come back next year," she said. "We need to get you into the Halls since this is your only chance."

They received their bracelets and wands past the red door. The space was massive, larger than the auditorium, and went up just as high. Hundreds of obstacles hung above their heads like a floating modern art installation.

She grabbed her sister and moved towards the far corner. "Let's at least put some distance between us and them for when this starts."

They took position behind a concave wall that looked like a spoon was sticking from the wall.

Pi pointed to squares on the six walls. There were about a half dozen on each side.

"What do you think those are?" she asked.

"I think we should stay away from them," said Aurie. "Professor Delight warned that the other students wouldn't be the only danger."

Violet and her gang had collected to the right side. There were twelve initiates, including the guy in the martial arts uniform, which was disappointing for more than the obvious reasons.

No one dared to camp near Violet's group for fear of getting caught in the crossfire, or being the next targets.

Aurie grabbed her sister by the shoulders. "We're going to do this, Pi. At the end of this, we're going to be the last two standing."

"I'm totally going to fire this wand right into your back if it's just us two at the end," said Pi, winking.

They shared a brief laugh. A countdown started.

Aurie took a quick glance around. She spied a floating sphere with holes in it near the top of the arena.

"See that up there," she told Pi. "As soon as we can, fly up there."

"But it's right next to one of those squares on the wall," said Pi.

"Just trust me," said Aurie.

The starting gong hadn't finished reverberating before

Aurie and her sister were flying up towards the holey sphere. Wand blasts zipped past as Violet's gang tried to shoot them out of the sky.

Aurie was almost to the sphere when she was hit in the back. The pain made her lose control as her body seized up. Pi sensed Aurie's immobility and grabbed her arm, dragging her the final distance into the sphere. They threw themselves against the inner wall, protected from the hailstorm of wand blasts.

"That wasn't as bad as I thought it'd be," said Aurie, rubbing her back.

"Look." Pi was pointing at her arm. There were three hearts on the inside of her wrist. The third one was empty.

Violet's gang was flying upwards, firing their wands as they went. The rest of the battle was on the bottom floor, as most of the initiates had stayed below.

Aurie fired a few shots through the hole, not really trying to hit anyone, but to slow them down.

Pi fired her wand, then threw herself back into the sphere. She said, "I'm not afraid of heights, but this is ridiculous. We must be three hundred feet up."

"Don't think about it. Just keep firing," she said.

Their attackers had slowed down due to the suppressive fire, but Aurie didn't think it would be long until they were upon them. She wasn't sure how two were going to win against twelve, especially when they hadn't hit even one of them yet. Every time she leaned out to fire, three bolts came flying her way.

Pi screamed and fell back into the sphere holding her arm. She'd been hit. The third little heart on her wrist was empty.

Violet's gang was nestled in the obstacles directly below them. Aurie could see the martial arts guy hiding behind a floating pyramid to her right.

"Should we make a run for it?" asked Pi through gritted teeth.

Right after, a light tone rang into the arena. The wand fire slowed as everyone glanced around.

When the squares on the walls slid open, six-legged insects the size of a small dog came flowing out like a chittering madness. Each side had released a different color of insect. The initiates closest to the holes were overrun before they could take to the air. When those initiates were knocked out of the game, a protective white cocoon formed around them, to keep them from further attacks.

Everyone still on the ground flew upward as fast as they could. It looked like a host of grasshoppers had taken to the sky. Those initiates above them fired into the fleeing ranks. Dozens of initiates were knocked out of the game in the ensuing chaos.

From below them, Violet cried, "Ignore the insects, keep firing. We've got them."

The assault on the sphere continued, though less voraciously, as her gang had to worry about the initiates flying upward. Aurie used the opportunity to catch one of the pale Scandinavian twins in the face with a wand blast.

On the walls, the insects had spread out. Nearest her position, they had orange chitins. Aurie watched as a large specimen leapt from the wall to an oddly shaped block. Other insects followed.

Aurie fired her wand at an insect on the wall. The wand blast turned it to dust.

She leaned out to fire again, and she got hit in the side. Violet had moved to a flanking position. She was crouched on a block about thirty feet away. Aurie curled into a ball for a few seconds before resuming the fight with gritted teeth. She was one hit from being knocked out. There were still far too many initiates left in the arena.

"We have to get out of here," said Aurie. "They've got us surrounded."

Pi ducked a blast, and nodded.

Other insects were making tentative leaps to floating blocks, distracting Violet's gang as they had to clear them off before refocusing.

Pi leapt from the inner wall and flew against the other side, knocking the sphere through the air a few feet.

"They move!" said Aurie. "You're a genius, sis."

"About time you noticed," said Pi.

Aurie flew through the middle of the sphere as fast as she could. She hit the inner wall. It felt like she'd dislocated her shoulder, but it knocked the sphere a good twenty feet in the opposite direction of Violet.

A wand blast nearly took Aurie's head off. She fired back, hitting the cute initiate in the martial arts uniform lurking near the wall. An insect came around the block he was hiding on and leapt on him. Both initiate and insect went careening into the center of the arena, spinning. Multiple wand blasts hit both insect and initiate, knocking them both out of the game.

Their new position put them away from Violet's gang, which had lost a few members by this time, but they were close enough to the wall that the six-legged insects were leaping towards their position. Aurie spent more time keeping them away.

Something impacted the outside of the sphere. It suddenly flew towards the wall, right into a knot of insects making a bridge.

"Get out. Get out," screamed Aurie, dragging her sister through a hole. They escaped out the side and flew towards a cluster of smaller blocks before the sphere impacted with the insects. The crunch of carapaces echoed through the massive chamber.

They each used a block to hide behind while firing at Violet's gang. The mass of little blocks formed a partial shield, but restricted their view. Not being able to see made Aurie claustrophobic.

An errant blast hit one of the smaller blocks, throwing it forward a few feet. She hit it a few more times, turning it into a mini-projectile. The more faez she poured into the blast, the farther the block flew. This gave her an idea.

One of the pale twins found a flanking spot and fired on her. Aurie barely got out of the way. She used another block to shield herself.

Rather than fire back at the pale twin hiding behind the angled block, she directed her blast at the block itself, trying to spin it. A regular blast didn't move it much; she had to really focus her faez into a compact missile and give the shot some solidity.

When she poured in a good amount, the angled block spun, exposing him to their blasts. A cocoon of white formed over him as they hit him three times in succession.

They took out two more attackers before their opponents figured out what was happening. Aurie and Pi flew away from Violet's gang, which was at half the numbers it was at the start. The arena was filled with lots of cocoons, but not enough to make Aurie feel confident about her chances.

Pi had taken position behind a large monolith. Aurie found a curved sphere that resisted attempts to move it around with wand blasts due to the curved surface.

A group of curious insects had moved opposite Pi and were trying to form a bridge to reach her, so her sister started blasting them. Aurie helped with blasts of her own, wanting to eliminate the danger so they could turn their attention back to Violet's gang.

Destroying the insects took longer than she expected, and when Aurie looked around, Violet's gang wasn't where she thought they should be. They'd taken position across from the monolith that Pi was hiding behind.

The remaining five lifted their wands. Aurie knew instantly what they were intending. The wand blasts would spin the block around, exposing Pi. Except the monolith was too close to the wall for that maneuver and would crush Pi like a bug. Professor Delight's warning about the unexpected dangers of the arena echoed through her frantic mind.

She couldn't lose Pi. Her sister was everything to her.

As Violet and her gang fired their wands, Aurie tapped the deep reserve of faez that she knew was waiting beneath the surface. She'd always been afraid to access the power that she knew she had, for fear of losing control like she had when they were younger.

But the fear of losing her sister overrode any other concerns. If she hit the monolith from the side before the other blasts, it would throw the block out of the way. She let the faez flow through her, and through the wand. A crackling ball of energy formed at the tip of her wand, like it'd gotten stuck.

She gave it a second push, and the wand exploded. Aurie felt a cool cocoon slip around her body as her consciousness disappeared within the enchantment. Aurie was out of the game with nowhere near enough points to survive the final cut. She would never get into the Hundred Halls.

14

It was Aurie's birthday, but she wasn't in her bed. Pi stood at the end with the present she wanted to give her. The bed hadn't even been made, which Pi couldn't remember ever happening. Ever.

Since the accident at the trial, Aurie hadn't been the same. She barely stayed in the apartment. Pi had wanted to give her the present last night, since she knew she'd be up early to leave for Coterie, but Aurie hadn't come in until late after Pi had fallen asleep.

More than anything, she wanted to take her older sister in her arms and give her the world's longest hug.

It wasn't supposed to be like this. Aurie was supposed to be the one getting into the Halls. Pi was practically choking on guilt. If she hadn't gotten sick a few years ago, Aurie could have taken the test last year, or the year before.

Pi wiped away a tear. "You tell me I never cry. See, I'm crying. But you're not here to see it."

Before Pi left, she made both beds—another first—and set the newspaper-wrapped birthday present on the pillow.

The lack of weight on her shoulders from her backpack

was a mixture of relief and disappointment. The Coterie had given her a list of things to bring, and to not bring. The list to bring was rather mundane—like shampoo and toothpaste. It could have been a sheet right out of normal university. The don't bring list, however, was more of what Pi'd expected. The only thing that surprised her was how extravagant some of the items were: personal demons, extra-dimensional rooms, sentient firearms, etc. At the bottom of the list, in bold and underlined, it said, "NO DRUGS." Which Pi thought was pretty obvious. If you were going to be dabbling in the world's most powerful magics, you wanted to have your noodle clear.

The Obelisk, the home of the Coterie of Mages, gave Pi chills when the obsidian structure came into view. The dark surface seemed to absorb light. It was grand, imposing, mysterious. It was a symbol of power. It was her new home for the next five years.

A line of black limousines idled in front of the Obelisk. A handsome guy around her age in a tailored white suit climbed out of the vehicle in front. He had short dark hair and the air of privilege.

She realized the others going in and out were dressed impeccably. She was reminded of her nameless sponsor. Her white cami top and pair of thrift store jeans suddenly felt out of place.

As she neared the entrance, the guy in the white suit snapped his fingers at her.

"Hey you, you're in the wrong place," he said.

She turned and stood her ground. "I'm a new initiate."

He let out a short condescending laugh.

She ignored it and offered her hand. "Pythia Silverthorne. You can call me Pi. Like the number, not the food. I scored number three overall on my Merlins."

He took her hand, looked her over as if he didn't know

what to make of her, and said, "Alton Lockwood. Fourth year. Who's your sponsor?"

The question caught her off guard.

"I...don't know his name.   We met through...an acquaintance," she said, trying to sound mysterious, but realizing it just sounded like she didn't know what she was talking about.

"Well, Pi, the number not the food, if you're being truthful, then welcome and good luck, but if this is some sort of subterfuge, then be warned that the Hall wards will make quick work of unwanted intruders," said Alton, the smile on his lips not present in his green eyes.

He released her hand and walked into the Obelisk without another word.

As more limousines released their charges, Pi took a cleansing breath and marched inside. As she passed through the double doors, a tingling sensation formed on her skin. For a moment, she thought the whole acceptance into Coterie was a trick, but the wards let her through.

The opulence of the entrance area took her breath away. Twin curved staircases climbed the outer wall. The mahogany and Persian rugs made Pi think she'd stepped into some kind of Venetian palace. It made her realize she was joining the Harvard or Yale of the magical world.

She was so enamored by the display, Pi barely realized there was a table sitting right inside the doorway, with two students sitting behind it.   She also realized that Alton Lockwood was nowhere in sight, even though he'd stepped through the doorway seconds before she had.

A guy and girl sat behind a massive tome that took up half the table. It looked like they were brother and sister with their similar oval-shaped faces and ruddy hair. They wore private school uniforms, styled younger than Pi expected.

The girl, wearing a name tag with Simone on it, waggled her fingers at Pi with a bored expression on her face. The pages on the massive tome flipped over.

"Pythia Alexandria Silverthorne," Simone read from the tome. "Give us your scribbles here."

"My what?" asked Pi.

The guy, name tag reading Derek, leaned forward and poked his finger on a line in the book. "What my darling Simone is asking is for you to write your name right here."

Pi grabbed the heavy pen and wrote her name. As she stood back up to ask where she needed to go, Derek leaned over and started making out with Simone.

"Well, then," said Pi under her breath, hoping they weren't siblings as she originally thought. "Uhm...where do I go now?"

Without breaking from her make out session, Simone made intricate finger gestures, summoning a ball of light. Pi was impressed she could manage the spell while locked in a heavy petting.

Pi followed the ball of light up the left stairs. Ornate elephants carved into the walls trumpeted their march upward. After a series of exquisite hallways she ended up at a mahogany door. Her name was etched on a gold plate. Pi traced it with her fingertip. Was it real?

She went inside to find a room bigger than her apartment, which elicited a tinge of guilt. The room looked straight out of a catalog of home furnishings: Ivy League edition. Pi dumped her belongings onto the king-sized featherbed. Her clothes didn't even fill one drawer. The few magical odds and ends she owned, including the rune from Radoslav, she placed in the rolltop desk. It looked lonely in a drawer by itself, so she threw a pair of socks in.

A female voice came from the hall. "I swear we're practically living in squalor."

The girl in the doorway looked like she should have been wearing a cheerleading outfit. The word perky could have been her first name.

After a brief silence, the girl marched over with her hand held out, straight and businesslike, as if she'd practiced the gesture until it was perfectly precise.

"Hi, Pythia. I'm Ashley Bellamy, but you can call me Ash. I'm sure we're going to be good friends," she said in a slight Southern accent, the kind used at cotillions.

Pi was taken aback, mostly because the sentiment sounded earnest.

"Hi, Ashley, I mean Ash. You can call me Pi," she said.

Their handshake lasted for an awkwardly long time. Ashley stood and smiled like a pageant queen, while Pi tried to figure out how to break the handshake. Eventually, Ashley bounced her shoulders and gave Pi a brief, peculiar hug.

"I'm so excited to be an initiate with you, Pi. Top three is really impressive," she said, then like a wave crumbling after its peak, her smile fell. "I'm real sorry about your sister. I heard there was some sort of malfunction with her wand. Is she okay?"

The tenderness surprised Pi, especially because she'd expected more hardcore attitudes, like Alton Lockwood's. She choked back a wellspring of emotion to present a stoic face.

"She's fine, physically anyway. The healers did a good job patching her up. She has a few faez burns on her arms," said Pi.

"That was her last chance?" asked Ashley, her face pinched with concern. "That poor thing."

Thankfully, the conversation turned to the exquisitely furnished rooms, which was mostly Ashley talking. Pi began to suspect that the earlier comment about squalor had been sarcastic, or at least she was hoping that's how it'd been said.

The other alternative was that Ashley was befriending her only out of curiosity and would ignore her as soon as she figured out the proper social order, so Pi kept her guard up.

A soft bell tone summoned them to a gathering. Ashley seemed to know where she was going, so Pi followed. The other initiates flooded out of their rooms. Pi was the only one wearing jeans.

They returned to the entrance area. The forty initiates were placed in a semicircle facing the balcony. The stairs and balcony were filled with Coterie students and professors.

The initiate on her left gave her a squint-eyed look and whispered, "Who's your sponsor?"

Pi stammered for a moment, then caught movement from the balcony. The shifting shield, like a haze on a burning highway, moved through the crowd.

She nodded upward. "Him."

The initiate's gaze widened. His lips flattened to white.

A younger man at the right of her sponsor in professor robes and thin-rimmed glasses stepped forward and held up his hand.

After clearing his throat and glancing at the man inside the shifting shield for confirmation, he began, "Greetings, initiates of the Coterie of Mages. You have been honored to join the most prestigious Hall in Invictus as a result of your Merlins, but now that those trials are done, forget about them. They'll never mean another thing to you.

"I am Augustus Trebleton. I will be the Master of Initiates for your first year. It is by my hand that you will pass or fail, so pay attention. And while there are forty of you at this moment, I do not expect to see all of you at the end. Frankly, I will not be doing my job if every one of you makes it. Be warned."

Professor Augustus paused for effect, then motioned towards the bottom of the stairs. The two students who had signed Pi in were waiting with a fabric pillow covered in pins. They moved into position in front of the first student in the arc.

"Now for the presentation of the hall pins. Afterwards, you will swear your allegiance to your patron," he said, then called out in a loud voice, "Brock DuPont, sponsored by Phillip DuPont the third."

A pin was placed on his chest. No one applauded. Another name was read off: "Orson Rutherford, sponsored by Vincent Thermopile."

The pins were presented with little fanfare, though sometimes the names of the sponsors were rewarded with a light amazement, as if the names meant something. Pi hadn't recognized any of them, though a few of the last names matched famous companies she'd heard of.

Pi stood towards the end of the arc, so she had plenty of time to watch the other initiates. The first thing that stuck out was that there were only six girls amongst the forty initiates. A similar ratio existed amongst the other students and professors.

She was contemplating the reason for the disparity when Simone and Derek, still dressed in their faux-private school uniforms, stepped in front of Pi.

"Pythia Silverthorne, sponsored by Eugene Hickford."

A trickle of laughter formed that quickly turned to a flood. Before long, the whole place was overtaken. The initiate next to her whispered, "Nice try. Eugene Hickford. Wow."

Pi glanced around. Some of the other initiates had tears in their eyes. The only one not laughing was Ashley. She kept her face as unreadable as possible. He'd said he'd find her a sponsor. She realized in that moment that he'd never said it would be him.

Professor Augustus cleared his throat loudly, and the laughter died down. Simone leaned forward and placed a pin in the shape of an eagle gripping a staff on Pi's white cami.

"Bentley Bishop, sponsored by Donovan Bishop."

The rest of the names were read without incident.

"Now you must swear your allegiance to your patron. Just as you did during the trials, raise your right hand and let the faez flow," said Professor Augustus.

Forty hands rose, and the man in the shifting shield stepped forward. When he spoke, she knew it was the man she'd summoned the demon for, but this time, his voice thrummed with power.

"Today you promise yourself to me, your patron." He paused. "A promise is a pact, a binding between two parties. A contract. I promise that you will learn to wield magics that can, and will, make the world tremble. You will learn things within these walls that others fear to even consider. Magic is a tool, a weapon to be wielded. But if you cannot master yourself, the magic will master you.

"For your part of the bargain, you promise yourself to me, and this hall, the Coterie of Mages. You promise to protect its secrets, your fellow students, and the Hall itself. But most importantly, you promise yourself to me. Your patron. Who gives you the strength to wield your magics without fear of madness. I am your shield, your protector. And you must do as I say, now and forever."

His voice rose to a crescendo, and he shouted, "I bind you to me!"

The sensation was not like the temporary binding during the trials. That one had been on the surface, and pleasant. It'd been like taking hold of a rope and letting oneself be led through a sunlit hedge maze.

As her every muscle seized up, Pi likened it to having low voltage current running through her body. It had echoes of the demon summoning as well, which worried her about the implications of the pledging. The binding went deep into her chest and wrapped itself around her heart.

A voice spoke in her mind: *stop fighting me.*

She opened her eyes a little to realize that most of the others had their arms down.

She knew she was fighting it because she wasn't completely sure about being a part of the Coterie. The phrasing of the pledge worried Pi that she was joining something she wasn't ready for.

Stop fighting me!

But this was what she'd been working towards. Power meant safety from those that would hurt her, or her sister. If she'd had power when she was ten years old, she could have stopped the strange man from killing her parents. Power meant that she'd never have to worry again.

Pi let go of her fears and completed the binding. For a few seconds, it felt like an elephant was sitting on her chest. Then, she could breathe.

Her arm fell to her side as the man in the shifting shield left the balcony. A part of her felt like it had gone with him.

Professor Augustus was speaking again, but Pi could barely pay attention. Through the link, she heard a name whispered in her head. She didn't think she was meant to hear it, which meant only one thing, it was the name of her patron.

Malden Anterist.

15

The Obelisk would be her home for the next five years. First-year initiates were allowed on the first five floors. No one told her how high the floors went, nor had she seen any stairwells or elevators to get there.

Classes didn't start for a few days, which gave the initiates time to read up on the hall rules and to get to know each other. This ritual was familiar to Pi after countless high schools in different towns with different families.

The only problem was that she'd never hung around the rich kids, mostly because her schools never had them, so she couldn't tell the difference between the layers of social hierarchy, except that she was at the bottom. Between her lack of wardrobe and the laughter-inducing sponsor, Pi hadn't expected anything else. The only surprise was that Ashley Bellamy hadn't abandoned her like she thought she would.

On the morning of their first class, the initiates gathered on the fourth floor in a round room called Telchine's Circle. This was, in the parlance of the hall, a safe room—meaning the magics practiced had to be of the lesser variety. Demon summonings, thaumaturgy, pyrokenetics, or other violent magics had to be performed on their respective floors. Danger, in this case, meant to the other students. Any magic—even the simplest cantrip—performed incorrectly could be dangerous, a known fact to even children.

Initiates were two to a table. They went around the room. A dais formed the center.

Pi and Ashley had taken one near the front, but not all the way. She wore her "Mages Do It with their Fingers" shirt because it was ironic, and hilarious, and if she wasn't going to fit in, she might as well enjoy herself.

Ashley chatted with the other initiates in a friendly manner. They greeted Ashley as an equal, but gave Pi sideways glances that made her feel more like a pet than a person.

While they were settling in, Ashley asked, "Do you have any trinkets?"

"Earrings? No," said Pi.

"No, trinkets. Magical ones." Ashley shook the bracelet on her wrist. It had interlocking ebony and jade stones. "This was my mother's. It gives me a small amount of protection against infections, or chemicals. Things like that."

"I thought that stuff was forbidden?" asked Pi, remembering the list of stuff not to bring.

"These items help to be a better mage. Brock over there has a power stone. It's a family heirloom. Probably three hundred years old. It gives him more access to his faez. Or Bentley, his necklace will shield him from any accidental blazes," said Ashley.

Pi opened her mouth to say it was cheating, that it gave some students an advantage over others. And considering that not all would make it through the first year, it seemed unfair. But she decided not to say it. Mostly because she liked Ashley and didn't want to insult her.

The conversations trickled to silence when Professor

Augustus walked in, trailed by the fourth-year student Alton Lockwood.

He winked at Ashley, who whispered low and husky, "Do you think he's attractive?"

Pi wasn't fooled. Asking if Alton was attractive was like asking if demons wanted to murder you. But yet, something about their meeting outside bothered Pi.

"He could be a model," she offered eventually.

Professor Augustus lifted a hand while adjusting his glasses with pinched fingers. He was younger than Pi had realized, maybe only in his late twenties.

"Fact. At least one of you will die this year," he said. "Look around at your fellow students. One of you will do something stupid. You'll try to impress your peers with a dazzling display of your magical prowess, pushing the boundaries of sense and magic, and pay the ultimate price for it. And I will applaud you for it."

A low-level chuckle flowed through the room. Pi wasn't sure if it was callousness or bravado. She hoped the latter.

"Limitless!" said the professor, raising his arm straight up like a rocket. "That is the motto of the Coterie of Mages. We do not put limits on ourselves, or our magic. We push. We dare. We do.

"At least one of you will die this year, because you will push yourselves." He tapped on his own chest. "*I* will push you. But today is not that day," he said with a cocked grin.

Pi found herself laughing along with the others. The whole speech felt a little rehearsed, but she appreciated the effort.

"Today, however, we are not going to kill anyone. At least I hope. To get to know your abilities, and to lay the groundwork for later lessons, we're going to talk about materials," said the professor.

He made a few gestures, and a circular desk rose out

of the dais. A variety of objects, including plants, metals, and liquids—most that she recognized—were on the table. Professor Augustus took a circuit around the dais before stopping next to Alton, putting a hand on his shoulder. Pi detected the twitch of annoyance on Alton's face.

"One of the responsibilities of fourth-year students is to teach and mentor first years. Alton Lockwood is one of our best and brightest. You should feel privileged to learn from him," said the professor.

Augustus pointed to Brock DuPont on the opposite side while simultaneously nodding at Alton, who lifted up a leafy sprig with berries on it.

"You, Brock. What is that?" asked the professor.

"Mistletoe," said Brock after a moment.

The professor made an agreeable nod. "What are its properties?"

"Can be used in summonings, antidotes for poison, protections against charms..." said Brock.

"Good enough for the start. But that was an easy one."

Augustus walked over to their table, and to Pi's supreme disappointment, he picked Ashley. Alton held up a hunk of silvery metal that had crystalline features.

Ashley answered right away. "Gallium. It's magically magnetic, so it can be used to set up perpetual levitation fields, like the ones the Japanese use in their Lev Trains. It cures warts, or at least reduces them, if properly attuned can be used for triangulation and locating, and can give the fungus folk a skin rash."

Augustus clapped his hands. "Wonderfully done. Does anyone know the proper ratio used when setting up a levitation field?"

Pi raised her hand, but the professor called on Bree Bishop.

"At the distance of one dragon, the proper ratio of gallium to target object is three to one."

Pi whispered, "Eight to one," right as the professor raised his hand and said, "Almost. It's actually eight to one. Congratulations, you would have immolated yourself in the faez feedback."

Bree looked a little embarrassed. A few disdainful glances were sent in her direction.

The professor pointed at Orson Rutherford. Alton lifted up a jar with a white sticky paste in it. He waved his hand, and a faint minty scent reached Pi's nose.

"Ear wax from the fae," Pi whispered to Ashley, who nodded appreciatively.

Orson drummed his fingers on his desk before answering correctly. Then he added, "It's an alchemical solvent used when making potions involving dragon's blood, it can protect against faez burn, and tastes great on toast."

Everyone laughed, including Pi. The professor continued with the game, pointing at a different student each time. Pi knew every one of them, though she didn't always know the full list of properties.

When Augustus tapped on her desk, a few muffled coughs of "Hickford Pi" went around the room. The professor duly ignored them and nodded to Alton.

Pi caught the hesitation as Alton almost lifted up a beaker of sea salt, which Pi knew intimately well, then reached for a different item. He lifted up a gray flat stone about the size of a child's fist.

She stared intently at the object in his hand. The other initiates chuckled lightly when she didn't answer right away.

The stone was suggestive of a codex rock, or possibly a titan's tear, but she knew it was neither. Pi tried to ignore the room full of eyes on her.

"Miss Silverthorne," said the professor, trying to sound encouraging.

Pi took a glance around the room. They looked ready to break into laughter. Next to her, Ashley was nearly in tears, which was the only thing keeping Pi from running out of the room.

She tried to remind herself that she'd summoned a demon lord not too long ago, but all she could think about was that she didn't know what the item was. She could handle sticking out. She could handle not having the same advantages they had. She could even handle their condescending glances and smug comments. But she couldn't handle not doing well. It was acid on her bones.

"Miss Silverthorne. We're waiting."

She concentrated on the stone as hard as she could, but it was like running into an invisible wall. A few more calls of "Hickford Pi" punctuated the silence.

"I'm sorry, Miss Silverthorne," said the professor eventually. "What was that again, Alton?"

Alton's lip tugged with amusement. "A paperweight."

The room erupted in laughter. Pi felt like she'd been packed in ice. It went on for over a minute. The whole time, Pi stayed perfectly still as if that would keep the shame away.

Eventually, the professor put order to the room. The questions went on, but the damage was done. Before, at least she'd been the girl who'd gotten third place in the Merlins. It was something she'd done better than they had, and it kept her from feeling like she was out of place, like she didn't belong. Now, she was the girl who didn't even know what a rock was.

16

The Golden Willow Clinic for the Sick and Infirm had seen better days. The brick building was in dire need of tuck pointing, and the west wall was overtaken with ivy, but Aurie knew it wasn't the building that mattered, but the doctors and nurses inside.

Aurie stopped at the guard station in the entry area. A heavyset man with a monkish hairline in a Dreadcore Security uniform sat behind a desk. His bushy eyebrows furrowed as she approached.

"You know you are not supposed to be here, Aurelia," said Herman the guard.

Every word was spoken with a distinct slowness in a monotone voice.

"Hi, Hermie," she said.

His face was wracked with confusion. "You are not on my list. Why are you here, Aurelia?"

"Hermie, it's okay. I just wanted to come visit. See how the kids were doing," she said.

"But you are not on the list," he said, rather emphatically.

"I was hoping...," she said, but realized Herman would

never be able to understand her request, so she left it unsaid. "I just wanted to stop by. Are the kids okay?"

"I am not on children floor for the irre...irre...irre...," said Herman, who appeared to be in pain trying to say the word.

"It's okay, Hermie. I know the floor," she said. "What about the kids?"

Mention of the kids brightened his face. "Eduardo was sent home last week."

"Great," said Aurie.

Eduardo had picked up a strange fungus from playing in the Potomac River. Dr. Fairlight had suspected industrial waste from the nearby alchemical plant, but there was no way to prove it. The fungus turned Eduardo's skin to lava when he got worried or excited. The first week on the floor, before they got the fungus under control, he burned up four beds.

She hesitated asking the next question, fearing the answer. "What about Emily?"

"Emily on floor six now," said Herman.

Intensive care was on floor six. Aurie feared it was nearing the end. Even if she'd wanted to see Emily, there was no way to get onto the sixth floor without a badge.

Aurie pulled a clear baggy containing slivers of lichwood out of an inside pocket. "Can you do something really important for me? Give this to Dr. Fairlight."

Herman looked confused, so she borrowed a piece of paper and wrote instructions on it. She'd been doing some research about Emily's condition based on her experience in the trials when she'd used the flight potion to absorb the growth steam. She'd had horrible joint pains after that and had drank some lichwood tea for relief. She hoped it might offer something similar to Emily.

After leaving the note and lichwood with Herman, Aurie went back to the apartment. She was sore from sorting Magic cards at Freeport Games for Hemistad. She'd been working double shifts to pay him back for the loan.

The drug dealers were standing outside of the apartment when she got there. They noticed her as she approached, and moved to intercept.

She poured faez into her fist, until the golden energy dripped from her knuckles.

"Touch me and find out what it feels like to have your bones catch fire inside your skin," she said.

The five guys held their hands up and backed away. "Hey, girl. We just playin'. No need for that business."

Back in her room, she let the faez go and checked her skin for signs of damage. Her arm felt heavy and sore from calling it up and not using it, but the skin had no burst veins or cracking.

"Stupid, Aurie," she muttered to herself, and flopped onto the bed.

The present Pi had given her sat on the desk. She picked it up and rotated it in her hands. She just couldn't open it. Doing so would acknowledge that she'd turned twenty, and would never get into the Hundred Halls.

After a few minutes of sulking, Aurie got up and prepared to inventory her magical books and supplies so she could sell them to help pay Hemistad back. She hated being in debt.

A knock on the door startled her. She peeked out the window to see the drug dealers still hanging around.

Her door didn't have a peephole since it'd been replaced a year ago from water damage, so Aurie put her ear to the wood. The second knock rang her ears.

"Who is it?" she asked suspiciously.

An older voice responded, though it was too muffled for her to understand the words. The only thing she got was an impression of Britishness.

Aurie unhooked the chain and cracked open the door, preparing to slam it shut if she didn't like who she saw.

A tall man with dark skin and graying hair, wearing an impeccable gray suit, stood outside.

"Patron Gray," she said, the words tumbling out of her mouth. "Is something wrong?"

First thoughts went to her sister, but then she remembered that Pi was in Coterie, so Semyon Gray wouldn't be visiting her for that. She had a guess that it had to do with the accident during the Merlins. After the healers had patched her up, they'd said that someone would visit her to learn more about the circumstances of the explosion, but she hadn't expected Patron Semyon Gray.

"May I come in, Miss Aurelia?" he asked.

"Yes, of course," she said, opening the door. "And you can call me Aurie."

As she turned around, she grimaced. *Call me Aurie? What am I thinking? He's a patron of the Hundred Halls, one of the most powerful people in the world.*

She recovered enough to have a polite smile when she faced him again.

"Can I offer you a seat?" she asked, picking papers off her chair.

"Thank you, Aurie," he said, and sat.

She took the spot on the bed across from him and tried to keep her knees from bouncing.

"Do you know why I'm here?" he asked.

"About the accident at the Merlins," she said.

He raised a single eyebrow and nodded.

"Would it be too much to ask if you would elaborate on the details of that event?" he asked.

Aurie suddenly worried that the reason Semyon had come to investigate her, rather than a lowly administrator, was because they were planning on taking preemptive legal action.

"What do you want to know? How it happened so you can prevent future accidents?" she asked tentatively.

"Of course," he said.

As she gathered her thoughts, she looked at Semyon Gray. While his gray eyes revealed the depths of his experiences, they did not suggest a hard man. Aurie found herself relaxing at this realization, the previous fears evaporating.

She explained the circumstances that had led to the wand explosion. When she started explaining, she was afraid she'd get teary-eyed, but she made it through in a calm voice.

He nodded appreciatively at the end.

"Had you ever been tested before? Standardized tests, I mean," he said.

"No. After my parents...we got moved around to different orphanages. Never stayed in one place for long," she said.

His kind eyes creased with concern. "I knew your parents. They were some of my favorite students."

Aurie wasn't surprised that Patron Gray had remembered her mother. "How did you know my dad? Since he was a healer."

"The halls work together frequently, or at least most of them do. It's one of the things that Invictus wanted of us. Second year is filled with mixed hall competitions," he said, then paused to smile. "Your mother was an extraordinary woman. She used the knowledge she'd gained in Arcanium to help your father find cures for ailments that were thought incurable. They were an amazing team," said Patron Gray.

Aurie knew the generalities of what her parents were working on, but to hear the importance of it from Patron Gray stoked fires of longing in her chest. At various times during her childhood, her mother would leave the country on trips to find artifacts, or scraps of ancient magical tomes, in hopes they could lead to new cures. Aurie always hated when her mother left, especially because her dad was always at the hospital. Even before their parents had died, she and her sister had spent their childhoods alone.

Semyon placed his hand on hers. She'd been squeezing them into fists. His hand was warm and rough with calluses. "I'm sorry, Aurie. I didn't mean to bring up old pains. Would you mind if I did a simple test? I need to understand your access to the faez."

She nodded. He took her hand in both of his.

"Pour as much faez as you can into your hand. Let it flow unbridled," he said.

"Are you sure? I thought we were never supposed to do that. Especially without a patron," she said.

He raised a mocking eyebrow.

"I promise you that I can protect you for this test," he said, a smile in his tone.

"Okay," she said, breathing deeply and preparing.

She kept her eyes open because she wanted to make sure she wasn't hurting him in some way.

Accessing raw faez had always been easy for Aurie. She'd always felt like it was a vast river behind a dam, as wide and deep as the Amazon, and that she just opened it up a little to let it out. She'd always been afraid to let it get away from her, feeling like the dam might break from too much power and wash her away.

After the first few seconds, Patron Gray barely reacted. The winkles around his eyes creased with effort, but he did not seem in pain. He was rechanneling her faez back into the place where it came from. Realizing she wasn't going to hurt him, she let loose like she never had before, and regretted it right away.

There was a brief moment, right when the flow increased,

that Aurie thought their hands would be forced apart, and raw magic would spray over the room like a busted water pipe. But Patron Gray clamped down and the moment passed.

When he nodded, she stopped and pulled away, feeling raw from the effort.

Semyon sat quietly in contemplation before speaking again. He seemed to be choosing his words carefully.

"Miss Silverthorne, you have a considerable amount of power. Much more than the average mage. Much, much more. Which explains why there was an unfortunate explosion. The wand wasn't constructed for the levels of faez you were able to give it, so it failed. Getting knocked out of the trial at that moment was not your fault. You should have passed and been placed in a hall," he said.

The news that she hadn't failed, that it had been the apparatus of the trial itself that had failed, was bittersweet. She felt numb and dizzy.

"It doesn't matter," she said, almost in a trance. "I'm twenty now. It's in the charter that all patrons are bound by, even you. The Hundred Halls can accept no initiates after the age of twenty. I've been twenty for almost a month now."

Semyon nodded along with her words. "Yes. That's true. It's in the charter and is impossible to circumvent."

Despite the seriousness of his gaze, his lips seemed to want to curl into a smile, or at least that's what Aurie thought was going on. Either that, or she was going insane.

"Miss Silverthorne," he said. "Aurie. Can you tell me again about the incident at the trials?"

She put her hand to her lips. Her face was tingly. "I already told you about that."

Semyon couldn't hold his smile back. His teeth were glimmering white.

"Tell me about the trial again," he said, as if there was

some message coded in the words.

"I don't under..."

Then it hit her. For a moment, she almost passed out, the emotions came on so strong. But she had to check, had to make sure.

"I'm not supposed to be able to talk about the trial. But if I can it means that the enchantment wasn't placed on me, and if so then the link...oh shit."

She clamped her hand over her mouth as she looked into his eyes for confirmation.

"Yes, Aurelia Silverthorne. I still have the link with you from the trials. Which means that technically, you were a part of Arcanium when you had your twentieth birthday," he said. "Due to your injuries at the time, and because I suspected that it might not have been your fault, I made sure you were not discharged in the normal way."

"But why...?" she asked.

"I told you before. I knew your parents. It was a tragedy that they passed. If I'd known that you and your sister had gotten lost in the social services programs, I would have reached out and had the alumni make arrangements for you and your sister. I failed in that regard. So when the accident at the trial happened, I made sure that you didn't fall through the cracks again," he said.

"Thank you," she choked out.

"You don't need to thank me. It was a failure of the trials," he said. "However, there are a few complications. All the spots in Arcanium were filled, and even at our best guess, your score at the time would have put you right on the edge of making it. So I will place you in Arcanium as a probationary member, which means that you have less room for error than the others. As well, you will be starting late."

"But you're the patron," she said, not understanding why

it mattered that she would be in probation.

"Yes, but as a first-year initiate, you are beholden to the Mistress of Initiates. It is she and she alone that decides if you pass or fail the first year. And know that she is a hard woman and any attention from me will only make it harder on you. It's best if you quietly slide into the program, keep your head down, and make it through the first year."

"I won't let you down, Patron Gray," she said.

"I know you won't," he said, patting her hand. "Now let's make this official and complete the link. You have a lot of catching up to do."

After he left, she practically floated against the ceiling. Her neighbors banged on the walls when she shouted for joy. The Hundred Halls. She'd finally made it. She was going to be a member of the Arcanium.

17

Pi brought the cell phone back to Ashley, who was modeling a new outfit in front of the mirror. Pi was pretty sure the thigh-length black jacket was more expensive than her whole wardrobe.

"Hey Ash, thanks for letting me use your phone," said Pi.

"So your sister really got into Arcanium?" asked Ashley, eyes bright.

"It's crazy. I don't quite understand it. But I'm happy. Though she's got a lot of catching up to do. It's already October. I guess if anyone can get caught up in a short amount of time, it's her," said Pi.

"I can't wait to meet your sister," said Ashley. "She sounds amazing."

A burst of pride filled Pi's chest. Her face was warm. "Yeah. After our parents died, she took care of me, like a mom. Sacrifices and everything."

Ashley honored the moment of silence, then her face cracked into a smile. "Are you going to the party tonight?"

"I don't think that'd be a good idea. I'll probably stay in my room and study," said Pi.

Ashley ran over and grabbed Pi's hands. "You should get out. It'll be good for you."

"I don't think the other initiates want me there and especially not the older students," she said. Ashley's face drooped. "Don't worry, my feelings aren't hurt. I can take care of myself."

"First. Not all the initiates think that way. Yes, there are a couple of jerks, but most of them are sympathetic to your cause. They think it's total bullshit the way Alton's been treating you in class," she said.

"Then why don't they stand up to him?" asked Pi, annoyed.

Ashley's nostrils flared with mischief. "Because they're soulless chickenshits. And second, you probably know this, but I'm going to say it anyway. You have to know people in Coterie to get ahead, hell, to survive. That's why you needed a sponsor to get in, and you'll need more help to keep moving up. Don't believe that it's only Augustus' word that gets us past the first year."

"They don't think I belong here," said Pi.

"Fuck 'em," said Ashley.

The foul word coming out of Ashley's plush lips with perfectly applied red lipstick made Pi laugh.

"You're always going to make enemies. And sometimes the right enemies will earn you friends," said Ashley.

"Fiiiine. I'll go. Thanks, Ash," she said.

Pi returned to her room and readied herself. Jeans, a white cami, and a little glitter on her shoulders wasn't in fashion, but she wouldn't have been comfortable in anything the other girls wore.

When it came time, Pi, Ashley, and a few other initiates snuck down to the entryway. First-year initiates weren't supposed to leave the Obelisk without permission, but that was seen more as a challenge than a rule.

The spell to disable the wards was complex, but Ashley performed it on the first try, releasing them onto the street. They ran, skipped, laughed their way to the Amber & Smoke. Typically, first years weren't invited to parties with older students, but Brock DuPont's father, who owned the bar, made it a condition of usage when it he closed it down for the night.

Music thumped and pulsed into the street. Inside, the volume invaded her bones. It was an herbal bar, and various brass incense censers wafted vaguely alchemical mixtures into the air. The students on the first floor had pleasantly dazed looks on their faces. Faint visions moved through the smoke like ghosts at a parade.

Pi grabbed Ashley's arm and dragged her up to the second floor, where it was easier to speak and there was no smoke. They got drinks at the bar; no one asked for an ID card. Pi had gotten whatever Ashley had ordered, a purple mixture that swirled under its own power, but didn't drink it. She had no intention of muddying her senses.

Ashley was adept at mingling with the other students, though they generally only spoke to fellow first years. Side rooms with Japanese-style paper screens held the fourth- and fifth-year students. A group of students were playing Five Elements in one corner of the second level. Their frequent cheers and laughter punctuated the noisy conversations. Pi hadn't played the game in years, though her fingers still remembered the forms. Just watching them play brought a tightness to her forehead that she pushed away.

As a circle of first years formed, Pi was included. She stayed mostly silent. She knew their names, and they spoke to her congenially. No one called her Hickford Pi, so she felt good about that, at least.

The night went on, and Pi took a few sips of the sweet alcoholic drink in her hands. Eventually, over her protests,

Ashley tugged Pi towards the game of Five Elements.

Simone and Derek were running the show, wearing their fetishy formal school outfits. Simone's was a nod to Japanese fashions with her pink Hello Kitty socks, while Derek was looking '70s' UK punk.

"Since we have a new group of combatants," said Simone, clapping her hands together, "I will explain the rules. The first one is that you must fight! No spectators. We're playing Five Elements head-to-head, and the winner gets to pick Shot, Shock, or Tongue."

Fellow first year Orson was the current winner. Someone pushed Ashley into the circle to much applause. She bowed and faced off with Orson like it was a boxing match.

"Wait, wait," said Ashley, waving her hands before she handed Pi her jade and ebony bracelet. No magical trinkets were allowed during the battle.

When Simone gave the signal, Ashley and Orson's fingers went through the complex gyrations of spell casting. Orson struck first with earth, but Ashley quickly countered with water. The match went on for a minute before Ashley broke through his defenses, scoring a win with earth.

Simone marched into the center and lifted Ashley's hand in victory.

"Shot, Shock, or Tongue?" asked Simone.

"Shot," said Ashley right away, much to the disappointment of the crowd.

Orson was handed a shot glass filled with something glowing red. It had a minor enchantment on it. After he drank it, he shook his head frantically and waved his hands in front of his mouth. Wisps of smoke and flame came out as he blew.

The game continued, and Ashley won the next four rounds. She gave them all shots, except for a second year who had turned her door into a living wall of tentacles as a prank.

She gave him the shock penalty. A glass ball containing a tiny lightning elemental was presented by Derek, who was wearing insulated gloves. The second year put his hand out, and the shock knocked him to his knees.

Next, Pi was pulled into the circle by Simone, who commanded that: "Everyone must fight!"

In the background, Pi heard her nickname whispered, but no one called it out. Ashley held out her knuckles, and Pi bumped them.

"Good luck, Pi. I'm not holding back," said Ashley with a grin.

"Neither am I," said Pi.

When the match began, Pi went right to spirit, which was a risky move since the fingerings took longer. But once she beat Ashley to the spell, the rest was over in about half a minute. It was the shortest match so far. Someone whistled appreciatively in the back.

Before Simone could even ask about the penalty, a chant of "Tongue" went up with the other students.

Ashley gave Pi a do-what-you-want shoulder shrug.

"Shot," Pi said eventually.

The guys in the crowd booed. Ashley flipped them all off.

The shot had something glowing and alive in it. The sprite-like creature swam in circles in the glass. Ashley downed it in one motion. Almost immediately, sparks came shooting out her mouth, nose, eyes, and ears. For a few seconds, she was a human sparkler.

"That was unpleasant," said Ashley, rubbing her ears afterwards.

The next few matches went even quicker than the one against Ashley. The other initiates were a little drunk, but Pi knew she'd practiced more than the others.

Once she'd given everyone in the circle a shot, Simone

shrugged and said, "I guess the game's over. No one left for you to beat."

The other initiates patted her on the shoulder, or gave her a respectful nod. A warm surge of pride filled her chest, right up until the moment she heard a new voice.

"This must be the worst group of second years of all time if an initiate beat you. I'll put her in her place," said Alton Lockwood, in his signature white suit.

The laughing died, and the other initiates looked away. Alton Lockwood, and a group of fourth years, had joined the circle.

"It's hard to believe that you could be that good, since you didn't even know what a rock was, Hickford Pi," said Alton.

Pi kept her mouth shut. She preferred to let him underestimate her.

Simone turned to Alton. "Isn't that a little unfair? You're a fourth year. She's barely an initiate."

"Why don't we ask Miss Hickford if she'd like to battle?" asked Alton with a cocky swagger.

"Of course," she said.

Alton squared off against her. He cracked his knuckles and did a few finger exercises to warm up.

Simone stepped forward and held her hand out. "Any trinkets?"

Alton's lip twitched with annoyance, but he complied, taking off an encrusted ring, a gold runed bracelet, an ebony tie clip, and a bone scrimshaw in the shape of an owl from a coat pocket. Simone left her hand out until he handed over a gold-plated tooth from the back of his mouth

As the sibilant sound of "Start" left Simone's lips, Alton began with the first element: spirit. He moved faster than she thought possible. Only her limbered fingers and the years of practice allowed her to keep up with him. The matches usually had a back and forth rhythm to them until one combatant finally outmaneuvered the other. This one was a staccato burst of gunfire, bullets flying in both directions with deadly accuracy.

Pi kept it up for over a minute. Not only did Alton move fast, but each element was reinforced with heavy loads of faez. It wasn't a match, but a siege, and Alton was bringing a battering ram the size of a steamship against her defenses.

When Alton finally struck the winning blow, Pi collapsed to her knees. She'd never been in such an exhausting game of Five Elements. The spectators were too stunned by the display to start chanting "Shot, Shock, or Tongue" right away. Alton's buddies were all cheering and clapping him on the back.

Pi was miffed by the loss. She was sure she would have been able to beat him. She'd seen him cast spells in class. He might have more experience than her, but she knew she was faster.

As the chants for "Shot, Shock, or Tongue" grew, Alton strutted up to her and straightened his tie.

"You know she wants the tongue," he said, playing to his friends.

Pi was demoralized, but didn't let it show, instead keeping a stoic expression.

"Let's get this over with," said Pi. "And someone line me up one of those dragon shots. I'll need to burn the taste of him out of my mouth."

"Come on, sweetie Pi," he said. "Let's just step into the room over here. Give us some privacy."

"I'd prefer not," said Pi. "Unless you want everyone to see me barf after we're done."

"Simone. Tell the first year how the rules work," said Alton.

Simone looked around uncomfortably. "Don't drag me

into this. Usually people pick tongue when they're going to hook up later anyway. Forced make out sessions are pretty gross."

Pi could have hugged Simone at that moment, but Alton didn't look dissuaded. She could sense his growing impatience and decided to just get it over with. She didn't want to involve anyone else in the skirmish.

"I'll go. I'll go," said Pi, holding her hands up. "Let's not make this any more than it is. My dog once put his tongue in my mouth when I wasn't looking, I think I can handle this."

She followed Alton into the side room. The table was set into the floor and cushions went around the walls. Dozens of empty wine bottles and half-eaten plates of food covered the table. He closed the paper screen behind them.

Pi turned around, ready to step into his arms. It wasn't going to be the worst thing that had ever happened to her, and she *had* agreed to the match.

"Let's get this—"

She heard the low speaking and noticed his fingers moving after it was too late. Her muscles seized up. He'd put a binding on her. The effect was too powerful for such a quick spell, but then she noticed the cuff links. He hadn't taken all his trinkets off.

"Well, Miss Pi. While I'm sure you were secretly wanting to kiss me, I'll let you know I had no intention of letting that happen. What I am going to do is inform you that you don't belong here, and that it would be in your best interest to leave the Obelisk tonight, or you might find it becomes your permanent home. Take your things and scurry back to whatever rock you crawled out of.

"To ensure that you are properly motivated, I'm going to put a little charm on you. You might find it's quite irresistible. It's my specialty. You'll find that you just can't control yourself tonight. Your inhibitions will be gone. Before the end of the night, the rest of the initiates will think you were either a stripper or a whore before you came here. They won't want to touch you, and neither will any more sponsors."

His grin was made of hate. He let her wallow in the realization of what he was about to do. It was clear this was a spell he'd used on other girls, but usually in the privacy of his room.

She refused to let it cower her. As he cast the charm, she knew she would have a brief moment when the new one overrode the binding, but hadn't completely taken hold. The transition would only last a second, not enough for a counterspell.

When her muscles released, Pi surged her knee forward, connecting directly with his groin. The impact disrupted the charm. Alton doubled over.

Pi used the distraction to cast the same binding he'd used, locking him into the bent position. She thought of about a dozen things she could do to him before she came up with a plan.

His eyes were wild with fear. The swagger had left him. Despite the rictus, his expression had slackened.

"I should take one of those bottles and shove it halfway up your ass." His eyes turned bloodshot. "Don't worry, I'm going to leave you here instead. I'll even pretend that you were a good kisser. But since you were a cheating fuck"—she took the cuff links from his jacket and put them in her pocket—"these are mine now. And if you try to get them back, I'll expose you as a cheater. Just imagine what people would think, sponsors included, if they knew you had to use these to take down a first year. They might question if you were worth the effort anymore."

Her words had a surprising impact on him. If he could

have moved his head, she thought he would have nodded. She mentally noted that she needed to understand the politics of Coterie better, since it appeared she was woefully underprepared.

"Have a nice night, asshole," she said, stepping out of the room. Pi cast a spell on the door that would release his binding the moment it was opened.

When she turned around she wiped her mouth off casually and gave everyone an it-wasn't-so-terrible shrug.

"I think he liked it more than I did," she called out, getting a bit of laughter from her fellow first years. "He wants to savor it for a while, so don't bother him."

She made a shuffling motion with her hand and winked at his friends. Then she walked directly to Ashley, who was standing at the bar chatting with Orson. Pi grabbed her arm and whispered under her breath, "We have to go. *Now.*"

Ashley nodded and marched-ran outside. As soon as they hit the street, Pi had Ashley get them a taxi back to the Obelisk. On the way back, Pi explained what happened and showed her the cuff links. The glossy look in Ashley's eyes at the end of the story put a stone in Pi's gut.

"When I said make an enemy to earn friends, I didn't mean like that, or with him," she said, sighing heavily.

"Is it that bad?" asked Pi.

"Alton's considered the top student in his class. But more importantly, he's got connections all the way up to the patron. Supposedly, his father signed off on major loans to members of the Coterie. Like Swiss-bank, offshore kind of loans, if you get my drift," said Ashley.

"What do you mean?" asked Pi.

Ashley turned to Pi and grabbed her hands, getting the serious girl-talk look on her face.

"When I decided to come to Coterie, my parents were

aghast. They'd always had a cold relationship with my grandfather, who's a famous alumnus and I thought it had to do with them not going to the Hundred Halls and eschewing magic. But when I asked my grandfather if he'd be my sponsor, he was super excited, and talked about how I could continue the glories of the Cabal for the family."

"Isn't that supposed to be like the Illuminati, or one of those other urban legends?" said Pi.

Ashley shrugged. "When I asked, he didn't say much more about it, but after a while he did talk about how much I stood to gain from membership. You see, my grandfather is a rich dude, but my parents aren't. They gave up their inheritance when they disowned him. I never really understood it until that moment. I almost decided not to go to Coterie, but if I didn't join this Hall, then he wouldn't pay for any of them, and it would kill me not be able to use magic."

"You still haven't explained the Cabal," said Pi.

"That's really all I know. But that's not the point. The point is that these rich and powerful people look out for each other and make sure they stay in power," said Ashley.

"Great," said Pi, "and I have no connections to make me valuable and Alton has tons."

"If you really did summon that demon lord, and get the patron to find you a sponsor, you might have more friends than you think. Magic is a form of power, and you're crazy good. Don't underestimate yourself," said Ashley.

They arrived at the Obelisk and went back to their rooms. Pi couldn't help but feel like she'd fallen out of the safety of her nest into the dangerous jungle and everything wanted to kill her. She also decided she needed to learn a lot more about the Coterie of Mages so she'd be more prepared. Luckily, she knew the perfect person for information, and besides, he'd summoned her for another job.

18

The inside of Arcanium smelled like heaven to Aurie. The massive building reminded her of a monastery crossed with Notre Dame, but the heart was the Library of Alexandria. The Arcanium, besides being one of the first founders of the Hundred Halls, had the largest collection of magical tomes in the world.

Illuminated dust motes from stained glass windows high above shone down on the rows and rows of books before her. Aurie reveled in the musty smell of paper and ink.

Patron Gray had told her how to find the initiate's quarters in the west wing. She moved through the rows at a leisurely pace, touching the bindings with her fingertips, reading titles such as *Gritziski's Catalog of Garden Spirits*, *Aracnomancy*, and *One Thousand and One Magical Uses for Honey*.

She crossed through the map room. A massive globe, half covered in shadow, floated in the center of the room. She'd heard that looking at it was like seeing the earth from space, much like an astronaut. The description did not prepare her for the quivering joy she felt.

Aurie found where the city of Invictus was located on the

east coast, resisting an urge to touch for fear of upsetting the magic that sustained the globe. Peering up close, the city came into view, as if she were zooming into Google Earth. The tiny Spire looked like a needle sticking out of the hub-like city.

Leaning back, she took in the continent. The southwest was covered in an eternal brown, a result of the decades-long blight. The Rockies were kissed with snowfall. She walked around the sphere towards the dark side. Lights speckled across the surface. Major cities like Beijing and Tokyo sparkled like jewels. Forest fires in eastern Russia smoldered like burning leaves, the smoke obscuring nearby cities.

On the far wall was a map of Invictus that stretched from side to side. She thought a nest of ants had taken residence on it until she realized they were tiny cars and gondolas, moving across the surface.

Aurie heard a woman giving a lecture from an open doorway at the back of the next wing. She peeked her head through to find a sunken auditorium. Seats went down for thirty rows.

Professor Mali was an older woman in a wheelchair with a thick head of steel gray hair tamed into a braid. Her pants were folded over around the knees where there were no more legs. She was rolling back and forth in front of the seats, her hands busy adding flourishes to her speech while her chair moved on its own.

"...the city fae, or maetrie as they are commonly called, fall into one of three courts: jade, diamond, or ruby. Unlike their counterparts, they interact freely with humans, especially in Invictus. Some even going so far as joining a hall, though that is rare..."

The professor's wheelchair came to an abrupt stop. She gazed up the incline to where Aurie was standing.

"Who are you and why are you standing in my class?"

asked the professor like a drill sergeant from the Marines.

Twenty heads turned to face her. The sudden wave of attention made her want to crawl back out of the room. She held up her hand, then realizing she didn't know what to do with it, shoved it behind her back.

"I'm Aurie. I joined Arcanium today," she said, cringing at how stupid it sounded as the words left her lips.

"You're late," said the professor.

Aurie jawed at the air for a moment. "You see, at the trials, I, uhm..."

"Not the trials, girl. Today. Semyon informed me that I would receive a new student. At the beginning of class. You are late. If this is how you plan to treat your studies, you won't last long in Arcanium," said Professor Mali.

Aurie would have explained that Patron Gray had said nothing about when she was supposed to arrive, but could see that the professor would only take excuses as a negative.

"I'll try to do better next time," she said.

"Try?" said the professor, looking like she'd just eaten a spoonful of manure. "You'll do more than try. You'll fucking be on time or you won't be here. Do you understand me, initiate?"

"Yes, ma'am. I mean professor," said Aurie, and she quickly grabbed a seat.

"I didn't say you could sit. Since you weren't here at the beginning of class, you can wait outside until we're done. Then I'll show you the initiates' quarters," she said.

If she'd had a tail, she would have tucked it between her legs as she slunk out of the door. The class continued while Aurie stood outside. She listened intently, not wanting to miss anything.

Despite the dressing down, Aurie was buoyant. She'd spent so many years teaching herself magic from books she got at the library that listening to a lecture, even from outside of the room, was a treasure.

About an hour later, class was dismissed. As the other initiates filed out, she saw a few familiar faces from the trials, including that cute redheaded guy that had partnered with Pi. She received mostly friendly nods. She could see the curiosity in their gazes.

Then Aurie was struck by an expression so sour, it made her double take. Violet Cardwell stormed out of the auditorium, her perfume choking Aurie as it wafted past.

Aurie couldn't believe it. How did Violet Cardwell end up in Arcanium? She didn't have long to contemplate before Professor Mali came rolling out. The professor waited until the other initiates had left before speaking.

"Semyon told me you were an exemplary student. He's been known to have moments of poor judgment. I hope this is not one of those," said the professor.

"I promise you I will work as hard as I can," said Aurie, annoyed at the pleading tone in her voice.

The professor wheeled down the hallway, her voice trailing after, "Your words are meaningless to me. I will believe it when I see it."

The professor explained the layout of the three wings and various floors, the rules, and the expectations for class. It was clear that she had this speech memorized, but she did not sound bored. She gave them as if Aurie were the President coming for a tour.

"As for your room, your addition is something of a problem. We are completely full at the moment. Already initiates are two to a room; therefore we'll have to improvise," said the professor, rolling to a dingy brown door tucked away in the back of the dorm wing.

At the professor's urging Aurie opened the door to find a

janitorial closet. Brooms, buckets, and cleaning supplies filled the messy room. It had the smell of old dirty mops.

"You can drag whatever's in the room into the hall. I'll have someone take it away. A bed will be brought up before evening. Do you need anything else?" asked Professor Mali.

"No," said Aurie. "Thank you. I'm happy to be here."

"Happiness is not a requirement for my students. Success is," said the professor, before rolling away.

Aurie threw her backpack against the wall and started hauling supplies out of the closet.

Once the professor had left the wing, the other first years came out of their rooms like frightened woodland animals checking to make sure the hunter was gone.

"She can be pretty rough," said the first initiate to arrive. It was the guy in the martial arts uniform from the trials. "The name's Deshawn."

"I'm Aurie," she said, then rolled her eyes. "Yeah, you probably already know that."

The other initiates introduced themselves. The names were a blur: Jacqueline, Xi, Drake, Daniel, and so on. Aurie only counted thirteen. She had a good idea where the rest of them were since Violet hadn't shown her face.

"So what was your pick order?" asked Deshawn.

"Pick order?"

"The halls. That accident didn't rattle anything loose, did it?" he asked.

Mention of the trials reminded her that Deshawn had been on Violet's team. She recognized another member of Violet's squad amongst the group. Deshawn seemed to react to Aurie's sudden discomfort.

"Hey, sorry about that. I was just optimizing my chances of getting into the Halls," he said.

"It's okay. It was a strategically sound move. Arcanium

was my only pick," said Aurie.

The other initiates reacted as if she'd just sprouted a second head.

"Are you nuts?" asked Deshawn. "You signed up for this?"

"Of course," said Aurie. "Didn't you all?"

It was clear by their faces that Arcanium hadn't been their first pick, and probably not even in their top ten. They each explained that they'd only put Arcanium on the list to make sure they got into a hall, but for each, it'd been near the bottom. It explained Violet's presence at Arcanium, as well.

"Where'd you all finish?" she asked.

"Yeah, we thought of that. All over the place, really. We can't make sense of it," he said.

"What hall was your top pick? Enforcers?" she asked him.

His lip twitched. "Dramatics. I thought the uniform would help me get picked in any team events."

Everyone else added their first choices—they were all from minor schools.

"Dinner's soon," said Deshawn. "Let's get you moved in."

The group made quick work of the janitorial closet. While they were cleaning it out, a fourth year came walking down the hallway with a bed balanced on his hand like a serving platter. He set the bed into the back of the closet, whispered to it, and left the room with no further comment.

Afterwards, she joined them at dinner, which she thought meant that she would be eating. When they led her into the kitchen and put her on dish duty, her stomach groaned in protest. After the older students were finished with dinner, Aurie was finally given a chance to eat. It was the best meal she'd ever eaten.

19

Light jazz haunted the Glass Cabaret. The booths were filled with customers, but Pi couldn't make them out. An enchantment obscured their voices and faces, which gave her an idea of the kind of people that frequented the bar.

She waited at the end, knowing full well that Radoslav had seen her. He was talking with a trio of men in sharp suits that looked like they needed Tommy guns tucked under their armpits. They rippled when she looked at them. It wasn't like the shield that the Coterie patron used, but she had to concentrate to see details.

After they left, Radoslav appeared at her end of the bar. At first glance, his eyes were night black, but after she looked a second time, they were gray.

"What court?" asked Pi, with a nod towards the other side of the bar where the trio had been.

Radoslav's lip collected a well-honed sneer. "Would you ask a woman her age?"

"The Jade Court, then," she said, knowing she was right when he changed the subject.

"Was our bargain worth it?" he asked.

He was handsome. Model handsome, the kind in a perfume ad that glowers at the camera with a detached amusement.

She felt compelled to speak right away, but fought it on principle.

"You said you had a job for me," she said, staring him straight in the eyes.

"You're no fun," he said, idly wiping the table with his pristine white rag. Pi wondered if he had all the surfaces enchanted to resist dust, because everything gleamed.

"I need something delivered," he said.

"Isn't that rather mundane? You could get a courier to do that," she said.

He leaned forward. A puff of breath hit her face. It had a metallic tint to it. Suddenly, the words she'd held back before came tumbling out despite her revulsion.

"For now, but I have to survive first," she said, fighting the words as they came out.

After the compulsion was over, he said, "I need to be able to trust said courier. Since I can make you answer me truthfully, among other things, I will not lay awake at night wondering."

"I didn't think you slept," she said. "And I wouldn't do that."

"Spare me the innocent act," he said. "You signed up for Coterie, which implies a certain moral flexibility in your quest for power."

The accusation stung more than a slap across the face. She wanted to think that she would use her power differently than the others, but until she proved that, no one would believe her.

"Speaking of Coterie. I'd like to trade for information," she said quietly.

He snapped his fingers and the air around them

shimmered, obscuring their conversation. "Trade?   What could you have that would be worth a trade?"

"What if I told you the name of the Coterie patron?"

He gave a dismissive shrug. "It's not so difficult to attain if you know where to look. And I already have."

"That name is a fake, attached to a fake history," she said. "I checked. This is his real one. It took a bit of digging to verify once I acquired it, but I'm certain."

He showed his perfect white teeth. "How did you acquire it?"

"During the binding, when I joined Coterie," she said.

"You shouldn't have been able to do that," he said, gravely serious.

"That's what I thought too.   While it's not uncommon for little details like a craving for their favorite food or speech patterns to transfer over during that moment, something that important should have never reached my mind," she said.

"Then how do you explain it?" he asked.

"I don't," she said. "But I have the name and I want to trade it for information."

He surged forward and did the trick with the air in her face. "Tell me his true name."

Pi gave him a cat-bird smile. "I added a little protection of my own. You won't be getting it that easily."

"I had to try," he said. "But if you want your information, I need to verify that the name is real. Think of it as a credit check. You give me the name, I check it out. If it is real, I'll answer your questions, whatever they are."

Pi knew that she was underselling the patron's name, but it was worth it to be generous with Radoslav, and to remind him that she could be useful.

"Deal," she said, and leaned forward and whispered it into his ear. A strange look passed across his face before he nodded.

"The delivery?"

He shoved an ornate box across the bar. The edges had gold filigree runes. There was, no doubt, a binding on it. Something small and light shifted inside, bumping against the inner walls.

A piece of paper was tucked into her hand. An address in the second ward was listed in a neat scrawl.

"I don't want to be transporting drugs or anything illegal," said Pi.

"You should have thought of that before you signed up," he said.

Pi pushed the box back across the table.

Radoslav snorted lightly. She hoped he was amused. "I acquire things. In this case, something is being made for a client. I'll need you to come back and deliver another one every six weeks, four total."

She collected the box and slipped it into the canvas carryall hanging over her shoulder.

Radoslav held her with his eyes. She waited for the eventual comment.

"Before you go," he said, glancing around to make sure no one was watching. He put a spell on her. Not like a human mage with gestures and voice shaping the magic. He was city fae. His womb had been concrete and steel and glass. Smoke leaked from his lips as if he'd just taken a drag off a cigarette, then he blew it out, enveloping her in his magic. The smell reminded her of gasoline and skyscrapers.

"I didn't know you cared so much," she told him, trying not to cough.

"Keep your hood up," he said without a trace of inflection. "Make the delivery. No messing around."

It wasn't until she was a few blocks away near the train

station that she understood the nature of his enchantment. She bumped into a guy in a Ramones T-shirt with big round white headphones on, and when he looked at her, he reacted with surprise as if she wasn't supposed to be standing there.

On the train, she traced the outline of the box through the canvas bag. Radoslav had assured her that it wasn't illegal, but she didn't know how much she could trust him. But there were too many people on the train for her to pull it out and examine the protective magics.

Pi had never been to the second ward because it was the entertainment district, and they'd never had the money to enjoy the sort of events that went on there. When famous bands visited the city, they played the Glitterdome.

Evening brought out the tourists, who wanted to experience the city of sorcery. They carried little replicas of the Spire that lit up like colorful icicles, or threw illusionary powder into the air—summoning the images of Siberian dragons, or swamp hags, or sea giants.

The buildings gave Pi the impression she was at an amusement park. The Great Garbanzo, Master Illusionist, was playing at the Orpheum Theater, which took up a whole block. Jillian Garbanzo was the Dramatics Hall most famous alumnus. After a worldwide tour, he'd set up shop in the city.

She found her destination at the edge of the first ward, as if the owner had wanted to be a part of the old money district but hadn't been allowed. The building looked like someone had dropped a pile of steel pylons into the earth, then connected them with glass.

A couple of muscular security guards wearing sunglasses— despite it being nighttime—stood outside the estate. They looked right through Radoslav's enchantment, staring at her the whole way up the path. When she saw the pins in the shape of a club on their lapels, she knew why. They'd been trained by the Protector's Hall.

Pi flashed her rune. The nearest guard pulled down his shades. His eyes glittered with magic. She guessed he could see in multiple spectrums. He whispered into his lapel, then nodded her towards the entrance.

The inside of the building was no better than the outside. A stuffed pink poodle on a pedestal stood inside the doorway. Orange question marks hung on the hallway wall. Pi had the feeling that the owner thought the experimental art pieces displayed culture.

"What the fuck do you mean I've got a delivery?" came a voice from somewhere deeper inside.

Heavy footfalls made her tense up. Pi suddenly realized that this delivery wasn't as simple as Radoslav had made it out to be. She pulled the hood tighter around her head.

She knew him as soon as he came around the corner. His crew cut, track suit, and nearly seven-foot frame were unmistakable. It was Bannon Creed. His company, Blackstone Security, provided magical protection to high-ranking government officials, heads of major corporations, or anyone else with enough money. His face had been splattered over the media a few years back when Blackstone Security had been accused of providing services to warlords in the east African conflicts. He was also the patron of the Protector's Hall.

"Who the fuck are you?" he asked.

It took a moment to recover from the entrance. He had a forceful presence. "I work for Radoslav."

When she started reaching into her carryall, Bannon's hand went to his hip while the other was held out.

"Not another fucking move," he said.

Bannon bristled with awakened magic. A glance into his crazed eyes revealed he was on drugs, or illicit magics. He looked ready to unleash something horrible. The sharp smell of ozone was in the air.

Pi held her hands up. "I'm here to make a delivery. From Radoslav."

A trio of women's voices called to him from the other room, enticing him to come back or miss the fun. Pi resisted a shiver of revulsion.

"It's in the carryall. Let me just take it out and give it to you," she said. When he didn't move, she added, "Your guard outside checked me out, or he wouldn't have let me in."

Bannon blinked, waking from his daze. The magic slowly receded.

She pulled out the ornate box and held it out. She regretted not just sliding it across the floor to him when he moved to accept it.

His massive hand curled around the box and her fingers. She couldn't pull away fast enough. Bannon's eyes were not on the box, but her.

With the tip of a finger, he pulled back her hood, revealing her short black hair, shaved on one side, and streaks of indigo hanging in the front. A revolting smile lingered on his lips.

"And who are you, delivery girl?" he asked.

"No one," she said.

"Would *no one* like to make a little extra money?" he asked, though she didn't think it was a question. Fear rippled up from her gut. She was more afraid than when the demon lord had escaped his circle.

Bannon Creed moved his meaty hand to caress her face, but a spark leaped out and shocked him. He stepped backwards, his face creasing with anger for a moment, before switching to wry amusement.

The women called to him again. He gave Pi a long, skin-crawling look before returning to them. Pi thought he said, "Fucking Radoslav," on his way back.

Pi didn't breathe again until she was safely on the train back to the Obelisk, her obligation to Radoslav complete for the moment. If the next delivery in six weeks was back to Bannon Creed, she wasn't sure she would be able to convince herself to step back into his house.

20

An early November tropical storm battered the eastern coast, bringing sheeting rain to the city of sorcery. The winds were bad enough the gondolas had to be grounded, not that she was allowed to ride them.

Aurie sat with her classmates in the room next to the Verum Locus, waiting for Professor Mali while gusts battered the home of the Arcanium. Violet sat up front with her gaggle of friends, playing Five Elements while they waited. Aurie tried to ignore the sounds of the game by concentrating on the storm.

When the professor wheeled into the room, she was soaking wet. She looked uncharacteristically distracted, though it didn't last long. As soon as she noticed the class staring at her, she snapped her fingers, which squeezed the water from her clothes and hair and deposited it in a glass on the table.

"Truth magic," she began in an elevated voice. "The Arcanium was founded on the idea that knowledge is power. Knowledge is gained through the seeking out of truth, no matter how inconvenient the answer. But before you can master truth magic, you must master yourself. Today we begin that task.

"Through that door is the Verum Locus, the room of truth. In there, you will relive the most eventful moments of your life. If you cannot master them, you will not be able to master the magic of truth. Without that, you cannot be a member of Arcanium."

A wash of vertigo overtook Aurie. *Relive her memories?* For the first time in her life, she actually questioned joining Arcanium.

"I see that look in your eyes, the slackness of your faces," said the professor. "You're suddenly doubting why you came here in the first place. This is natural. We all have moments in our lives that we never want to return to. When I was an initiate, I was forced to relive the moment I lost my legs. But once I overcame that fear, I no longer wanted to have my legs magically grow back."

A surge of unexpected rage filled Aurie's chest, bringing water to her eyes. She pushed it back down until it choked her.

"One by one, you will enter the room of truth. I cannot tell you what you will encounter there, and only you will know what happened. But know that you cannot fake your way out of this. I *will* know if you are engaging the truth or a fabrication of your own making."

The professor took a long look at everyone. Her gaze was sympathetic, which worried Aurie more than any yelling could.

"One last thing," said the professor. "Remember that we are at our greatest power when we give up control."

The professor let it sink in before tapping Deshawn on the shoulder. "You're first."

Deshawn got up, glancing back at the class as if he were a prisoner on his way to execution. After he was gone, the room fell into a sullen silence. Violet and her friends tried to resume their game, but it sputtered to nothing but lip biting and feet tapping.

It seemed like it was forever before Deshawn returned. It seemed like it was only a few seconds.

He came back ashen. He wouldn't meet anyone's gaze and took a seat on the far side away from everyone else and held himself.

Professor Mali sent Xi into the room next. The Chinese initiate came back sobbing twenty minutes later. The professor gave him a comforting nod.

One by one, they went in. Everyone came out affected by whatever experience they had in the room. Each time, Aurie mentally begged to get sent in, wanting to get hers over with, but was then relieved when it was someone else.

When Violet went in, Aurie found herself wishing that it was an awful experience. But when the blonde initiate came out in tears, and ran out of the room before anyone could stop her, a wave of guilt hit Aurie.

"Aurelia," said Professor Mali.

Aurie startled, kicking the seat in front of her, receiving a withering glance from Jacqueline.

The professor gave her a terse look as she went by. Aurie found she could hardly swallow as she entered the room. The door clicking shut felt like a tomb closing over her.

It was an ordinary room, except for one feature. It was filled with the golden speckled light of faez. The raw magic made her skin tingle as if she'd been dipped in mint.

She waited a moment, but nothing happened. She turned, facing each of the four directions. She rubbed her eyes, wondering if something was wrong.

"Maybe—"

The words were ripped from her lips as the world dissolved

around her. The colors of a different life painted in as the old one faded. They were the shades of memory, of dreams.

She was in her old house—the three story with the brick front. It was an idyllic spring day. The kind you visited in your memories of childhood.

Aurie sat in the living room playing a game of Senet with her sister, Pi. Her hands moved without thought, lifting the smooth stones from one bowl on the board to another. Aurie remembered that her mother had brought the game back from Egypt as a consolation prize for being gone so long. She'd been on a research trip investigating ancient artifacts.

Adolescent rage filled her like a balloon, then popped with the thoughts of what would happen that day.

You know nothing about rage yet, Aurie told herself, *but you will.*

Across from her, the ten-year-old version of Pi moved her stones. She wore her hair long, past her shoulders. Wisps of curls haunted the edges, especially around her face. That fierce spark was in her sister's eyes—buoyant beyond reproach.

She'd forgotten how different Pi had been before the accident. It made her skin itch and she wanted to tug at her hair, but the vision wouldn't let her. She was being marched down the path of the worst day of her life. Why would they do this to her? What kind of school forced people to relive events like this?

It wasn't like she needed to see this day again. Aurie knew this day like the beating of her own heart. It was the day their parents died. She wanted to reach out and gather her sister in her arms and hold her tight, to protect her against what was to come.

"Do you think they'll let me take Scratches to Arcanium?" asked Pi as the orange tabby weaved between her feet.

Scratches was an old cat with gray around his muzzle.

The younger version of Aurie gave the cat a long look before answering, "Yeah, Pi. I'm sure they'll let you."

It won't matter much longer.

Aurie tried to get her body to move, even a twitch like yanking on a string of a marionette, but she was trapped in her own memory. A cold dread filled her chest, made her face numb. She vacillated between fear and rage. This was worse than watching a movie of it, because she could feel her emotions at the time, yet also feel her own present day ones.

Pi tilted her head. "I'm not an idiot. I know the cat's old, but I was hoping you could help him live longer. Maybe Dad could help you, since you're gonna be a healer like him."

Their mother, Nahid, stepped into the room. Even before Aurie turned her head, she wanted to scream: *No! Get out! Get out now!* But as soon as she laid eyes upon her, those feelings were swept away by the longing to be held by her mother again.

Aurie had forgotten how beautiful she was. Her crackling blue eyes contrasted with her dark hair laid out like a silky waterfall upon a floral scarf. Her intelligence was held like a sword before her. Aurie had watched many a man be skewered on her wit, thinking she was an assistant or secretary. Though she could display moments of cold calculation, her heart was as warm as a summer day.

Aurie found herself trembling. She wanted to rush into her arms, smell the lilac perfume she wore, bury her face in her shoulder, and let the pains and agonies of the last few years pour out in a torrent. She felt like a starved dog chained to an old post with salvation within sight. It was an ache that went down to her roots, until she felt like her chest was going to cave in from the pressure.

Memories bubbled up: huddling in bed with her mother and Pi, reading adventure novels and giggling with abandon, sitting in her lap as a small child watching storms light up the night sky, mother chasing her around the kitchen with a scoop of icing on a spoon to dab on her nose.

"Girls," said her mother with a faint Iranian accent. "Your father and I have work to do in the basement. It's very delicate and we cannot be distracted. So you'll need to play quietly up here until then. Now would be a good time to do your homework."

"Yes, Mother," they said in unison, while the real Aurie screamed, *NO!*

"*Dooset daram,*" said Nahid, her love coming through the phrase.

"*Dooset daram,*" the vision girls repeated.

Nahid left the two girls to their game of Senet.

No, Mother. Don't go. You won't come out again. You won't come out at all.

But then she remembered she would come out as a charred and broken body. Aurie remembered sitting on the back of the ambulance getting questioned by a police officer about what happened when they'd pulled her mother's body out of the remains of their house. The smell of death choked her.

Eventually, young Pi said to Aurie, "I'm bored with this game," and gave a shrug before moving towards the stack of homework on the kitchen table.

"I don't want to do homework," said young Aurie.

Pi had her hands on her binders. Little colored tabs stuck out from the papers. Pi was looking out the front window. Her head was slightly tilted.

"Wanna play Five Elements? The real way, with faez?" asked young Aurie.

Pi's forehead scrunched. "But Mom said we're not allowed to play it that way. We have to play finger exercises only."

"Come on, Pi. Everyone at school plays with faez. Don't

be a chicken, bawk-bawk," said young Aurie, flapping her arms, elbows out.

Pi put her hands on her hips. "I'm telling Mom and Dad you called me a chicken."

"You heard her. She said not to bother them. Now come over here and play me, or are you afraid you'll get beat again?" said young Aurie.

Pi's face went through contortions, caught between her sister's mocking taunts and the desire to listen to their parents. The origins of her sister's persistence were glimmers in her eyes.

No. No. No. Don't listen to me. Go get them. You shouldn't let me bully you like that. She shook her invisible head. *Dammit, I forgot how much of an idiot I was.*

Pi plopped down in front of Aurie, her expression one of fierce determination. They went right into a match of Five Elements.

The surge of faez surprised Aurie. She didn't know if it were the vision Aurie or the real one using magic, but it felt raw and uncontrolled. She was sure sweat had beaded up on her brow back in the truth room, but she couldn't wipe it off.

Pi, despite being younger by three years, beat Aurie three games in a row. Then she got up and made a face.

"See. I'm not afraid. And I'm better than you," said Pi.

Aurie remembered the rage coursing through her veins like hot lead. It felt just as bad the second time.

"I was letting you win," said young Aurie. "Best out of seven."

"I don't want to," said Pi.

"Fine, but I'll tell Michael that you like him," said young Aurie.

Pi threw her arms to her side and sat across from Aurie again. This time she looked mad enough to spit.

The game began like the others, but this time, young Aurie tapped into her well of magic and hammered her sister with it. Inside the vision, the real Aurie was swallowed by the overwhelming feelings of angst fueled by the potent raw stuff of magic. The more she fed her feelings, the less in control she was.

It wasn't fair, she told herself. *I was young and everyone did it. How was I supposed to know what would happen?*

But she did know. The dangers of magic had been drilled into her again and again. At school. At home. The government mandated safety classes for all children who could wield faez beyond the barest spark.

She knew, she knew, she knew. This thought sat on her chest like acid, burning into her soul. Through the haze of tears the vision persisted. The feedback loop kept growing. Fountains of raw faez flowed from Aurie. She lost the understanding between the vision and reality.

The world whirled around her, spinning out of control. She was no longer playing the game, but fighting against the wave of magic flooding from her body.

When the fire came rushing in, she instinctively formed a shield around herself and Pi. The blast threw them out of the building.

Later, the investigators would tell her that the uncontrolled magic had hit a gas line and triggered an explosion. These types of accidents were not uncommon. Youngsters with access to powerful magics was like giving a toddler a gun, they reminded her afterwards. As if she didn't already know.

This did not reassure her like they thought it would. But what did they know about comforting a thirteen-year-old girl who just caused the death of her parents?

Aurie became aware that she was back in the room of truth. She felt strangely numb, drained. Salt lines crisscrossed her face. She rubbed the scar on the inside of her left forearm where shattered glass had cut her. A section of lumpy flesh along her ribs ached from the memory of the explosion. The raw faez had warped her flesh as it flowed from her body.

After collecting herself, Aurie exited the room, squeezing her arms around her chest. She desperately wanted to see her sister.

But she didn't make it far. The pinched lips and hard, distinctive jawline on Professor Mali stopped Aurie in her tracks. The words came hissing out above a whisper, loud enough for the rest of the class to hear: "If you're not going to take this seriously, then you're not going to even last until the winter break."

Aurie stumbled out of the room, her insides barren as ground zero of a nuclear blast. In a daze, she wandered through the wing until she found a dark corner in one of the Hall's many libraries. She shoved herself into the corner, as far as she could go, until the shelves bit into her back. Then she curled around her knees, pulling so tight she could barely breathe.

When that wouldn't do, she punched the floor hard enough to break the skin on her knuckles. And again. And again.

"It was my fault. It was my fault. It was my fault."

She kept repeating the words like a spell, hoping that somehow admitting her mistakes might bring forgiveness, and more importantly, her parents back. But that wouldn't work. Nothing would. They were gone. Buried in the ground seven years. She would never see them again, not even in that room, because she was never going back there again.

21

Orson Rutherford stood in front of the class naked as an imp. Wisps of white material hung over his muscular body. He was doing his best to cover himself with his hands, but given the circular nature of the classroom, he had to practically cup himself.

Ashley elbowed Pi in the ribs and whispered, "I told you he has a nice body."

"Thank you, Orson," said Professor Augustus, speaking loudly to be heard over the laughter, "for demonstrating what poor finger work does to a simple transfiguration spell. Please have a seat."

Pi grinned at Ashley. "Poor finger work?"

She rolled her eyes in extravagant fashion.

As Orson waddled back to his table, he asked, "Can I go get a new set of clothes?"

The corner of the professor's lips crept up in a mischievous smile. "Feel lucky you only lost your clothes. Had you formed your hook-and-claw gesture with any less rigidity, you'd have turned your silk shirt into a blanket of brown recluse spiders rather than a spider's web."

Orson looked mortified at what his mistake could have caused and took his original spot, pressing himself against the table for covering.

"He does have a nice ass," whispered Pi, noting the way his cheeks dimpled.

Professor Augustus clapped his hands at each syllable of the first word he said: "Specificity. Say it with me class. Specificity.   Without proper enunciation, without proper gesturing, without proper faez shaping, you will Fuck. It. Up. You are mages, not short-order cooks throwing together a batch of scrambled eggs for a couple of truckers in bibs. Need I remind you that your classmate Bentley is still at the hospital, breathing through his ribcage with his skin turned to slime? Laugh if you want, but there's a good chance we'll never see him again, and I suspect that even if we do, it won't be in Coterie."

Someone in the back, Pi couldn't tell who, muttered, "It'll be in the sewers."

The professor, without turning around, said, "Rather than make jokes, Brock DuPont, you might consider relying less on your trinkets and learn how to be more exact, or you might be sharing a sewer with Bentley. Because I've learned over the years that those that rely on their magical devices rather than honing their skills are usually the first ones to go."

Pi was sneaking a look at Brock's face when she heard her name: "Pythia! Front and center. You're next."

She strode to the dais. The squeak of her sneakers cut through the silence. She bit her lower lip as she waited for the instruction.

"Miss Pythia," said Augustus. A few whispers of Hick Pi echoed around the room. "I would like you to transfigure the daisies in that vase to a more extravagant flower."

As Pi approached the desk, the door wheezed open. Alton

Lockwood marched into the room. His expensive shoes clicked against the hardwood. He adjusted the lapel of his white suit with practiced disdain.

"Sorry I'm late, Professor," he said without a trace of apology in his tone. "I had business with the patron."

"No need to apologize," said Augustus. "Miss Pythia was about to show us a proper transfiguration, since Orson failed spectacularly in all regards."

Alton met her gaze, but gave no indication of his enmity. She'd encountered him a few times in the Obelisk. He'd been cordial, which worried Pi more than anything.

She pushed Alton out of her mind and concentrated on the transfiguration. Changing one thing into another took more than just memorizing a spell and performing it flawlessly. Even similar items were different enough that it created complications. It made it more difficult that the flowers were a living thing.

Essentially, Pi had to reform the structure of the flower while not destroying the living cells. In this case, knowledge about flowers and their makeup was required. Luckily, last year Aurie had been on a horticulture kick when she heard a rumor about potion mixing during the trials, and had made them both memorize the useful parts of common flowers, so Pi was well versed.

"We're waiting," said Alton from behind her, making her think back to when she'd misidentified a common paperweight.

Pi set her hands on either side of the bouquet of daisies and cracked her knuckles by squeezing her hands into fists. The flowers drooped over the edge of the vase, having been sitting in tepid water for days.

First, she let faez flow into the flowers. They twitched with the added energy. The next part required deft dexterity. She manipulated the spell, pulling and tugging as if she were making dough.

Pi had an image in her head of what kind of flower she wanted to create, but she noticed the other students yawning with boredom or checking their cell phones and thought about what Ashley had said after the Amber & Smoke about making friends. These kids understood the politics of power. To get them on her side, she had to prove that she was a force to be reckoned with.

Pi decided she needed to do something even more spectacular than she'd first planned, but she didn't have enough living material to create what she wanted. While keeping the daisies in a malleable state, she searched the room with her eyes. Once she had identified the additional living material, she performed a one-handed levitating spell on the creeping philodendron on the back wall, drawing it towards her.

A few in-breaths signaled an increased interest, but Pi wasn't done yet. With the philodendron draped over the daisies like a bad wig, Pi added even more faez, softening up the plant material to be transformed.

Shaping was more artistry than engineering. Once she had broken down the material, she had to rearrange it into the desired shape. As she worked, the other initiates leaned forward against their desks.

Feeling ambitious, she levitated a chicken bone from the reagents tray and added it to the transfiguration. She tried to ignore the whispers as her classmates tried to figure out what she was trying to do. She was coming to the most delicate part—she had to get the parts to fuse together.

Pi was moving through her fingerings, dancing the faez around the plant material like a master seamstress stitching a dress in midair. The new plant was beginning to take shape: it had a bulbous body with a parted mouth lined with bone teeth and cowl of leaves. She was at the most difficult part—she had to convince the whole structure to meld together—when something hit the floor, making a loud noise and breaking her concentration.

The delicate lattice of magic and plant material snapped. The plant-flower-bone hybrid collapsed on the desk in a sludge of green muck. It hissed and bubbled. Captured faez dissipated into the air.

She spun around expecting to find that Alton had dropped a tome on the floor, ready to skewer him with a vicious insult, only to realize that the book was lying at Professor Augustus' feet.

His gaze was a mixture of disappointment and something else she couldn't decipher.

"Thank you, Miss Pythia, for demonstrating the next most common failure point for mages: unearned ambition," he said. "While the buildup was impressive, you have to be capable of carrying through or pay the price. I thought Orson was a shoo-in for worst performance today, but you won today's lowest grade, and have earned an evening cleaning out the alchemical vat. Thank you, class, you are dismissed."

Pi stood stunned while green goo dripped on her sneakers. A hiss of noxious fumes escaped the mixture. She felt her face grow bright crimson.

Ashley squeezed her shoulder as she went by. "That was shitty of the professor. Whatever it was you were making looked like it was going to be spectacular."

"Thanks, Ash," said Pi, staring at the green slime dripping from the table.

She caught an amused snicker from Alton before he left the room.

The professor was tidying up his materials when Pi approached him.

"Professor Augustus, may I ask a question?"

His right eye twitched as he adjusted his thin-rimmed glasses with pinched fingers. He cleared his throat. Standing so close reminded her of how young he was, maybe not even into his thirties.

"You may," he said.

"Why did you interrupt my spell?" she asked.

His gaze went to the floor, then he glanced at the door before returning to her. "Are you asking for special treatment?"

"No," she said forcefully. "I wouldn't do that. I just want to know why you did that to me and not any of the other initiates."

She wanted to ask if the patron didn't want her there, but wisely.

"Why do you want to be in Coterie?" he asked, chin raised.

"I want to learn magic, and Coterie had the best reputation," she told him confidently.

His eye twitched again. She couldn't figure out why he seemed disappointed.

"You would probably be the only one of your class who is here for those reasons," he said.

She opened her mouth to refute him, but wondered if he wasn't right. Even Ashley was only in Coterie because she had no other choice if she wanted to be a mage.

"Why did you join Coterie?" she asked.

His eyes creased with mirth. "For the same reason as you."

"I don't understand," she said. "You've done very well in Coterie. You're Master of Initiates."

"Ahh, yes. That's true," he said, but he didn't seem to believe his own words.

His ambivalence made her uneasy.

"Where does your last name come from? I've never heard

Silverthorne before," he said, his brow furrowing.

"It's made up, kinda. My mother didn't want to take my father's last name, so they compromised by taking an amalgamation of each of their last names. We're the first, you could say," explained Pi.

"And how many generations of DuPonts, or Bishops, or Lockwoods do you think there are?" he asked.

"Many generations, I would imagine," she said, and when the professor frowned, she added, "probably further, I guess. To the founding of the country."

"My last name is much like yours," he said, his eyes taking on a sympathetic cast. "Trebleton is a new name, or at least new by their standards. My five years as an initiate with that name was a living hell. So if you think they're going to allow you to show them up in their own Hall, you're either a fool or blind."

"But if I keep getting low scores, I won't make it to second year," she said.

His face took on a hard mask. "Then maybe I will have saved your life."

He swept out of the room before she could say anything else, leaving her to clean up the mess and ponder his warning.

22

Aurie spun a twenty-sided die on the counter at Freeport Games while she waited. The plastic piece whisked and jumped across the glass surface. Her dark hair hung over her face. She just didn't care enough to move it back behind her ear. Inside the glass case were bowls of dice and counters, and at the end, sitting on a velvet holder, a swirling indigo glass ball.

"Aurie!" cried her sister.

She barely turned before Pi tackled her in a hug. Her sister made purring noises as she buried her face in her shoulder. The grin on Aurie's face almost hurt, she was smiling so hard.

"Oh god, Pi. I missed you," she said, squeezing her sister in a smothering hug. Pi was a little shorter, so her head tucked neatly beneath her chin.

"I'm not letting go, like ever," said Pi.

Aurie feigned a choke. "I'm dying, I'm dying."

"You're not dead yet," said Pi in an English accent.

Eventually Aurie pulled away. They sighed at the same time, which released a couple of giggles. Pi's ensemble of designer jeans, polka-dot silk shirt, and form-fitted black jacket surprised Aurie. Her hair was missing its indigo streak.

"Does Coterie give you a fashion stipend or something?" she asked.

"Ash got them for me. Said they were her younger sister's," she said.

Aurie raised an eyebrow. "It's not like you to try and fit in."

A bit of darkness passed across Pi's gaze.

"It's hard to explain. Coterie is...well, it's Coterie," said Pi, sort of shrugging her shoulders. "How's Arcanium? Top of the class as expected?"

Aurie wanted to spill the truth, that she was performing terribly. All the years of studying, expecting Arcanium to be about books and knowledge—which it was, there were plenty of wonderful, musty, old tomes—but it was more than that, it was different. But if she started talking, then she'd have to bring up the truth room, and their parents' death, and she didn't want to ruin their reunion.

"I'm doing okay," said Aurie.

Pi punched her sister in the arm. "You're so modest."

Further discussion was cut short when Hemistad shuffled into the room. He jingled faintly as if he were hiding bells in his pockets. His eyebrows wagged on their own like two bushy caterpillars trying to escape.

"The Silverthorne sisters. What a joyful day that you're both under my roof at the same time. I was beginning to wonder if you were just one person, maybe a doppelgänger or a fetch. I was preparing a ward to protect myself," he said, the mirth coming through his voice in warm tones. "Are we ready for a little task?"

Pi glanced to Aurie, deferring. "What do you need us to do?"

He frowned a little when he noticed Pi's clothing. He hooked a finger in their direction. "Come with me."

He led them into the back. Aurie thought she knew the store layout well, but he took them through an unfamiliar hallway into a room with a well in it. The diameter of the stone ring was at least ten feet. A stainless steel mechanical winch was fastened to the ceiling. A steel wire went into the hole.

Aurie shared a glance with her sister, who made an I-have-no-idea face. Hemistad grabbed a yellow pendant with black buttons on it. His discolored thick nails clicked against the hard plastic. He pressed the bottom button, and the winch whirled into life. After about thirty seconds, steel grating appeared. Hemistad stopped the platform right below the edge of the stone.

He climbed onto the platform with the remote in his hand, looking at them expectantly.

"What are we doing?" she asked.

Hemistad blinked hard as if he didn't understand the question. "You needed help and I provided it. Now I would like your assistance in some matter of importance to me. Are you unwilling?""

Aurie's thoughts went back to a previous visit, when Hemistad had momentarily let her see his true self. Was he luring them into a basement to murder them? Pi seemed to have the same reservations.

"No. Not unwilling. Just curious to what we're doing,""said Aurie.

Pi spread her hands out. "Come on, Hemistad. Don't you think it's fair that we ask?"

The momentary confusion on his hunched brow broke like a wave crashing in understanding. "Ahh, yes. I thought you had intuited where we were headed. We're going into the Undercity."

"But we're initiates, we're not allowed in the Undercity," said Aurie.

Pi added her agreement. "It's one of the first things they tell us. Even the older students are warned about the dangers and to only go in large groups, or with experienced mages."

"Rules? I'd hardly call it a rule. I think they're just trying to keep from losing too many foolish initiates. But you'll be fine. You're with me," he said. "Come, quickly. I'm on a schedule."

Aurie shrugged and joined Pi on the platform. The winch clicked into reverse, and they lurched downward. The shadows from the well quickly overtook them. Aurie touched her earrings, and light bloomed into the space. Pi added a wisp moments later.

The platform went down for a good minute. Aurie was beginning to wonder if they'd ever reach the bottom when the walls disappeared and they were plunged into a vast space. Pi's exclamation was quickly swallowed by the emptiness.

The platform hit the bottom with a solid thunk. Hemistad tucked the remote into a holder on the side and mumbled something about needing to change the batteries. Then he headed off directly as if he knew exactly where he was going. Aurie and Pi fell in behind him.

The ground was rocky, but relatively flat. It felt like they were in a large cave, but she hadn't seen any walls. Their wisps bobbed along with them. Aurie glanced back at the platform, realizing that if they lost Hemistad, they'd have no way to get back.

Later, rocky walls appeared out of the gloom. They entered a wide brick-lined tunnel that turned their footsteps to echoes. Brown seepage dripped down the walls. Aurie had an itchy feeling between her shoulder blades, but shook it off as her imagination.

Side tunnels went off into the darkness, but Hemistad stayed on the wider path. Sometimes they heard sounds from those openings: human voices, water dripping, other uncategorizable noises, including one that sounded like a chainsaw on helium.

They took turns occasionally. Aurie kept a mental map just in case, though she doubted she could get them across the cave back to the platform.

Hemistad led them out of the tunnels and into another wide space. It was colder here. The ground traveled deeper into the Undercity. They'd been underground for at least an hour.

Aurie thought she saw a faint glow in the distance, but when she turned to look, it was gone. Hemistad hadn't noticed, or at least gave no visible sign, so she stayed alert.

A deep growl reached out through the darkness, putting a shiver into Aurie's back. It wasn't nearby, but it was close enough.

Hemistad stopped and grumbled. "Consarn it."

His black eyes glistened in the darkness. They took on an otherworldly quality. He seemed uncertain of what to do next, looking in different directions.

When they heard the growl a second time, he mumbled, "Horse cocks," before turning to them.

The veneer of the old man had disappeared. He seemed stronger, more alert, hardier.

"We've encountered an unexpected complication. You must stay here while I go and deal with this. Do not try to help. Do not come after me. In fact, do not leave this spot no matter what. Your life depends on it."

He gave them no time to respond and marched off into the darkness like a man about to deal with his unruly hound, fists held at his sides.

The growl reverberated through the darkness from a different direction than before.

"What the hell is that?" whispered Pi. "Nothing normal can make that noise. It sounds like the belly of a dragon rumbling in hunger."

"Like that, but worse," said Aurie. "I think I would be relieved to find out it was a dragon."

"Any ideas?" asked Pi.

She shook her head. "Nothing that I've ever studied. It could be something unique to the Undercity. All the unused faez leaks down here, creating strange and terrible things."

They stood close together. Even when she couldn't hear anything, Aurie had the impression of a smothering darkness somewhere beyond the edge of the light. She thought about quenching her earrings, but standing in darkness seemed much worse than being a beacon.

When nothing happened for about ten minutes, Aurie began to relax. The presence of danger seemed to have moved on. She expected Hemistad to come back soon.

"I really wish we were in the same hall together," Aurie blurted out. "I feel like we're already growing apart, especially with your Coterie friends and all their connections."

Pi snorted derisively. "It's not like that. And I have to find my own way eventually. You can't be my mom forever."

A wave of guilt almost knocked Aurie over. She felt like she'd been plunged back into the truth room. "That's totally unfair. I never wanted that to happen."

"That's not what I mean, Aurie," said Pi, raising her voice. "We're different people. We can't be together always."

"But you're all I have left," said Aurie, ashamed of the way her voice cracked.

"It's not that," said Pi, her face wracked with anguish. She fumbled at her words. "Coterie is way more complicated than I expected. You just don't understand. It's not easy for me like it is for you at Arcanium."

"Easy? You have no idea. I'm not sure I'm even going—"

The words "to pass" were poised on her lips, but they stayed there when she heard a girl's scream. Pi's wide eyes showed that she'd heard it too. Aurie was about to ask, when she heard it a second time, more clearly.

"That sounded like someone's in trouble," said Pi, looking ready to jump into action.

"We should go help," said Aurie, imagining the girl who had screamed as Emily from the hospital.

"Hemistad said to stay," said Pi, though it was clear she didn't agree. She was practically running in the direction of the scream without actually moving.

"But he's not here, and I don't think he expected that to happen," said Aurie.

A concerned look passed across Pi's face. "What if that thing we heard is making that sound to lure us away?"

Aurie couldn't help but agree with her sister. There were many supernatural creatures that mimicked human voices to catch their prey. "Then we'd better be ready."

They moved in the direction they'd heard the sound. Her breath was loud in her ears. She wished she'd known they were going to the Undercity. She would have researched a spell that could have let them see in the dark. The bobbing lights gave away their position.

A young girl came stumbling out of the darkness, jeans ripped at the knees from falling. She looked a few years younger than Pi. Her Buffy T-shirt had blood on the sleeve, presumably not hers. She was shaking.

"Holy fuck," she said, face white with terror. "Please tell me there's a way out nearby."

"What's going on?" asked Pi. "What made you scream?"

"I don't know. And I don't want to know. But we'd better get the fuck out of here." The girl's face screwed up as she looked at Pi. "Are you doing some sort of fashion shoot down here? No wait. I don't care. Can we get out of here?"

She was trembling and hanging on to Pi's sleeve, looking all around as if she were expecting monsters to come jumping out of the darkness.

"There's no way out nearby," said Aurie, trying to sound calm even though inside her heart was trying to climb out of her chest. "So we need to understand what it is so we can help. We're mages."

The girl's lower lip trembled. "You know that feeling that you get when you're walking in the dark and you feel like you have to run, like right now. That's what it is, except with teeth. And it's hungry, really fucking hungry."

At that moment, something growled. It went right through Aurie's stomach. It was the same thing Hemistad had gone after.

Pi leapt into action. She had a packet of salt in her pocket. She made a circle on the stone. She didn't have a lot of salt, so the line was thin and ragged.

Aurie placed her fingers on her throat. Her veins were throbbing. She drew the magic up, whispering over and over until her neck was glowing. Then she spat her words out, sending them into the darkness like a sparrow to find Hemistad.

She joined Pi and the girl in the circle. Pi chanted a protection spell, her voice coming out with a tremor. The thing in the darkness growled again. It wasn't far beyond their bobbing wisps of light.

The salt line bothered Aurie. It looked too thin to hold up. She leaned down and started whispering to it, telling the line that it was thick and strong and would hold up to even a demon lord. She didn't know if truth magic worked on the materials of magic itself, Professor Mali hadn't taught them that, but she was out of other ideas.

She kept the faez flowing, not into the protection circle—Pi was doing that—but into the line of salt. It looked thicker by the time she was done whispering.

When the thing in the darkness came into the light, the impact shook the ground. The circle nearly collapsed around them. Aurie lent her sister strength as Pi fell to her knees.

The girl they'd rescued was screaming. The kind of mindless terror that burst eardrums.

The creature hit the circle again. Aurie had no immediate impression of it, except that it was made of darkness, and teeth, and hunger. It hit the circle harder than Pazuzu, the demon prince, had hit.

Aurie knew better than to look at it, but she wanted to stare into its horrible maw. It surrounded the circle, swallowing all light except the cylinder around them. Their protection was crumbling.

A hale voice called out in a strange language. The hunger in the darkness responded as if struck by a flaming whip. Hemistad had returned. His voice rose and fell like a symphony, each word acting like a hammer strike to the creature. He drove it back from the circle, marching after it.

Aurie had a vague impression of someone larger, superimposed on Hemistad, as if she were seeing his true self. He was a giant of a man with fists like granite. Then he disappeared into the darkness.

The girl had passed out. She lay stretched across the rock, mouth agape. Pi was heaving with breath. The salt had blackened, the force feedback from the creature's impact searing the circle.

A great roar filled the air, forcing them to put their hands over their ears.

Then a few minutes later, Hemistad returned, looking

more like the old hoary shopkeeper than a giant.

His lips were white with a quiet fury. "I told you to stay where you were."

"She was in danger," said Aurie, looking down to find the spot where the girl was lying empty. "Wait? What the hell?"

"The Hunger creates visions in your mind to get you to come to it. I'd placed a ward on you back there, but once you'd left it, you were unprotected," said Hemistad.

"So the girl wasn't real?" asked Pi. "You were using us for bait? Without telling us first?"

An uncomfortable emotion passed across his face, making him momentarily old again.

"Is this true?" asked Aurie.

He cleared his throat and glanced into the darkness. "I had planned on telling you, but it seems it had gotten loose and I had to act quickly."

Instinctively, she believed him, but she didn't like it.

"You could have told us on the way there," said Pi.

"Humor an old man who was readying himself for a difficult task," said Hemistad. "And there would have been no danger if you'd listened. Next time I tell you to stay put, you stay put." Then he seemed to realize his tone and sighed. "You did good when you called for me, and the circle. It shouldn't have withstood the Hunger, but it did. You girls are more resourceful than I expected."

"What is the Hunger?" asked Pi.

Hemistad retreated into himself, wrestling with what he had to say. When he looked up at them, his eyes reflected the pain and misery of a thousand wars.

"You understand karma?" he asked, his voice hushed and low. "Magic can be like a rubber band. Little magics have only a small effect, a tug here, or a tug there. Nothing that can't be dealt with. But once you start dealing in the greater magics, the rubber band gets stretched, pulled so taut until it either snaps back into place, or breaks. That's what the Hunger is."

He marched into the darkness, the weight of the events tugging his shoulders down. Aurie and Pi fell in behind him as they returned to the platform and back to Freeport Games.

Aurie mulled Hemistad's words about karma and rubber bands, and the vision she'd seen of him. She wondered what the Hunger really was, and why it had chosen that girl to draw them into danger. But mostly she couldn't help but have the impression that Hemistad had just gone through his own room of truth, and that one day soon, she would have to go back into hers.

23

The second delivery for Radoslav was in the third ward. Pi stood in the antechamber of an English-style mansion. A painting of an older woman in a silver gown and holding a bubbling blue potion stared down at her from the wall. It creeped Pi out, and she tried not to put her back to it, but the security had let her in a side door and told her to wait, explaining that the mistress of the house was having a party and that it might be an hour or so. She'd have pulled it off the hook and turned it around if it wouldn't have caused trouble when the owner arrived.

The long road to the house had been lined with limousines and magically propelled carriages. A giant shimmering bubble had floated down and deposited a middle-aged woman in a chartreuse gown with puffy sleeves on the front steps.

Pi spent a few minutes fiddling with the box before she realized that she didn't have the right tools to get past Radoslav's protections. Annoyed by the wait, and wanting to get away from the painting, she decided to venture into the house.

Pi crept past the hard backed study chairs before the

great hearth. The sounds of the party—glasses clinking and people chattering—could be heard faintly from the next room. She kept herself tight as a spring, ready to leap back towards the antechamber should she hear anyone approaching.

Pressing her nose against the double doors, she could see through the crack. Men and women in formal dress milled about the large area. She thought about enhancing her hearing with a spell but decided they might have sniffers to make sure everyone was behaving. It wasn't like she couldn't use the old tried and true method of jamming her ear against the wood, which she did.

It took a moment to pick out the individual voices. There were so many people, and every one of them seemed enamored by their own talking. She wasn't sure how they actually had conversations. Most of it was a series of thinly veiled bragging.

Then she heard a voice that rose above the others and nearly made her flee back to the antechamber. His deep baritone and liberal use of the word "fuck" gave away the presence of Bannon Creed.

Hearing him made her really want to see who else was in the party. Since she couldn't actually get into the filigreed box, knowing more about the people it was going to seemed like the next best thing.

Pi turned the handle and leaned her shoulder into the door, opening it as slow as a glacier, until she could see into the room. She didn't recognize most of the faces at first, but eventually she saw a few she knew: Jillian Garbanzo, the master illusionist who headlined the Glitterdome on a regular basis, and Camille Cardwell, who owned the *Herald of the Halls*. The rest were well dressed, magically enhanced, and generally what anyone would think of when they said the word elite.

Then she saw the shimmering shield moving through the

party, attended by the woman from the painting. It was her patron, Malden Anterist.

Pi opened the door wider, trying to hear what they were saying. When Pi heard the woman's name, everything clicked into place. Celesse D'Agastine. She was the patron of the Order of Honorable Alchemists.

The two patrons wandered near enough to the door that she could hear their conversation.

"It's been thirteen years since his death," said Celesse. "The bastard hid his secrets too well, and his lackey Semyon has stayed loyal, despite my generous offers."

"We have other plans in play," said Malden. "Some short term, others with a longer timeline. I will not be denied what is mine."

Celesse gave him a condescending laugh. "The rest of the Cabal is getting impatient and you're getting foolish. Many things have withered on the vine in these twelve years, putting other stratagems in danger. We must double our efforts."

When Malden spoke, it was with great restraint. Pi didn't know if Celesse was that oblivious or didn't care. "Be patient, my dear."

Pi heard nothing more when a hand grabbed her by the shoulder, yanking her backwards.

"We've caught ourselves a spy, gentlemen," said a familiar voice.

Pi spun around to be confronted by Alton Lockwood in his signature white suit, along with a few of his fourth-year buddies.

"You?" he exclaimed, then his expression turned hard with the thoughts of what he was going to do. "Miss D'Agastine is going to have a field day. How the hell did you get in here?"

"I'm supposed to be here," said Pi, shouldering off the hand on her arm.

"A likely story." He grabbed the filigreed box out of her hand. "What's this? Some sort of magical bomb?"

She reached for it, but one of his goon buddies grabbed her wrist.

"I *told* you, I'm supposed to be here. And I wouldn't mess with that or you're going to be the one Miss D'Agastine has a field day with. That box is for her," she said.

He wasn't dissuaded by her warning, instead using the opportunity to puff up like a peacock, thrusting his chest out and stepping right in front of her.

"I know your shtick, Hick Pi. You're a fast talker, and that's gotten you out of trouble before, but not this time. Hold her. I want to see what else she's got on her," he said.

That he didn't use a spell proved to her that they had sniffers, which meant she couldn't use one to defend herself without getting in trouble with the lady of the house. But that wasn't going to help her as they grabbed her arms. She also knew he wasn't just checking to see what else she had. He wanted his cuff links back, but he wasn't going to find them, because she'd turned them into earrings. He'd been looking at them the whole time and hadn't noticed.

He pulled back with Radoslav's rune in his hand. "What's this?" And then his eyes widened with understanding, but also, not understanding. "Who are you really?"

It was luck that she hadn't reacted. She'd been busy eyeing up a second shot at kneeing him in the groin when he spoke, so she'd been a little distracted.

"You didn't think I really got into Coterie because of Eugene Hickford, did you?" she asked, getting up in his face. "I've never even met the man."

She hid her surprise when he actually backed up. She could see the wheels turning behind his eyes. He was a bully, but a smart one. He'd thought he'd found a lamb, but really it was a tiger, or at least that's what Pi wanted him to think.

Someone handed her the rune, which she shoved into her pocket. Alton actually handed her the filigreed box, concern above his head like a cloud.

"Alton, dear," said Miss D'Agastine from the doorway. "That's no way to acquire a girlfriend. Really, has your father taught you no manners?"

Pi froze, expecting Malden to come through the door after Celesse.

"Miss D'Agastine," said Alton, flashing a winning smile. "I was just admonishing one of our Coterie initiates for spying on your party. She works for Radoslav."

As he held the box up, Pi snatched it out of his hand. She marched to the alchemist patron and handed over the filigreed box. Celesse had a quirk on her lips, ready to fly into a witty remark.

"My apologies, Miss D'Agastine," said Pi. "I wanted to make my delivery so I could return to my studies."

Patron D'Agastine held her long blue fingernails beneath Pi's chin. "Well, you are an interesting specimen. How did you come to work for Radoslav? Have a bit of fae in you?"

"I get results," said Pi.

D'Agastine was delighted by the answer, cawing and giving a clap as she sneered at Alton and his friends.

"And what is your name, dear?"

"Pythia, but I go by Pi," she said.

"Pythia. What a lovely name," said D'Agastine, considering Pi as if she were deciding on buying the ruby encrusted bracelet *or* the diamond coated one. Then she seemed to remember that Alton and his friends were standing there. "You may leave, gentlemen. And Alton."

He turned back for a moment. "Yes, Miss D'Agastine?"

"If you try one of your fucking tricks on my guests, I will

make sure you accidentally get a dose of a slow and painful poison that will rot off your dick and give you a life-long case of hemorrhoids," she said as sweet as cotton candy.

When she was done, Alton was as white as his suit. He walked stiffly back into the party.

Patron D'Agastine turned her attention back to Pi as if nothing had just transpired. "How is Radoslav? Does he still think he's better than everyone else?"

"Isn't that all of the maetrie?" said Pi.

She cooed. "Yes, but he's a particularly condescending prick. I'd still fuck the attitude out of him, but he's as old as the city. He hasn't tried to sleep with you, has he?"

"No," said Pi, almost adding ma'am, but deciding against it.

"You may call me Celesse," she said. "Why did you join Coterie? I have a feeling you would have done wonderfully in my Hall."

Pi lied and said, "Alchemists was a close second, Celesse."

She reached out and pinched Pi's cheek. "Oh, you're so adorable. Well, I suppose I must be getting back to my party. I'm the host and all. But if you decide that Coterie isn't treating you right, you're welcome in my Hall anytime. Just see me personally."

Pi didn't know what to say, so she smiled like she was in on the joke. Celesse strutted back into the party.

Not wanting to risk Alton's return, Pi escaped outside and back to the train station.

Her thoughts were a whirlwind in her head. The Cabal was actually real, not some urban myth to scare kids. There were at least three patrons at the party, indicating the Cabal was made of members of the Hundred Halls. The conversation between Celesse and Malden had sparked many thoughts for Pi. Thirteen years ago, the head patron and founder of the

Hundred Halls, Invictus, had disappeared, presumably dead. Malden had indicated that he knew he was dead, if it were Invictus they were speaking of. These plots might have seemed ludicrous to her if she hadn't heard them herself.

All of it made her worried about what she was getting herself into by joining Coterie and working for Radoslav. She needed to know what was in the filigreed box. It seemed like it was a key to understanding what was going on. Radoslav would have another box for her in six weeks. If the pattern held, she'd be delivering it to another patron of the Halls, who would also be a member of the Cabal. Which meant she would have to break into the box before she delivered it. The magical protections on it were quite strong, and she hadn't really even tested them. She had a lot of work to do if she was going to be ready.

24

Arcanium Hall felt like a monastery to Aurie during the winter break. She wandered the halls, mostly alone, usually with a book in her hand and the earrings providing golden light.

On this day, she was sitting in the corner of the Serapeum, her back propped against the wall, surrounded by books she'd pulled from the shelves. She was reading a book on Egyptian magical history called *Mummies, Mayhem, and More*, looking for ideas that might help Dr. Fairlight with Emily's curse. Through email, Aurie had learned that the lichwood tea had stabilized Emily, but required higher dosages each time for the same effect. Dr. Fairlight had confided that she couldn't use much more lichwood without risking an overdose.

Aurie read through the whole tome and slammed the book shut when she was finished. The rows of books swallowed the noise, making the action less cathartic than she desired.

She put her face in her hands, letting the book slide through her knees and fall to the floor.

"Five straight days of reading and I've found nothing. Not one damn thing," she said to herself. She was so used to talking with her sister that she'd been thinking out loud, forgetting no one else was around. Which made her miss Pi.

She poked the stack of books with a finger. They weren't going to go back onto the shelves themselves, and she was too tired to spell them back up there. Professor Mali would have disapproved, anyway. She liked to lecture about the importance of not relying on magic too much.

She was about to climb to her feet and start putting away the books when she noticed an inscription on the inside of *Mummies, Mayhem, and More*. The book had fallen open to the title page. A note was written in the margin:

To Nahid. I wish I could go with you to Egypt. But since I cannot, I'm sending along the next best thing: this stack of books to help you find what we've been looking for. Love, your bawdy lad. —Kieran

If she hadn't been sitting she would have fallen. It was a book from her father to her mother. They'd lost everything in the fire. Nothing had survived, including all the notes from their artifact research.

Except this book.

Aurie trembled as she lifted the tome. She studied the scrawling handwriting as if it were a spell that could bring them back. Both her mother and her father had held this book. She squeezed it to her chest and then inhaled the musty aroma.

Why was it here? Were there any others? Maybe they'd had too many books at home and Nahid had brought the extras to Arcanium. Aurie looked upon the rows and rows of books like a starving child upon a delicious feast.

The book could give her a link back to her parents. Maybe it would help her deal with the room of truth. Or maybe some other book her mother had owned might help with Emily's curse. Hope bloomed in Aurie's chest like a mountain sunrise.

She went back through the book, this time scouring the pages for information that could lead her to other books. She made notes on the references in the margins, then ran to the Biblioscribe, her boots echoing in the empty hall. The paper crinkled in her hands as she addressed the brass golem.

"Scribe, do you keep a history of the books that have been checked out?" she asked.

The Biblioscribe had a serene look on its metal face. Aurie thought it looked like it had just passed gas.

"Yes, Aurelia. I keep records on all transactions within the Arcanium."

"If I give you a list of books, can you tell me if Nahid Silverthorne checked any of them out?" she asked.

"Affirmative," he said.

She was tingly with excitement. Aurie took a deep breath and read them off. When she was finished, the golem stared at her blankly.

"Scribe? Any matches?"

"Negative," he said.

"Dammit," she said, crumpling up the paper into a ball and slamming it into the wastebasket.

She tapped on her lips, not ready to give up. "Can you tell me about the books donated to the library by Nahid Silverthorne?" she asked hopefully.

"Affirmative. Nahid Silverthorne donated the following books: *Monsters of the Adriatic, Slow Wind, The Short Guide to Royal Tomb Protections, The Artifacts of the Kings, Scarabs Are Spells, The Final Dimension, Zoroaster Magic, The Life of Darius the Great,* and *Magians Not Magicians.*"

Aurie had the Scribe give her the locations, and went on a scavenger hunt. The Scribe could have levitated them to her, but that feature wasn't available to first-year initiates. She wasn't even really supposed to be using the Scribe. She found all the books and piled them onto a table and started reading, keeping an eye out for notes.

It wasn't until she was reading *The Short Guide to Royal Tomb Protections* that she found more evidence of her mother. Nahid had beautiful penmanship. As a young girl, Aurie had treasured the postcards she sent from across the ocean. The i's were dotted with a tiny diamond and the ends of sentences had wonderful flourishes that looked like they'd been made with a calligraphy pen, even though they weren't, an artifact of her mother's childhood in Tehran.

Nahid had marked the spells and enchantments that she thought were most useful for exploring tombs. Aurie spent a little time memorizing the spells before she remembered there were more books and set it aside for later study.

Aurie did a lap around the table when she opened *The Artifacts of the Kings*. The text was filled with her mother's handwriting, at the bottom, in the margins, even in the spaces between the sentences. Her father's wild scrawl could be seen here or there, as if they'd each read the text multiple times and left each other notes and thoughts. She read the back-and-forth in their voices, hearing the warm tones and affection they had for each other. Even though the material was quite dry, mostly dealing with the trivialities of the arcane, she could feel the love and respect they had for each other in the notes. They were a terrific team.

It seemed they thought some ancient Egyptian artifacts from the time of kings could be used at the hospital. They had identified a number of candidates, but the section that had the most writings from her parents was about an artifact called the Rod of Dominion.

Aurie did a double take the first time she read the name of the artifact. It was the same one that Pi had summoned the demon Pazuzu to ask about. Pi's sponsor at Coterie had wanted to know where the item was. The answer came back to her: *beneath the city of lights in the halls of the dead.* Or at least that's what her Infernal translation was.

The notes indicated they'd narrowed down the location where the artifact might have been kept, but ancient magics in the Valley of the Kings prevented them from exploring further. They brainstormed ideas on how to bypass the magic. Most of the terms were advanced concepts Aurie had never heard of, like transdimensional legerdemain.

Aurie was so busy with the books and her parents' notes that she didn't hear the approaching footsteps until it was too late.

"Good evening, Aurelia," said Semyon, in his formal robes. He had heavy bags beneath his eyes as if he'd been up for days.

"Patron Semyon, hello," she said, startled, then glanced at the darkened stained glass windows. "Good evening?"

"Accomplishing a little studying?" he asked with an eyebrow raised and a finger poking into the opened *The Short Guide to Royal Tomb Protections* near the edge of the table. "This doesn't look like anything Professor Mali would have assigned."

"Just killing time during the holidays," she said, trying to sound nonchalant.

He plucked the book from in front of her, a frown on his lips.

"I see," he muttered as he reviewed the text.

"Is something wrong, Patron Semyon? Am I not allowed to read these?" she asked.

"No," he said, clearly troubled. "I'd just forgotten what your parents were working on at the time of their passing. These are very dangerous artifacts they pursued. Many of them have terrible curses associated with them. I always worried that they might awaken one in their pursuit. I hope you're not messing around with this?"

"No, not at all," she said. "I found it by accident."

"Accident? Be careful, Aurelia, the world of the arcane does not exist upon accident," he said. "And you should be focusing on your studies with Professor Mali. She's very disappointed in your efforts thus far."

Aurie opened her mouth to refute it, but realized it would be foolish. He'd given her a chance by letting her in.

"I'll double my efforts, Patron Semyon," she said.

"Very good," he said, though he sounded distracted. "You have a lovely winter break, Miss Aurelia."

He gave the book back and meandered away.

"You too!" she called after him, then buried her face in her hands.

What was she doing? She should be studying truth magic and preparing herself for the next time in the Verum Locus. But the homework didn't seem like magic at all. Professor Mali had assigned them each to write about their experiences in the room and meditate on what they learned. How was this helping with becoming a member of the Arcanium?

So Aurie had decided to make her time useful. If she couldn't meditate, she could at least find a solution for Emily's curse. This had seemed like the proper course until Patron Semyon had arrived.

Aurie stared at the piles of books, the notes, the smudges of ink on her fingers.

Then she made a declaration to herself. "Better that I find a solution for Emily's curse than to become an initiate in the Arcanium."

She threw herself back into the books, quietly hoping that she was doing it for the right reasons.

25

Professor Augustus strolled around the twenty-by-twenty-foot-square room, tapping on the exterior glass walls. His lips were set at a grim line. Smoke swirled between the two panes of glass. A faint keening could be heard when Pi placed her ear on the smooth surface, making her nose wrinkle in disgust.

"These are what are affectionately called 'kill rooms,'" said Professor Augustus once he'd made a complete circuit around the room. "You will be spending the next two weeks in one of these."

Various tables and other equipment filled the space: small melting furnace, chemical shower, reagents shelf, trays, pouring ladle, and other items. Each room was repeated on both sides of the long hallway. The cube-shaped rooms were separated by double panes of glass. The smoke was faint enough that seeing from one cube to another wasn't difficult.

Alton stood at the back of the room, picking lint off his jacket. He was humming to himself with a satisfied look on his lips.

"These rooms are designed for the safety of your fellow students. For the next few weeks, you'll be creating runic switches, which can be used for higher-level constructions, including translocations and *le mystère de la pendaison*," he said, evoking a chuckle from the students.

"Between the panes of glass are deathgeists. A particular geist bred for their attunement to danger. They can sense future mass deaths through the temporal matrix. Or in other words, they can narrowly see into the future. If they believe that you're about to create a fatal incident that could endanger the rest of the class, the glass will break and they will kill whoever is in the room, thus eliminating the cause," he said.

The professor pulled his glasses off to wipe them against his robe. The squeegee sound could be heard above everyone's heartbeats. When he was finished, he replaced them and beamed a big smile.

"Now that we're done with that unpleasant message, let's get to work. Any questions?" he asked.

Orson cleared his throat. "How often does the glass break?"

Augustus adjusted his wire-rimmed glasses. "I think we only had one last year. It was a good year. But I must warn you that runic switches are much more difficult to produce than what they were making at that time. This year's task is by special request from your patron."

There was a lot of swallowing and brow wiping after that. Pi entered her cube at the same time as the rest of her classmates. The glass door magically sealed behind her, forcing the air out in a whoosh. Ashley mouthed the words good luck from the next cell.

Pi slipped on the leather apron, tying it tightly around her midsection. The goggles pressed against her face, making her nose itch. She poked at it a few times before realizing it was just going to be uncomfortable.

The professor's voice came through the speakers: "I almost

forgot. Each student will be expected to make one hundred runic switches within the two-week period. You may only use the tools and materials in the rooms. You will be graded on your speed and their quality. Myself or Alton can verify if you think you've made a proper switch. I suggest you make a small batch first before continuing, or you'll waste a considerable amount of time due to the inevitable mistakes."

The instructions were given on an electronic pad that was positioned near the table so they could read and scroll easily. Pi studied the directions, reading through them multiple times for context and nuance.

In the next cube, Orson hurried through his motions, his dusty blond hair swaying in front of his face. Pi cringed at the way he clinked his beakers together. His leather apron had come loose in the back.

The rest of her class, even Ashley, had thrown themselves into the task. Though it was hard to see through the successive panes of smoky glass, she had the impression of a hive of bees in the honeycomb.

At the moment, Pi was bottom of the class in ranking and had no sponsor for her second year lined up. She would have contacted Eugene Hickford, but he'd disappeared into the Ozark Mountains years ago and no one had heard from him since.

She had to climb the rankings, or she'd get booted out of Coterie at the end of the year. Just doing well wouldn't be enough. She had to score enough points to catch up to the others, and after studying the recipe, she knew playing it safe wasn't an option.

The process for making a runic switch took three days. Which meant that after the test batch, if she only did one batch at a time, she'd have eleven days or three batch cycles to finish the rest, making around thirty to thirty-five each time.

Or at least, that's how the other initiates would probably make theirs. The equipment and setup suggested that course of action. Pi had no intention of following the standard path.

The first step was casting the switches. Each one looked like an oversized dog tag with piston and cup connecting ends so they could be snapped together. The runes would have to be meticulously added after the blanks were prepared with an acid solution. Runic switches were used to create magical fields that could be used in all sorts of different constructions.

Pi turned on the melting oven and set up the pig molds, which were iron trays with impressions in them to pour the lead. She only had enough ingot to make one hundred switches, which meant any extra material had to be remelted and poured again, wasting valuable time.

Using a hunk of molders clay from the bench, Pi formed little dams on the mold and enchanted them with some fire protection. It would require pouring each one individually, rather than dumping the metal into the main channel and letting it fill each impression like a miniature river way. The mold held ten impressions, so she'd have to repeat the process ten times to make a hundred switch blanks.

Once the electric furnace was hot enough, Pi used the leather gloves to place the lead ingot bars into the pouring cup in the oven. Rather than let the venting system remove the dangerous fumes, Pi put a charm on the pipe to collect the lead smoke rather than pull it out, so the furnace would stay hotter and she could melt faster.

While she waited, Pi dumped sand into the pouring ladle and practiced so that she didn't spill any when it came to the real task. By the time the lead was liquid, she was ready, only spilling a few grains of sand each pour.

Pi cleaned out the mold, put all the sand back into the dish, and put on her protective face shield. After pulling the small crucible out, Pi scooped the impurities off the top and dumped them into a slag bin. Then she hooked the handle to the crucible to pour. When she lifted it, the end of the ladle sagged from the weight. The sand was nowhere near as heavy as the lead. She compensated by grabbing further up the handle, but that made pouring less precise.

Setting the ladle lip against the mold impression, Pi tipped it over, releasing a stream of orangish-silver liquid. The metal sizzled in the mold. Tiny smoke balloons released from the surface. Pi held her breath even though the face shield was enchanted to protect her from the lead fumes.

She repeated the process until the ten molds were full. Then she put new ingots into the crucible and returned it to the furnace. When the blanks were cool enough, Pi popped them out and threw them into a pile of sand.

While she waited for the ingots to melt, Pi reformed the clay barriers and repeated the whole process.

After the fourth batch, the room sweltered with heat, forcing Pi to wipe the sweat from her forehead before it ran into her eyes. The iron mold was popping as it cooled, deforming back into shape. She tied a towel around her forehead to hold the sweat back.

The other initiates had moved past the lead pouring and were preparing their blanks for the next stage. Professor Augustus tapped on the glass door and raised an eyebrow. Pi gave him a thumbs-up before pouring the next batch.

On the sixth batch, her mold cracked, spilling lead over the ceramic tiles. Pi used sand to make a dam before it damaged the floor. Once she had the molten lead contained, she eyed the smoke in the glass walls. Swirls of crimson floated between the panes, signaling the deathgeists' interest in her mistake, but they quickly returned to colorlessness.

She turned off the furnace and let the remaining lead

cool in the crucible. She'd have to clean it up and repair the mold before continuing. Many of the other initiates had left for dinner, which reminded Pi how hungry she was.

After examining the mold, she realized her mistake. By pouring one batch after another without the proper time to cool, the mold had gotten successively hotter until it had cracked. She could repair it with magic, but it would take hours.

The repair took half the time because she poured faez into the mold at double the safe rate. Her clothes were soaked and smudged. She attempted to set up the next batch, but her hands were shaking from hunger, so she gave in. After a detour to her room for a change of clothes and a chocolate bar, she returned to the glass room.

While she waited for the furnace to heat up, she examined the blanks only to find that a third of them had defects. She'd have to do a better job removing the impurities before pouring next time. Pi dumped them back into the crucible and sighed, squeezing the bridge of her nose between her fingers.

"Two steps forward, three steps back," she muttered.

The other initiates were giving her questioning glances and shaking their heads. Even Ashley seemed worried every time they made eye contact.

When she resumed the blank operation, Pi used water to cool the mold between pours. This was dangerous for two reasons: the sudden cooling could crack the mold again and moisture left on the mold could turn to steam when the molten lead hit, throwing hot metal everywhere. The deathgeists keened and sparks of bloodred formed in the smoke while she performed the operation, making her nervous.

When she finished, it was near morning of the next day. She'd made one hundred and five blanks, using all the available lead. Exhausted, she opened the door to let the heat out and curled up on the tile floor to sleep for a few hours.

While she slept, the other initiates returned to the workshop. The symphony of grinders woke her. The other initiates were grinding their test blanks into the proper shapes.

Pi spent a few minutes stretching, ate another energy bar, and started mixing the etching material she would need later for the runes. The directions said to grind the blanks first, but she thought it was a waste of time. The etching mixture would have to sit for thirty hours, so she could grind while she waited.

Like the lead blanks, the etching mixture was designed to be made in batches. The bowls could only hold about a fifth of the acid solution. With a thirty-hour window, Pi didn't want to repeat the process, so she scoured the tables for larger containers. Eventually, she settled on using the stainless steel sink as her bowl.

She started by removing the drain pipe and soldering a smaller bowl over the opening. Then she removed the spigot to remove the possibility of errant drops of water upsetting her acid solution.

The sink wasn't designed for mixing solutions, so Pi reinforced it with some runes and protections. If there was any point in the process that was going to get her killed, it was this one, so she went over the sink multiple times until she was absolutely certain she'd sealed it.

The container of concentrated hydrogen peroxide splashed into the sink, releasing sharp fumes. These concentrations were used in rocket propellant, so she had to be careful with spark sources, or bring the wrath of the deathgeists. Next she added copper sulfide and a half dozen other chemicals, weighing each one three times before adding it to the hydrogen peroxide.

Since the mixture in the sink was an explosive, the next part could only be performed with magic. Pi cast a series of transfigurations that turned the mixture nonreactive before she heated it with faez.

With one hand churning the large wooden spoon and the other making counterclockwise motions over the yellowish mixture, she heated it, bringing it to a rolling boil.

"Double, double, toil and trouble. Fire burn, and cauldron bubble," she said, feeling quite wicked.

She stopped adding heat after five minutes of stirring. The liquid bubbled, forming a whitish froth along the edges. She kept the clockwise motion of the spoon, expecting the rolling boil to subside, but it kept going. Her gaze went straight to the smoky walls when she realized that the concoction was headed for a reaction. Blotches of crimson bloomed around her.

"What's wrong?" she muttered in a panic, examining the sink as if it had the answer written on it. If the mixture didn't cool down by the time the enchantments wore off, the whole thing would explode. The deathgeists hadn't killed her yet, but they appeared to be readying themselves. She had to find a solution, and fast.

Pi tried adding cold to the mixture to counteract the heat, but the boil kept rolling. The heat seemed to be innate to the liquid. She didn't dare try to dispel the whole construct either since that would lead to disastrous consequences.

At the near wall, Orson had noticed the growing redness of the smoke and was watching intently as he moved towards his door. A few of the other initiates' heads had bobbed up. Her death felt imminent. Sparks of bloodred rippled through the glass, testing, teasing. Everything she'd tried should have worked. She'd thought through the procedure multiple times before she attempted it.

She was down to seconds before there wouldn't be enough time to cool it before the reversion. All four walls had turned red. The deathgeists were ready.

The professor stood outside her door. His face was drawn down, his lips white with concern.

For a moment, she thought about fleeing, but because the mixture was on its way to a chain reaction, realized that the deathgeists would kill her before her hand touched the door.

Alton Lockwood wasn't in the workshop area, which led her to believe that it was sabotage. This gave her hope that whatever the cause was could be stopped. Pi searched for the source of the added heat. The wooden spoon was still in the sink. Pi yanked it out, and the liquid stopped boiling right away.

Before anyone could draw conclusions, Pi dropped the spoon and faked a spell on the mixture. A tiny tug like a string pulling on her breastbone announced that the transfigurations had reverted. The walls quickly faded to pale. Pi shuddered with relief, then gave everyone a thumbs-up. She'd avoided disaster by mere seconds.

Realizing that the danger was over, the other initiates went back to their work, except for Ashley, who was wiping away tears. Pi wanted to go out and hug her, but the etching mixture had to be completed. The professor stopped in front of her glass wall and mimed wiping his forehead off.

Pi threw herself back into the work. After another hour of adding reagents and a few more minor enchantments, the mixture had been reduced to an inert state. It took all her self-control to make it back to her room so she could collapse in private. Her hands shook like a junky in search of a fix for a good twenty minutes before she could finally get them back under control.

She thought for a while about telling the professor about the sabotage, but decided the word would only get out, and she preferred to keep her battles quiet. Pi returned to the workshop after a quiet meal in the dining room alone.

With the etching mixture sitting for the next twenty-four hours, Pi threw herself into the boring task of grinding the blanks into switches. She ground the edges and shaped the cup and piston connections with a pencil grinder. After the first twenty, she had to take a break because her hands cramped into useless claws.

She worked through the second night because once everyone had left she was afraid that Alton Lockwood would return and sabotage something else. She figured that while the workshop was full, he couldn't mess with her equipment. As a precaution, she checked all her equipment and materials for hidden charms so there were no further incidents.

When the etching mixture was finished, Pi set up an assembly line. Each switch would have to soak for twenty minutes before having three separate spells cast on it. Then she would draw the runes using gold-flecked paint.

This last part Pi enjoyed the most. She only wished that Aurie was there with her. As orphans, they didn't have much money, but they could spend hours making crafts with the leftover colored pencils and construction paper that the schools usually threw out.

Pi took her time. Once the rune was on the switch, it couldn't be changed, and each one required faez to bond it to the lead. She also recognized around the fifth day that there was no way she could redo the switches if something was wrong. Only five switches couldn't work, or she'd fail the class and be out of Coterie at the end of the year.

On the seventh day, with all eyes on her, Pi marched up to the professor and informed him she was ready for the final examination.

"I hope you're sure about this," he said, following her back to the room.

The professor made a big display of examining the runic

switches, all lined up on the table as if it were a cooking competition show and she'd made designer cupcakes. She half expected him to pick one up and bite into it.

After the initial visual inspection, he cast a few spells to confirm no dangerous defects. Once he was satisfied that he wasn't going to be maimed by a faulty switch, he pulled a master switch out of his pocket, picked up the first switch Pi had made, and connected the two together. When the runes on both started to glow a warm, honeyed light, he nodded and set it back down.

He tested each switch, nodding when they passed muster and marking down the level of intensity. Pi's heart tried to climb out her throat the whole time.

When she passed the halfway point without a defective switch, Ashley gave her a thumbs-up. Pi thought she was in the clear and had started to relax when he found a defect on the fifty-seventh switch.

At first, she wasn't worried. It'd taken that long to find the first one. Surely there couldn't be many more in the second half? But her confidence dipped when the fifty-eighth was also bad. Then when the runes on the fifty-ninth didn't glow either, she crossed her arms around her chest and hugged herself tight.

The other students were at least as concerned as she was, except for Alton, who had come in after the first few and was watching from the side with faked disinterest.

When the sixtieth switch was good, Ashley raised her arms, then shoved them back under her armpits. Pi's foot bounced nervously as she neared the end. Two more bad switches were found, and the remaining twelve had to be perfect or she would fail.

Pi dug her fingernails into her palms. She didn't know what she was going to do if she got kicked out of Coterie.

Then the worst happened. The final switch didn't glow when the professor connected them.

"I'm sorry, Pythia," he said, a frown tugging his lips.

Pi started to panic until she saw faint illumination emerge. She pointed rapidly, like a child finding her first Easter egg.

"It's glowing! It's glowing!" she exclaimed.

He looked down and a smile broke across his face. "Why, you're correct. Congratulations, Miss Pythia. You completed the assignment."

The professor held up the final glowing switch, and the class gave her a round of applause. She couldn't read the nuances of their smiles, but she didn't care. She'd survived.

"Great job," he told her before leaving. "I didn't think it was possible to finish this fast, and the quality was generally above average. Unless someone finishes the perfect batch, I don't know how you won't be first in the class for this assignment."

Afterwards, Pi cleaned up the workshop, taking care to wipe the enchantment from the wooden spoon so that Alton wouldn't know why it hadn't worked. She wanted him to question his sabotage so he might make a mistake at a later time.

After a sleep, a long shower, and a quiet feast in the dining room by herself, Pi spent the remaining time studying. While she'd finished tops in the assignment, the result only put her into the middle of the class. She wasn't safe from being expelled from Coterie at the end of the year, by any margin, nor did she have a sponsor. But she hoped her audacious performance might draw at least reluctant interest. She only wished that she could celebrate her success with Aurie.

26

It wasn't until late January that the first-year initiates of Arcanium returned to the room of truth. Their eventual return had been a source of discussion between the initiates, drawing nervous laughter and boasts of conquering their fears, but upon arrival the cocky laughter fell to silence.

"You must master yourselves before you can wield magic with any confidence. To do otherwise is to court disaster," Professor Mali began as she wheeled in the front of the seats. "These events in your life are like hairline fractures that must be repaired before you are whole enough to tackle real magic. Violet, you're first."

Violet trudged into the room, giving everyone a backwards longing glance. To bide the time, Aurie had brought *The Artifacts of the Kings* with her. She'd been reading and rereading the text and her parents' notes for clues. As far as she could decipher, they'd been planning an expedition to retrieve the Rod of Dominion before their untimely death.

Each time she read those passages, Aurie thought about how, due to her parents' death, Emily had lost out on a cure. Shame pasted itself on her face in blooms of crimson, darkening her olive skin, which only made the promise of the truth room more daunting. When it'd just been her family's life that she'd impacted, it felt like she was being properly punished. But now that she understood what her parents had been working on, she felt like she'd deprived the world of a cure.

They hadn't specified exactly how they were going to remove the Rod from the Valley of the Kings. A fatal curse had protected the artifact from previous attempts, leaving a swath of dead explorers in its wake. It was clear from the tone of their discussions that they felt they would be successful, but they made no mention of how they might avoid the curse. Those notes had probably burned up in the fire that had claimed their lives.

Aurie was so deep into her tome that she hadn't realized that Violet had returned from the Verum Locus and was softly crying a few seats behind her. It was initially hard to muster sympathy for the girl who'd almost kept Aurie from the Halls, but the continued sobbing broke down her resolve.

Aurie climbed over the seats as Violet blew her nose into a handkerchief. Her eyes were puffy and red.

Violet shot daggers at Aurie as she settled into the seat across from her. Aurie almost returned to her original seat, but lingering guilt made her stay.

"Do you need anything? A glass of water?" asked Aurie.

Violet said nothing. Her shoulders shook. Aurie glanced longingly at her seat before turning back to the blonde girl.

"Even though I don't know what you went through in there, I can tell you're strong. Much stronger than I am. Last time I went in there, I failed miserably. I'll probably fail again," said Aurie, quietly.

The muscles in Violet's face spasmed as multiple emotions tried to break through. A wheeze escaped out of her throat. She put a hand over her mouth.

Aurie sat for a while trying to think of something else to say. Realizing that Violet didn't want to talk, she started to climb over the seats again.

"I don't know why I'm here," whispered Violet in an anguished tone.

Aurie stiffened, not wanting to spook Violet, but realized she needed to say something. "You're here because you did awesome at the trials."

"But why am I not in Alchemists? Arcanium was practically last on my list, barely above those theater geeks," she said, wiping her nose with her handkerchief. "My mother hates me. She thinks I betrayed the family on purpose."

"It's not like you can't study alchemy in Arcanium," said Aurie. "You can make that your specialty in the fifth year."

Violet shifted in her seat, as if she didn't know why Aurie was being nice, and it unnerved her.

"I lost all my old friends," said Violet, under her breath.

"But now you've got new ones," said Aurie, head nodding towards the knot of girls near the front.

Violet's face wrinkled with suspicion. "Why are you being nice to me?"

She was going to give a saccharine answer, but given the looming assignment, switched to the truth instead.

"I don't know," said Aurie.

Violet struggled with speaking, before the words came out laced with apprehension. "How is that girl? The one from Golden Willow? She was cursed or something?"

A hole opened in Aurie's heart. "She's alive...for now."

They fell into a contemplative silence, each girl staring at her folded hands, until Aurie was called for her turn.

Violet might have told her good luck, but the words were lost as Aurie's fears whirled into action. She dreaded what was coming, but also looked forward to it, because she hoped to learn more about the Rod on this second visit to her past.

Professor Mali grabbed Aurie's wrist before she could enter.

"I know this is hard, but you must give up control. Let the vision show you the truth," she said.

Aurie didn't bother responding and marched inside.

The vision came faster and harder compared to the last time. It was as if she'd been hit by a train. One moment, the air was golden light, and the next she was sitting at the kitchen counter while her dad was cooking bacon on the stove, dancing around as the grease popped.

She felt the wounds of regret, the longing for comfort, well up in her chest until she was choking on her emotions. She forced them down, gasping, until she could breathe again.

It was earlier in the day than last time. Pi was sitting at the dining table with her face in a book and papers spread around her.

Aurie wanted desperately to jump off the stool and tackle her father in an embrace, but she was trapped like a visitor on an amusement park ride. She missed the way he could hug her for days, wrapping her up like a warm blanket.

Her father whistled a tune as he hopped from foot to foot, poking at the sizzling bacon.

"Hey, Dad?" asked the vision Aurie.

"Yeah, sweetie," he responded. He had a melodic voice and sometimes sang his spells. Her mother often said it was his voice that had first attracted her.

"Do you think I can go over to Natalie's tonight?" asked Aurie.

He tensed up slightly before setting the spatula down. He slid the pan off the burner and switched it off. He leaned against the other side of the counter. He had the most wonderful freckles that she'd loved to count when he would read her bedtime stories, though those days were long past.

"Your mother and I had a talk about you and Natalie last night. I'm not sure you can go over there unsupervised," he said.

"But she's my best friend," said Aurie.

"You can keep in contact over the internet, using whatever you kids use these days," he said.

Tears flooded to Aurie's eyes, but the real Aurie didn't feel sadness, only forgotten shame as she remembered this moment.

"But why?" asked vision Aurie.

Her father glanced to Pi before resolving to speak. "We know you two were practicing magic. It's just too dangerous without a patron."

"But the other kids do it, too," she said.

As the words came out of her mouth, the real Aurie shrunk inside, and not because of the heavy sigh her father had just given her.

"And other kids get hurt all the time. Even if nothing tangible happens, it's a bad idea. You have to learn to control yourself first before you can control such power; otherwise, the faez will drive you mad," he said.

The echoes of the professor's comment hit her in the chest like a spear. She felt stuck to the spot.

"So until you've earned our trust back, you're grounded. You can use the time you'll be spending at home preparing for your piano recital. It's only a few days away," he said, then went back to the bacon.

It felt like someone had tied ropes around her gut and was cinching them tighter. Aurie went into the living room. Pi stuck out her tongue, then followed her into the next room, taking position on the opposite couch.

A fit of rage claimed Aurie. Why did she have to relive

this day again? Couldn't she have visited a happy memory like when they'd gone to the beach in Florida and they'd built castles using wet sand, then at night they'd eaten fresh seafood at open air cafes?

The rage turned to an ache that went all the way into her bones as she was forced to sit on the couch while her father was in the other room. She wanted his approving gaze, his laughter and smile, but all she'd gotten was his disappointment in her.

When her mother got home, Aurie was too busy sulking to notice until she heard a snippet of the conversation waft into the living room, snapping her upright.

"I picked up that book of charms you were talking about. Most of them are pretty useless, but there are a few gems," said her mother.

"What about the remaining switches to finish the construction? Do you have those?" he asked.

"Someone will be delivering them tonight, Kieran. We've got everything now. We're prepared as we're going to be," she said.

Her father's voice lowered, and Aurie had to strain to hear.

"I'm just worried, is all. Since the both of us are going, and the curse," he said.

"Which we've prepared for. Our solution will work. Have you spoken with Dr. Hothwitz?" she asked.

"Aye. He's quietly lining up candidates for the Rod. Only the most pressing ailments until we understand its capabilities. There's a young boy who might not last until the end of the week who could desperately use it," he said.

"Then we'll go tomorrow morning," she said.

"Are you sure?" he asked.

"What's the point in waiting any longer? We're as ready as we're going to be," she said firmly.

"What if it's not there?" he asked. "It wouldn't be the first time that a tomb had already been looted."

"Then it's not there and we start looking somewhere else," she said. "We can't wait until everything is perfect. Sometimes you just have to trust yourself and take a leap of faith."

"You're right, Nahid. You're always right, but I'm just worried," he said. "I know you do this stuff all the time, and I always worry when you leave, expecting that you'll never come back, but this time seems much worse. That curse is serious business, much more dangerous than anything you've ever faced."

"I know. Which is why you're coming with me. It's going to take the both of us to bring back the Rod," she said, then a moment later she added, as if she knew it was the last moments of her life, "*Dooset daram.*"

"I love you too," said Kieran.

Their voices lowered to the point that Aurie couldn't hear anymore.

Aurie reeled in confusion. She didn't remember this conversation at all. Was it real? Or was this something she wanted to hear based on the tomes she'd been reading? Maybe the professor was right, and she was controlling the vision, making herself see something that had never happened.

Her nose itched, so she scratched the end with a fingernail. As her hand moved, Aurie realized she was fully in control of the vision. She tested it by standing up and moving towards the kitchen. A faint looking Aurie was still seated on the couch. Aurie had broken away.

But she felt a tension on her like pushing on a spring. The further away from the vision Aurie she got, the higher the tension.

Her parents were still whispering in the other room. She wanted to hear what they had to say. She knew it was something important, but each step towards them increased the pressure by double.

Or was that really what she wanted? Was it just a desperate need to see her parents alive again? Is that what this investigation into the Rod had become?

Aurie forged into the kitchen, the resisting force becoming unbearable. Her parents were speaking quietly, nearly nose to nose, while their hands were entwined. If she could have a picture of that moment to take back, it would have lightened the darkness in her heart.

Aurie spoke before she remembered that it was only a vision. "Don't go."

Like a bubble popped, the vision collapsed around her, sending her back into the real world. She staggered at the sudden dislocation, vertigo whirling through her head. Aurie fought back the rising bile in her throat. The golden speckles of faez sparked with annoyance upon her return. Aurie had upset the room of truth.

Outside, the professor's grim countenance was confirmation that she had failed again. Aurie took her seat, pulled the tome to her chest, and hugged it as she contemplated the memory of her parents.

Why can't I see the truth? she asked herself. *How much of that was real?*

Every day since her parents had died, Aurie had wanted to go back in time and fix it. Every day she wanted to erase her mistakes so that her parents would live. Every day she was beset with the guilt that came with never being able to make it right. No matter how many times she sacrificed for her sister. No matter how many jobs she'd taken to keep Pi fed and warm. No matter home many times she held her sister as she cried to sleep at night in some random foster home.

Nothing would ever bring them back. Nothing would ever let them wrap their arms around her, squeeze her tight, and tell her everything was going to be okay. Nothing would fix the unfixable, erase her mistakes, give her and Pi the lives they had before the accident.

Nothing would ever be the same, and it was Aurie's fault. Even being successful in Arcanium had lost its meaning. Why should she enjoy the Hundred Halls when so many kids had been deprived of their lives when her parents had died?

Aurie knew of only one way that she could ever even come close to fixing what had happened. She had to complete the task that her parents had been about to embark on. She had to find the Rod of Dominion.

27

The doors of the Glass Cabaret closed behind Pi, leaving her on the busy street as cars rumbled past, windshields glinting in the Saturday afternoon light. She turned the ornate box over in her hands, hearing a faint noise as the object inside hit the soft sides. Radoslav had seemed distracted, which had been fine by her. The more she learned about him and the Cabal, the less she liked the arrangement with the city fae.

She wasn't entirely sure he was a part of the Cabal, as the maetrie weren't known for interfering with human affairs. They had their own politics to deal with between the three courts. Radoslav had no known allegiance, but that didn't mean he wasn't connected to one of them secretly.

It left her feeling like a pawn in the larger game, a problem she was going to rectify, starting with the ornate box. Pi hurried to an alleyway, where she'd left a pile of magical investigative tools in a backpack hidden behind a dumpster.

Last time, when she'd delivered the box to Celesse D'Agastine, Pi had learned that Radoslav put a time signature on the box that would notify him how long it'd taken to deliver it. She wasn't sure how much of a delay would make him suspicious, a few hours at best, so she had to hurry.

Pi pulled out the scanning disc that she'd borrowed from the initiate labs in Coterie, and after whispering a spell, waved it over the ornate box. The air around it bloomed into colors like a flower garden had burst into existence. Each color represented a different spell. The layers of protection bothered Pi. Either Radoslav was just naturally paranoid, or the object in the box was particularly valuable.

She pulled a pair of welders goggles out of the backpack and slipped them on. They were slightly too big and hurt the bridge of her nose, but Pi ignored it and pulled the box into view.

She'd enchanted the goggles to maintain the investigative spell while she teased apart their purpose. There were five separate spells: the timer on delivery, a lock that was keyed to Radoslav and the recipient, an anti-scrying enchantment, a nasty defensive spell, and a final one that was so entwined with the others that she couldn't determine its purpose. The final spell was like a thin webbing that connected the others. She guessed that it was there to keep the other spells from mingling and causing unintended effects, a known issue with layered enchantments. After testing the amount of energy in the fifth spell and learning that it was only a small amount, Pi decided to attempt breaking into the box.

She pulled another item of her design out of the backpack: scaffolding to suspend the box by its six corners. The scaffolding cube had enchantments on it to keep the magic of the box tamed until she could unravel it. The idea was much like applying crosswires to a bomb before clipping other wires while defusing it.

With the protections in place, Pi went to work. The five entwined enchantments made for difficult work, especially because she didn't want to eliminate them. If she delivered an enchantmentless box to the third Cabal member, they would become suspicious.

Pi poked and probed the defenses, looking for a way to stretch them so she could open the box. After thirty minutes of determined study, she decided to give it a try. It felt like she was pulling back elastic webbing, using spells as her hooks and connecting them to the cube scaffolding.

Crouched in the alleyway behind a battered blue dumpster, the first few minutes went as expected. It wasn't until she tried to unentangle the defense spell and the thin webbing that things started to go wrong.

As she unhooked them, a chain reaction started to form. Like lightning in a massive thundercloud, the magical energies pulsed with danger. Pi tried putting it back to the original position, but the energies continued to propagate, headed towards a disastrous conclusion.

Pi yanked the stasis bag out of her backpack and threw the scaffolding containing the box into it, freezing the chain reaction for the moment.

"Shit," she muttered, realizing that she'd screwed up royally.

Once the chain reaction had started, she'd understood the purpose of the fifth spell. It had low energy because it was only a trigger. The remaining power came from the other spells, especially the nasty defensive one.

The stasis bag could delay the reaction, but only for a short while, no more than twenty minutes, she guessed. She had to solve the problem or it would trigger. She thought about abandoning the box, and fleeing the city, but an innocent bystander might get hurt. Nor did she want to give up her position in the Halls.

As the cars went rumbling past the alleyway, Pi squeezed her face in her hands, mentally reviewing the five spells to figure out a solution. She manipulated them in her mind as if they were a Rubik's Cube and she were preparing to solve it. It wasn't long before she realized there was no possible way to get past the enchantments, at least in the way she'd originally planned.

Throwing everything, including the stasis bag containing the box, into her backpack, Pi took off at a run. She found a blue police phone and put a spell on it so she could call a different number: the one inside the Arcanium initiate ward.

"Hello," she said when a girl on the other side answered. "Can I talk to my sister, Aurie? It's an emergency, like fast."

The sounds of doors opening and closing came through the phone until she heard her sister's voice.

"Pi? Is everything okay?" asked Aurie.

"I need your help. Can you meet me at"—Pi pictured the train lines crisscrossing the city and figured a location on the way to her destination—"that stop by the gondola station shaped like an onion?"

"I'm not supposed to be out in the city," said Aurie. "How urgent is this?"

"Really bad," said Pi.

"Okay, I'll be there," said Aurie.

"Thank you. Please hurry," said Pi, and hung up. A few passersby gave her strange looks because she was on the blue police phone. She ignored them and took off at a run to make the next train, which was about to leave.

She slid through the doors and found a seat away from everyone else, peeking in her backpack to check the stasis bag. The energies were building up, but still manageable.

By the time she reached her destination, the bag was barely holding it together. When she ran off the train, Pi started shouting her sister's name to locate her.

After a frantic minute, she found Aurie, grabbed her

hand, and went running towards the nearest bathroom. A few businesswomen were milling around the sinks, checking their makeup or clothing when they crashed in.

"Everyone out, now," said Pi.

"Excuse me?" said a woman in a power suit. She looked like a CEO straight out of central casting, with hair that made her look like a cobra.

Pi produced a ball of flame in her fist and showed it to the woman, who quickly changed her tune.

"You girls are crazy," she said, leading the pack out of the bathroom while pulling out her cell phone. She'd be most certainly calling the cops. Pi might have been concerned, except that if they failed to contain the box, the police would be the least of their worries.

Aurie put an enchantment on the door to keep anyone else from coming in, while Pi checked the stalls, which were thankfully empty.

"No time to explain why, but I need your help defeating these enchantments," said Pi, dumping the stasis bag on the dirty tile floor.

Aurie pointed at the goggles on Pi's face. "Do you have another pair?"

She shook her head. "I wasn't planning on this taking two people. Can you do something?"

Aurie whispered to her fingers, then placed them against her closed eyes. When she opened them, they were completely shimmering blue, even the whites.

Pi explained the plan in hurried phrases. Her sister nodded along.

"Ready?" she asked, holding the stasis bag as if she were going to dump out a pack of angry badgers.

Once she removed the scaffolding cube, Pi had to clamp down on the enchantment before it got away from her. Then she let Aurie take control, freeing her up to manipulate the spells. It was like doing open heart surgery and defusing a bomb at the same time.

The work was delicate. Pi had to tease apart the webbing, stretching until she could hook it to the scaffolding. After a few tense minutes, Pi finally defeated the enchantment. She was free to open the box.

While holding her breath, she lifted the lid. Inside the gilded box lay a gallium coin covered in runes.

"What the hell?" said Pi, underwhelmed.

"That's all it is?" asked Aurie. "Why did you need to get into this box?"

"Let's get out of the bathroom and I'll explain on the way. I'm sure that lady called the cops," she said.

Pi memorized the runes on both sides, then closed the box and slipped the enchantments back on. When she was finished, she examined the spells to make sure there was no sign of tampering. She shoved the stasis bag, scaffolding, and goggles into the backpack before they left the bathroom.

They were back into the crowd when a group of three police officers came running up to the bathroom to bang on the door.

"Fix your eyes," she told Aurie before they got on the next train.

On the way, Pi told her sister about the boxes, the Cabal, and Radoslav, including all her concerns.

Aurie sat quietly for a moment before saying, "You should give up Coterie."

"No way," said Pi.

"Everything you've told me about them isn't good. Why do you want to be a part of that?" she asked.

"They're not all bad. Ashley's a good friend, and Professor Augustus, though misguided, has been trying to help me.

There's good and bad everywhere, Aurie.   Coterie is no different," she said.

Aurie squeezed her lips together and cast her gaze askew. "I'm not sure about that, but I can't make you quit."

Pi took a good look at her sister. The dark bags under her eyes had their own bags they were so heavy.

"Are you okay? You look like you're not sleeping," she said.

Aurie's lip twitched. "I'm fine. Just doing a lot of studying."

Pi knew it was a lie, but she didn't want to press her sister, not after she'd come to her rescue at a moment's notice.

"Mine's the next stop," said Pi, reluctantly. "I miss seeing you."

They stood up as the train neared the station, the rapid clacking slowing.

"I miss you too," said Aurie, who wrestled with her words before continuing. "I'm working on some things I learned about Mom and Dad's death."

"Aurie, you need to let that go. You didn't do anything wrong," said Pi.

"It's important, Pi," said Aurie, looking her straight in the eyes. "If I ask for your help, can I count on you?"

The train lurched to a stop. They grabbed the nearby pole to keep from falling over.

"Of course, anything. I'm there for you," Pi said as she moved towards the open door.

Aurie gave her a terse wave as the door closed. Pi regretted she hadn't gotten a hug from her sister. She could have used it.

The destination was a few blocks away from the train stop in the fourth ward. When Pi came to an empty lot, she checked the address twice, wondering if she'd gotten it wrong.

Then a dark-skinned guy a few years older than her,

but clearly a student of the Halls, appeared not far from her location, though she hadn't seen him arrive. He had spiderweb tattoos on his arms that seemed to move when she wasn't looking at him. He was handsome, with stark blue eyes.

"You shouldn't be here," he said.

Pi produced Radoslav's rune. He gave her a once-over, before shrugging.

"I'll take the delivery," he said.

"I can only give it to one person, and you're not her," she said.

He didn't look impressed. "Fine. Close your eyes and hold the package out."

"Not while you're around," she said.

He held his hands up and retreated backwards. "Your wish is my command."

He winked, and a clap of thunder from behind her made her spin around. She realized right away she'd been tricked. He was gone when she turned back.

After confirming she was alone, Pi closed her eyes and held out the box. She started to wonder, then felt electricity across her skin.

A silky feminine voice whispered, "Tell Radoslav he owes me dinner."

It took a few moments to realize the box was gone. Pi opened her eyes to an empty lot. Irritated by the subterfuge, she stalked back to the station. She had to get back to the Obelisk to return the items she'd borrowed before the professor realized they were missing.

In addition, she wanted to research the runes from the gallium coin. Their simple nature had surprised Pi. She'd been expecting something more malevolent that might indicate the Cabal was up to no good.

Despite her denials with her sister, Pi had considered

leaving Coterie more than once, and not just because Alton Lockwood was trying to kill her. In a way, she'd hoped that the item in the box might help her finally decide, but the mundane nature of the coin only confused her.

But nothing was ever simple, or black and white. Maybe the coin was a gift, and had no nefarious purpose. And maybe the Cabal wasn't a sinister group bent on world domination, but a partnership between some of the patrons of the Hundred Halls. It wasn't like she had any proof otherwise.

She wasn't going to give up looking though. She'd start with the runes and pester Ashley with questions about her grandfather. It might not be sinister, but there was something going on, something that she was determined to figure out. Something that would help her understand if she should truly stay in Coterie.

28

The storms of March had left the air hazy with ozone. Wisps of mist rose from the glistening street like apparitions, while water dripped from the green nose of the copper dragon into the rain-filled basin.

It'd been seven months since Aurie had last visited the Enochian District, but it felt like seven years. She'd thought that once they made it into the Hundred Halls, everything would get easier.

Pi came striding down the street, the glittering Spire rising above her in the distance at the city center. The smile on her sister's face coaxed laughter from her own lips. They embraced, neither one wanting to let go.

"I missed you," Aurie whispered in her sister's ear.

"Of course you did," said Pi with a wink. "I've missed you too. I didn't realize it would be so hard to be apart."

Aurie pulled back and tussled her younger sister's hair. It was shaved on the sides and the tips were purple. She looked like a fashion magazine's version of punk rock.

"What's with the hair? I thought you were going all Coterie?" asked Aurie.

"Fuck 'em. I realized that I wasn't going to get ahead by playing their game," she said.

"Is that working?" asked Aurie.

"I've got some interest for a second-year sponsor. Things have been looking much better the second half of the year," said Pi.

Aurie smiled for her sister even though she was disappointed. She'd secretly hoped that Pi would give up Coterie.

A cat went streaking across the street with a screech, chased from the shadows by something that hadn't revealed itself.

"Who's there?" asked Aurie, feeling dumb for even asking.

It felt like she had eyes on her.

"So," began Pi, distracting her, "I know you didn't bring me here for the ambiance. I assume this has something to do with Mom and Dad?"

Her sister's gaze fell upon the singing stone that contained their voices. Her lips remained stoic while her eyes glistened with memories.

"I want to complete their legacy," said Aurie.

Pi's forehead wrinkled with confusion.

"Before they died"—Aurie paused and took a deep breath. It was hard to speak of that day to the only person that knew the depths of her shame—"they'd been preparing an expedition to retrieve a fabled artifact that could help the dying. The Rod of Dominion."

"That's the item I asked the demon about," said Pi, putting her hand to her mouth. "Wait. When I gave the news to the patron, he seemed surprised by my success, and mentioned that other forces were at work. Maybe this is that magical karma that Hemistad spoke of."

"I'm not sure about that," said Aurie. "Believing in

magical karma is kind of like astrology. I think it's more straightforward. The Rod is an ancient Egyptian artifact that helped the pharaohs maintain power. I think your patron wants the Rod for the same reasons."

"Then why would you want to retrieve it?" asked Pi.

"It was also a force of good in those times, giving the pharaohs the power to heal diseases and remove curses. Imagine all the people that could be saved using the Rod," she said.

"What if the wrong people got ahold of it?" asked Pi.

"The world is filled with dangerous things. Nuclear bombs. Spell plagues. As long as the right people have them, they're not dangerous," said Aurie. "So if we don't get it first, they might. Why else did your patron ask about the Rod?"

"Alright. So the Cabal is looking for the Rod. Do you actually know where it is?" asked Pi.

"Not entirely," said Aurie. "I think I know where it's at, or at least where our parents thought it was. In the Valley of Kings in Egypt."

"But the demon said it was *beneath city of lights in the halls of the dead.* We both thought that meant the catacombs of Paris," said Pi.

"It still could, but I don't think so. The Rod is protected by a curse that affects anyone who tries to take the artifact from the boundaries of the tomb in Egypt. I think it's still there," said Aurie.

"Then how are we going to get it? We can't get to Egypt. Not while we're in the Halls," said Pi.

"Mom and Dad said something that day," said Aurie, but when Pi gave her a strange glance, she added, "Don't ask how I know, I just know."

It was more than just not wanting to explain her failures in the room of truth. She also knew it was possible that knowledge was a fabrication of her mind, and she didn't want Pi to doubt her.

"But anyway, they said something about going to retrieve the Rod, but they also planned on attending our piano recital a few days later. There's no way they could fly to Egypt, raid the tomb, and fly back in time. Which meant they were going to create a portal into the tomb, bypassing the curse," said Aurie.

"No way," said Pi, shaking her head. "The energies required for a portal are enormous. You can't just place one anywhere. There has to be enough latent energy to draw from or the structure will collapse. Otherwise, someone would have used a portal a long time ago to break into the tomb."

"What if Mom and Dad found a place with enough latent energy?" asked Aurie.

"Fine. Where?" asked Pi.

"Here," said Aurie. "Well, not exactly here, but near here. Invictus is called the City of Sorcery for a reason. Nowhere else in the world has so much magic concentrated in one place. Why else do people stay out of the Undercity? The excess faez collects down there, creating terrible things, probably like that weird Hunger that almost killed us when we were with Hemistad. And that Infernal translation. It could have just as easily been *beneath the city of sorcery*. The Infernal word for light is similar to magic."

"You think we can build a portal to Egypt down in the Undercity?" asked Pi, who didn't appear to believe Aurie.

"No. I think Mom and Dad had the portal already built. They were just missing a few items to complete it before they could use it," she explained.

Pi put a fist to her mouth. Her eyes held grave thoughts. "You remember that box you helped me open with the runed gallium coin inside? I think I understand it's purpose now. Gallium can be used for a lot of things like levitation or wart removal. It's magically magnetic. The coins are made to locate a particular magical field. It's looking for a gate of some kind, which means the Cabal are looking for the Rod, too."

"Your patron did give you that task, so it shouldn't be a surprise," said Aurie.

"Yeah, but I thought he'd given it to me to get rid of me. Like it was impossible or something. And maybe it was, except for our magical karma. Once I gave him the answer, he was surprised. It was only after I gave him the news about the Rod that I started delivering the coins for Radoslav. The timeline makes sense," she said.

"Have you delivered all the coins?" asked Aurie.

"One more to go, in a couple of weeks. I assume it'll go to my patron. He's the last one," she said.

"They'll be able to go after the Rod once they have it," said Aurie. "Which means we have to find it first."

"I can always *not* deliver the coin," said Pi.

Aurie crossed her arms. "Which will only slow them down for a few weeks at best and put you in danger. Better that we get the Rod before them. That way they'll never know."

"So why again are we here? We could have met anywhere," said Pi.

"In Mom and Dad's notes, they reference the location as the place where they first expressed their true love. I thought that could have been anywhere, but I realized they meant the singing stone. I think it's in the sewers beneath this street. I checked that manhole cover before you got here. There's a ladder."

"You want to go down there?" asked Pi, incredulously. "You realize this isn't the safest of areas."

"That's why we're here in the daytime. We've got a few hours to search before we need to leave," she said. "But I don't think we'll need it. I'm certain it's here."

Aurie and Pi went down the ladder into the sewers beneath the street. Wisps followed them, providing light. The tunnels were wide and relatively dry, despite the recent rain. The pipes rumbled as they carried water to other parts of the city.

She'd placed a beacon on the ladder to keep them from getting lost and then another on her sister, over her protests, in case of separation. Aurie assumed the portal was located nearby, or they would have picked a different entrance.

They explored the sewers, going up and down each passage methodically, marking the walls with chalk so they knew if they were covering the same ground again.

Aurie had expected to find the portal or signs of their parents pretty quickly, so after the first fruitless hour, she started to get discouraged.

A few hours later, Pi found the first chalk mark, signifying that they had thoroughly explored the area.

"I'm sorry, sis," Pi said. "Maybe it's not here, or you're wrong about the translation. Like you said, Infernal is tricky."

"Maybe there's a secret door in a wall or something that we missed," she said.

"Somehow I doubt that Mom and Dad built a secret door. I think if it was going to be here, we would have found it," said Pi.

"It's okay. It's not like we were going to go through the portal today. We still need to get some runic switches," said Aurie, discouraged.

Pi reacted strangely to the news. "I know where I can get some. The patron had us make them in class a few months ago. Another sign that they're going after the Rod."

"What are you going to do? About Coterie?" asked Aurie.

Pi crossed her arms defiantly. "I'm not giving it up. Yet. I have to know for certain. Plus, I'd be useless without the protection from my patron."

"What if he figures out what you're doing through the link?"

"It's a risk," said Pi, reluctantly.

"I was certain it was here," said Aurie, slamming her fist in her other hand.

"It's okay. At least we got to hang out again," said Pi. "I really miss this."

"Me too," said Aurie. "I love you, sis."

"I love you, too," said Pi. "Now, let's get the hell out of here. Wandering around in the sewers is creepy."

Together they left the sewers while daylight still ruled. Aurie bid farewell to her sister after a long hug with promises to continue searching in their free time. On the train back to Arcanium, she tried to piece together how she'd been wrong about the sewers. She'd been certain that they'd find the portal beneath the singing stone. She'd study her notes again, but worried they'd offer no further ideas. If they couldn't find it in the next few weeks, the Cabal would have the last coin and would be able to locate the portal, and thus the Rod of Dominion.

29

The city of Invictus buzzed like a hive in early April as spring brought the approach of finals for the students and the promise of fresh air for its residents. Tourists from all over the country and world had descended upon the second ward for the Auntie Andy's Amazing Aeromancy show at the Glitterdome.

Crossing the street, a car full of teenagers with a swarm of enchanted paper airplanes—bombers, three-wing Fokkers, and other assorted craft—in close pursuit swerved, and Pi had to leap out of the way to avoid the shiny bumper zipping past.

"Watch where you're going!" she yelled from the safe confines of the sidewalk. She resisted the urge to send a fire jet after them to burn the paper airplanes out of the sky.

The rhino-faced bouncer at the Glass Cabaret let her inside with a nod, not even asking for ID. Light jazz wafted through the air in a dream. Pi ignored the stares, as she was wearing jeans and a hoodie with a backpack while everyone else wore designer clothes.

Radoslav wasn't behind the bar, so she took a stool at the end. After she made the delivery, Aurie was supposed to meet her at the Enochian District so they could make one last sweep. They'd been exploring the sewers every day before evening, trying to find the portal.

When Radoslav came through the curtains, holding his expression into practiced disinterest like a fine dry red wine, he stopped, turned his head, and uncharacteristically tilted it.

"I'm not here on the wrong day, am I?" asked Pi, suddenly feeling like an idiot.

"No," he said, "not at all. But I sent along a note that the delivery was unnecessary. The last box was picked up two days ago. My apologies that you did not receive my note."

A cold dread descended on her. "No apology necessary. I work for you after all."

His face was normally unreadable, but she detected a hint of something lurking on his lip, a twitch that wouldn't quite fire, nor go away.

She'd turned to go when he spoke again.

"Be careful, Pythia. The streets are particularly restless today," he said, his gray eyes revealing a momentary slip of—concern?

Before she could say anything, he disappeared into the back, the curtains swaying gently at his passing.

She left the Glass Cabaret with the distinct feeling she was being monitored. Radoslav had given her a warning, which meant he knew something, or had determined it.

The note, she realized. It should have made it to her. If Malden had retrieved the final gallium coin two days ago, and had not delivered the note, it meant that he knew what they were up to and didn't want to tip her off.

It also meant that she was in terrible danger. If the Cabal knew they were trying to find the Rod, they would have no problem killing her.

The only bright spot to the situation was that she'd learned something about Radoslav. He clearly wasn't a member of Cabal, or he wouldn't have bothered warning her. Discreetly as she could, Pi cast a few defensive enchantments.

On the train to the Enochian District, she couldn't shake the feeling that someone was following her, so she slipped off the train before the doors closed at the stop before her destination.

She hurried to the concrete stairs, then took position at the bottom to see if anyone had followed her. Behind her, a saxophone honked out tunes for loose change and the occasional crumpled bill.

Once she was certain no one was following, Pi took to the street. It was only a few blocks to the dragon fountain, and she was early since she hadn't needed to make the delivery.

The streets weren't busy like the other locations. The majority of traffic consisted of delivery vans and taxis, usually heading to other wards. Few cars were parked along the curb.

Pi kept her head down and moved at a brisk pace. Once she got to the Enochian District, she planned to set up in a secluded area and watch for followers. When Aurie arrived, they'd have to decide if they were going to go after the Rod. It was possible that the Cabal already had it, but if they didn't, it was their last chance.

Pi dodged around a delivery van. A couple of movers were carrying boxes into an unmarked warehouse with a rusted door and broken windows. They gave her strange looks as she went past, watching her as she marched away. Only after she was about thirty feet up the street did they continue into the building.

That was when the spell hit her. Her muscles seized up until she was as stiff as a statue. The forward motion sent her tipping over. A broad-shouldered man in a blue track suit caught her, dragged her into the alleyway, and dropped her heavily on her side.

The street smelled like old urine and vomit. Pi's head rested near an oily puddle with a dented empty beer can floating in it.

A wave of fear rose up in her chest, making her vision waver. This was it. This was the end. There was nothing she could do about it, and there was no way that Aurie would find her, since she wasn't at the meet up location.

Her captor leaned down, almost within vision. Recognition came slowly, but when it hit, she wanted to scream.

"Hello, sweetie Pi," said Alton Lockwood, sneering from his crouch. "Are we uncomfortable? Good. Things are going to get a lot worse from here on out."

He pulled out a handful of long zip ties and bound her arms and legs together.

"I learned my lesson last time," he said. "You're a tricky bitch. But those days are at an end."

He leaned down and picked her up, throwing her easily over his shoulder. He carried her into a nearby building, opening the door with a spell. It was a ratty old apartment with a pea-green water stained couch. He threw her onto it facing the tube television sitting on a battered milk crate.

"You know," he said, sauntering over to her, "for a girl, especially a brown girl, you really are impressive. If you'd learned to keep your pretty mouth shut like your friend Ashley, you might have survived Coterie, maybe even excelled. But we just can't have uppity bitches on the loose, making our Hall look bad."

His words enraged her, until she was practically choking on her spit. She fought the binding, but couldn't break it.

A car door slammed outside, making Alton stop in his tracks. A couple of male voices gave him pause.

"Excuse me," he said, adjusting his track suit jacket as if

it were his normal white suit coat. "I need to make sure we're uninterrupted for the next few hours."

He stepped out the door before the men arrived, mumbling a spell as he went.

Pi took a deep breath and concentrated on making her lips move. If she could access the defensive spells she'd placed on herself earlier, she could break his binding.

Shifting the faez to her lips, rather than her hands, took effort. She tried to ignore Alton speaking to the men outside, but it was hard because she knew what was coming.

After what seemed like forever, she shook the binding free. The zip ties held her down, but she was able to waggle her fingers and break them with a spell.

She thought about rushing outside and enlisting the two men's help, or at least taking the fight to Alton, but if he'd charmed them, three-on-one odds weren't good, even with surprise on her side.

So she ran to the back of the apartment, looking for a way out. She found a bedroom around the time she heard the front door open. As quietly as she could, Pi opened the window and put her leg out. A figure moved into the room.

When Pi didn't recognize the man, she threw herself out the window, only to find Alton waiting for her. He punched her in the face, knocking her backward onto the concrete. Her consciousness fled as he leaned into her vision.

30

Professor Mali faced the class like a queen addressing her subjects. Aurie sat in the back of class, knees nervously bouncing. She could barely concentrate. Despite the importance of the day, she could only think about the Rod of Dominion and their failure to find the portal in the sewers. Pi was supposed to deliver the final gallium coin, which would give the Cabal the last thing they needed to find the portal themselves. They'd argued for the last few days about not delivering the coin, but decided that it would put Pi in too much danger, either from the binding with Radoslav, or from direct attack from the Cabal. Better to find the Rod first, and spirit it away before they even knew that it was gone.

"Today is your final test in the room of truth. Some of you have worked hard to address the challenges in your past, while others"—the professor speared Aurie with her gaze—"have yet to even get started. Let me remind you that if it is your desire to be invited back to Arcanium as a second-year student, you must conquer your fears in the room of truth. Are there any questions?"

To the surprise of everyone, Aurie raised her hand.

"Yes, Aurelia?"

"May I go first?" she asked as demurely as possible.

She planned to sneak away after her turn to join Pi for one last attempt to find the Rod and wanted as much time as possible.

"A solid attitude," said the professor with a nod of approval. "Yes, you may go first. I hope this bodes well for you in the room."

As Aurie walked down the center aisle, the other students gave her encouraging smiles and a few thumbs-up.

Deshawn gave her a fist bump on the way past. "Go get 'em, Aurie."

"Aurelia," said the professor.

Aurie crouched down for instructions.

In a quiet voice, Professor Mali spoke to her. "I know this has been difficult. With your history, the orphanages, and so on, I can only imagine that whatever you're experiencing inside must be quite traumatic. But know that the magic practiced in Arcanium will put a heavy strain on you. If you have cracks underneath, then your studies will only tear you apart. You're a terrific student, one of the most promising I've seen since I've been the initiate instructor, but know that I will not pass you if you cannot master the room of truth. To do so would be to set a bomb loose in the world. So good luck. I truly hope you do well."

Aurie stayed stoic until she entered the room of truth, then her expression broke, already mourning the life that couldn't be.

Everyone had been so damn encouraging, every last one of them. It would have been easier if they'd hated her, or thought she didn't deserve to be in Arcanium.

It didn't even matter anymore if it'd been her fault that her parents had died. That had been a reason at one time, but since she'd learned about the Rod of Dominion, that reason mattered no longer.

She couldn't by any rights put her desire to be in Arcanium above the lives of Emily and the others at Golden Willow. The Rod of Dominion mattered more than any petty desires to be a mage, to experience the learning in the Hundred Halls, to have friends that shared her life.

But it didn't make it hurt any damn less.

As the golden sparkles of faez turned into the living room of her childhood home, Aurie choked back a sob.

Her mother, Nahid, stood in front of her with her hands clasped. The look of disappointment was a toxin to Aurie. Immediately, she knew this was not truth. This was her subconscious subverting the vision. The professor's warning echoed in her mind, but she was too far past her decision for it to matter. She'd never been more sure about something in her life that would simultaneously wreck it.

"You haven't kept your sister safe like you promised," said her mother.

"I've tried. I'm not perfect. Not by any measure," she said, then realized the normal rules of the vision weren't applying. This wasn't the vision Aurie speaking, but her, the real her.

Nahid shook her fist, anguish threading her voice. "You let her summon a demon lord, and join the Coterie of Mages. What have you been doing? How could you let your little sister do that? And now you're leading her into the sewers on a damned quest to find something that gave your father and I nightmares for weeks when we even considered going after it. You're a first-year initiate, Aurie. You should know better. Give up this foolishness. Pass your tests, stay in Arcanium."

Aurie knew it was her own mind pulling the puppet strings of her mother, but her heart couldn't distinguish between the two.

"I'm trying, Mom. I really am," said Aurie, holding back tears. "It's not easy. I miss you every day. I try to do right by Pi, but I can't be there every moment. She's her own person too."

"Then don't take her after the Rod. Leave it be. The curse is more dangerous than you can imagine. It got your father and I before we even stepped foot inside," she said.

Words chilled in her throat. Could that be true? Patron Semyon had warned her that the Rod was dangerous. What if her parents had woken the curse? Magic worked in strange ways. Some called it karma, others said it was like quantum theory. Was she a fool to take her sister after the Rod? Maybe.

"I have to. It's too important. You and Dad went after the Rod for the same reasons," said Aurie.

Nahid stepped forward, took Aurie's hands within her own. They were so warm! So real! She nearly swooned from the contact.

"Then wait, my darling. Wait until you're older. Until you can take on the challenges. You have time," said her mother.

"I can't," said Aurie. "I have to go now, or the Cabal will get it and Emily and the others will suffer."

A calmness overtook her, like the wind falling silent across a vast lake and the ripples stilling to glass. She'd come to peace with her decision. Now, she just needed to know one thing.

"Mom. I know this is all in my head. Just a vision recreated from my memories. This isn't you, but me. You're the reflection of my hopes and dreams. Professor Mali is right. I don't know what the truth is. I never have. I have no idea if I caused the accident, or if it was something else like the curse, or the strange man that Pi once told me she saw. I sometimes wonder if I *want* to have caused it, because then I would have a reason to feel so awful all the time. That I was being punished.

It would almost make sense that way. Almost. But I didn't come here for that. I didn't come here to learn what happened, because it doesn't matter. No matter what it was, you're still dead," she said.

Her mother looked like a rope ready to break, frayed in the middle and unraveling quickly. But there was something else, deep in the eyes, like jewels at the bottom of a dark pool. Buried in her memory of her mother was the overwhelming love that her mother felt for her and Pi. Never once in their thirteen years together did Aurie ever question how much her parents loved her. Those eyes held back a dam full of love, ready to burst and flood her with emotion.

Aurie pushed it back before it overwhelmed her. She took a deep, quivering breath.

"I've been going over these visions in my head. Reviewing them, trying to learn from them. There's something I'm missing. Something important that I've forgotten, lost amid the years and the fears and the tears. So I am asking you, asking myself really. What have I missed? There's something that day that matters, and I can't figure it out. What is it?"

Her mother stood silently for a long time. Aurie didn't think it was going to work. She mentally prepared herself for the price of failure. Then Nahid walked into the living room, slow and solemn like a priest leading a funeral procession.

Pi was sitting on the couch, along with a younger version of herself. Aurie knew this moment. She'd lived through it too many times in her head. She didn't need a room of truth for it.

"Girls," said her mother, not to the real Aurie, but to the fake one. The vision had slipped back into its routine. "Your father and I need to work in the basement. We don't want to be disturbed, so you'll need to play quietly up here until then. Or get your homework done."

"Yes, Mother," the vision Aurie and Pi said in unison.

Nahid went into the basement. Aurie's skin grew flush as she watched her mother disappear into the darkness.

Focus, Aurie.   Pay attention.   There's something I'm supposed to see.

"I'm bored with this game," said Pi, and moved to the table.

"I don't want to do homework," said young Aurie.

Pi was looking out the front window. Her head was slightly tilted.

"Wanna play Five Elements? The real way, with faez?" asked young Aurie.

But the real Aurie wasn't paying attention. She noticed what she hadn't seen the first time. Pi was looking out the window.

Pi's forehead scrunched. "But Mom said we're not allowed to play it that way. We have to play finger exercises only."

"Come on, Pi. Everyone at school plays with faez—"

"Shut up. The both of you," said Aurie.

The visions turned towards Aurie, both noses wrinkling with the annoyance of being disturbed from their play.

She pointed at her sister. "What do you see? What's out the window? Did you say something that day that might tell me who it is?"

Her sister looked out the window again. Her expression fell grim, her normally olive skin pale as a ghost.

"There's a funny man," she said.

"Funny how? Like a clown or something?" asked Aurie.

Pi shoulders tensed with annoyance. "Not a clown. Funny to look at. Like I can't see him all the way."

The words sparked a memory for Aurie, bringing with it a tidal wave of concern.

"What did you say that day?" Aurie asked herself out loud. "Something about a glimmer?"

Then words came out of Pi's mouth as if she were an

automaton. "He shimmered." She looked out the window. "He shimmers, even now."

Aurie remembered it now. She'd thought Pi was trying to say that she saw a city fae, a maetrie. Told her she was being ridiculous, since they lived in the suburbs. But it wasn't a maetrie she saw. It was someone using an identity masking charm. They were difficult to maintain, but she knew one person who had one on him all the time: the Coterie patron, Malden Anterist.

"Oh, shit," she said, feeling cold all at once. "Pythia. She's in trouble."

Aurie dismissed the dream, the return of the real world making her dizzy with vertigo. She fought through it to exit the room, only to find a sea of surprised faces. Professor Mali was nowhere to be found.

Deshawn spoke first. "Didn't it work?"

"What?"

"You just went in the room, like thirty seconds ago," he said. "Didn't it work?"

"I have to go," she said, and started moving towards the exit.

Deshawn stood up, along with a few other students, including Violet. "You can't go, Aurie. You have to pass. We need you in Arcanium."

"I...I can't stay. I have something to do that's more important," she said, trying to step around them, but they stayed in her way.

Deshawn's face wrinkled as he gathered his words. As he spoke his features smoothed. "If anyone deserves to be here, it's you. Don't throw your chance away. Go back in the room and confront your fears."

"It's not that," said Aurie desperately. She almost broke into an explanation of everything that was going on, but she didn't think they would believe her, and she didn't want anyone to try and help, and get hurt her because of her. "I just need to go. Please. It's important. More important than Arcanium."

"Someone get the professor," said Deshawn to one of the others. "She just went down the hall."

Everyone was looking at Aurie like she was crazy. She knew the moment the professor arrived, they wouldn't let her out of the room.

"I have to go," she said as calmly as she could. "Please move aside."

When Deshawn grabbed her wrist, gently but firmly, Aurie wanted to cry inside. "We're not letting you leave. We're your friends."

Everyone started nodding and adding their agreements. She'd never had so many friends in her life. It was agonizing. Whatever she did now, they wouldn't be her friends much longer.

"I'm sorry. I have to," she said.

Aurie couldn't take a chance that even one person could stop her. Pi's life depended on it, she knew that deep in her bones. Whatever she did, it had to count, but she didn't want to hurt them either. Drawing on her deep well of faez, she said in a calm and authoritative voice, the truth magic threading through like rich ore deep in the earth's crust, "You all suddenly feel very tired. So tired that you can't stay awake."

They each realized what she was doing, and their faces went through various stages of betrayal before their eyes closed against their will and they collapsed. The worst was Violet, who seemed to come to the understanding that Aurie was exactly who she thought she was.

With regret like a fever in her head, and barbed wire wrapped tight around her heart, Aurie ran out of the room. She had to get to Pi before the Cabal did. If it'd been Malden Anterist who'd killed their parents, then he'd known who Pi was all along. They'd been playing her, using Radoslav to deliver the very tools they would need to find the Rod, and now that they didn't need her, they could throw her away, just like they did their parents.

31

Pythia awoke on the battered pea-green couch, sitting straight up with her hands at her sides. Her head ached as if a train had driven through it. Alton had hit her in the jaw hard enough to break it. She didn't think she'd be eating meat or anything requiring chewing for quite some time.

She checked to make sure her clothes were still on, which didn't bring relief, only a sense of impending tragedy. Not only did she find her clothes were still on, but there were no bindings holding her to the couch. Her wrists and ankles were free, and Alton Lockwood was nowhere to be seen.

The door was unguarded a few feet away. She just had to get up and run out. She just had to move her feet. *Why won't they move?* Pi could flex her muscles, or tap her toes, but when she tried to get up from the couch, they refused to obey.

A toilet flushed in another room. For the first time, Pi realized a small table had been set up near the couch. An expensive briefcase was sitting open, revealing tubes of liquids and jars of reagents. It was a traveling alchemy shop.

Alton sauntered in. His face lit up when he saw she was awake, and in turn, Pi felt herself warm with excitement. She'd never realized how attractive he was, how finely his clothes accentuated his muscled form, how his eyes were like the glittering of a million galaxies...

What the fuck am I thinking?

She tried to shake those thoughts free, but moving her head back and forth brought agony to the lower half of her face.

"It's about time. I was getting rather impatient," he said, clasping his hands together. "I see you're fighting it, but don't worry. Now that you're awake, we can finish this properly. You won't feel conflicted about your feelings for me when I'm done with you."

Pi strained against the enchantments that held her on the couch, pulled and fought, even when it triggered pain in her jaw, relishing the agony because it was better than thinking about what was coming next.

But the enchantments were too strong and the pain too great, and she fell back, exhausted. She speared him in her sights, reminding herself of how much she hated him, trying to counteract whatever it was he'd done to her, while simultaneously trying to figure a way out. Her thoughts oscillated between fawning over his broad shoulders, and putting a knife in his belly.

Alton strolled over to the briefcase as if he were a salesman giving a demonstration.

"It was unfortunate at the Amber & Smoke that I was not able to subdue you properly. Enchantments alone are not always enough to affect the subject. I've found that the proper cocktail of potions, along with a few choice spells, can create a longer lasting impression," he said, his tone one of a scientist explaining his experiments.

He pulled out a little squat opaque vial out of the briefcase and held it up for her.

"Succubus tears," he said. "A powerful aphrodisiac that when combined with a few other ingredients, gives the enchantments a fertile soil in which to take strong roots. I gave you a touch of it while you were out so I could ensure that you wouldn't cause me any more trouble. A small amount makes a person highly suggestible for a short time, eight hours max. For longer periods, I need you to be awake. You see, once I'm done layering in the spells, I will have you drink the rest of this vial. To be honest, I've never given anyone this much, but this amount should make the spells effectively permanent."

He flicked his fingernail against the glass and gave her a snake's grin.

"Succubus tears are quite expensive," he said. "In fact, I'm going to blow a small fortune when I give you the rest of this. You see, this has been a little side project of mine. Not only am I going to put an end to your little power play, but I'll be proving a theory. When I show you off to the patron, he'll realize my worth and give me the proper position to utilize my talents. You see, this combination of spells and potions allows me to imprint you with whatever suggestions I want. I can make you love me, or be allergic to water, or think that you can fly. Anything. Permanently. With this formula, just imagine what I can do. Imagine the senators, or heads of state, that I can control. Or even other patrons."

He paused, lights of ambition flickering in his eyes. She saw him consider going it alone for a moment, before realizing it would be dangerous.

"When I'm done with you, you'll think I'm a god. You'll worship the very ground I walk. Every thought will be consumed by how you want to please me. I may not even bother with you after that, for that would give you what you want. I could whip you and you will thank me for it. Who knows what I'll do? Maybe it'll be nice to have a pet mage around. You can be my assistant. Just imagine the outfits I can dress you up in. Just imagine what you'll want to do for me," he said, his eyes alight with the possibilities.

Though it took every ounce of her will, and made her eyes water from the pain, she spoke through gritted teeth. "Fuck you."

"Soon enough, you little bitch," he replied with equal venom.

Alton pulled a leather-bound notebook from the inside pocket of the briefcase. He opened it up, holding it front of him like a choirboy about to break into song.

The smell of faez filled the room as he began the first spell. While words flowed from his lips, his free hand danced like a conductor at a symphony.

The first enchantment etched into her, silencing her. Like a drowning victim slowly sinking beneath the waves, she felt the spell smother her free will. Part of her wanted to give up and let go. She knew objectively that he was right. Once he was finished, she'd beg him to sleep with her, no matter how revolting it was now.

But she'd always fought, would always fight, would never give up. She hoped that maybe, deep down inside, she could bury her free will so that in some weak moment, when time put cracks into the enchantment, even decades from now, the real Pi would surge forth and enact her revenge.

The spell wove around her arms, her legs, binding her, keeping her from staying afloat. She fought and wriggled, doing everything she could to stay herself, but succubus tears had destroyed her defenses.

She looked at Alton, trying to memorize the hate she felt for him, trying to bury it deep, when something large and black rose above his head.

The cast-iron pan came crashing down on Alton's head,

crumpling him to the floor. Between the unraveling spell and the sudden visual change, Pi was confused, until she saw Aurie standing there with the black pan in her fists.

Aurie cast a few spells, releasing Pi from Alton's grip. When she no longer looked at him with longing, she knew that the worst was past.

Then Pi threw her arms around her sister, squeezing her tight. "Thank you, Aurie."

Aurie held her at arm's length. "You look like hell, sis. The right side of your face is black and blue. What happened?"

"He punched me," said Pi, rubbing her jaw.

"I was worried about killing him when I hit him with the pan. Now I think I didn't hit him hard enough," she said.

Before Alton could wake, they moved him to the couch and put a few bindings on him. Then they took turns explaining what they had learned. The revelations only made the danger more acute.

"How did you find me?" asked Pi.

"The spell we used in the sewers so we didn't lose each other," said Aurie.

For once, Pi didn't give her sister a hard time about being overly prepared.

"What do we do with him? We can't leave him here, but we need to go after the Rod," said Aurie, then she saw the look on her sister's face. "No. We can't kill him."

"I wasn't going to suggest that, as tempting as it might be," said Pi. "But I have an idea that might make him wish we had. We can't let him keep the knowledge in his head. It's as dangerous as the Rod."

Aurie agreed, and together they prepared Alton for the same enchantments that he was going to cast on Pi. When he awoke, he startled, then tried to move his arms, finding them immobile.

"Here's what we're going to do, asshole," started Pi, holding his notebook up so he could see it. "Since you took such excellent notes, we had no problem deciphering how to perform the permanency enchantment. So what we're going to do is this. First, we're going to put the suggestion in you that if you ever expose yourself to a woman, no matter if she honestly desires it or not, you will feel such exquisite pain in your nether regions that you'll wish you'd died. Second, you're going to quit Coterie and find an honest profession somewhere in the Midwest and never practice magic again. Third, you're going to forget the very enchantments that we're going to layer upon you, and finally, you're going to forget us forever, even if you see us again. It'll be like we didn't exist."

Together, Pi and her sister cast the spells detailed in the notebook. Then they dumped the vial of succubus tears down his gullet and poured out the remaining potions into the sink. Alton was in a comatose state by the time they were finished.

"It might take him a bit to snap out of it," said Aurie. "He can find his way back when he comes to. What are we going to do with his notes?"

"Burn them," she said, and they did, using a rusty grill in the alleyway for the deed.

"Shall we go back to the sewers?" asked Pi.

"No," said Aurie. "If the portal was there, we would have found it. I think we're close, but looking in the wrong place. I think the singing stone was a beacon to help guide our parents, but not in the sewers."

"Where then?" asked Pi.

Aurie held the words between her teeth before speaking reluctantly. "The Undercity."

32

They used the lift that Hemistad kept in the back of Freeport Games. He wasn't around to ask—he was away at a gaming convention—and he'd never told them not to, so they didn't feel like they were disobeying him. They left him a note so he'd know not to bring the lift up without them.

When they reached the bottom, Aurie cast a locating spell on the lift so they could find it again after they were finished. She hoped they would need it.

They strode into the darkness, boots echoing against the stone. They wore backpacks full of supplies. Wisps followed them dutifully, shedding meager light into the vastness of the Undercity.

From their time in the sewers, they were well acquainted with the beacon on their parents' singing stone. They used it to orient themselves, marching towards the area they hoped contained the portal.

After an hour of steady movement, Aurie stopped for a drink.

"It shouldn't be much further," she said, her voice falling to a whisper as she spoke. The darkness swallowed the words.

To their left, a faint light appeared momentarily, like someone flicking a lighter then snuffing it out. It happened a second time while they were watching, but it'd moved further away.

Pi whispered, "It looks like it's going the other direction."

When a third flicker confirmed, Aurie felt the tension in her shoulders release a little.

A while later, they came to a series of wide tunnels, much like the kind that Hemistad had taken them through earlier in the year. Unlike the others, these were bone dry. A layer of dust covered the stone surface.

"At least we know no one else has come this way," said Pi.

"Unless there are other ways to reach the portal," said Aurie.

Neither sister wanted to speak the obvious, so they moved into the tunnels. It was wide enough for the two of them to walk side by side without touching. The tunnels didn't always take them towards the beacon, so they had to double back at times.

Pi kept looking over her shoulder so much that Aurie had to stop and ask, "Do you see something?"

"Hearing," said Pi in a stage whisper. "I think, anyway. I can't decide if it's our footsteps echoing down the tunnels, or someone's following us."

Aurie shouldered out of her backpack while saying in a loud voice that echoed in both directions, "Don't let your imagination get the best of you."

"It's not my imagination," said Pi defensively, then seeing Aurie's face, nodded with understanding.

While Aurie dug through her backpack, she said, "If this weren't so serious, I'd remind you of the time you nearly burned down that haunted house."

"I'm sorry, but clowns are bullshit," said Pi.

When she stopped, Aurie made a rotating finger gesture to keep Pi talking while she searched. The contents of her pack had shifted during the hike.

"Haunted houses should come with a warning," said Pi, shrugging as she searched for words. "Like a rating or something. One clown means only clown-related materials on the premises. Four clowns means that Pennywise himself is going to drag you into the sewers."

When the smooth stone bumped against her fingers, she yanked it out. It was a piece of amber. While Pi continued on about clowns and haunted houses, Aurie put a spell on the amber to make it glow if anyone else was near.

She rotated in a circle, watching the chunk of amber closely. A faint golden hue formed on the far side, like it was turning to warm honey. But as quickly as it appeared, it disappeared, leaving the sisters to share bewildered glances. She tried it again, but the amber stayed inert.

"Could be someone following us, or could be a large rat," said Aurie.

"Could be a killer clown too," said Pi with a smirk.

It wasn't long after that they found the portal. The tunnels led to a large room. A stone arch had been built in the center. The bricks had been set unevenly, the mortar thin in some areas, thick in others. A piece of rod had been formed to the shape of the opening. Runic switches covered nine-tenths of the rod, the final gap only a foot across.

"They made this," said Pi in awe.

"And we're going to finish it," said Aurie, pulling her sister to her side. They relished the sight of something their parents had made for a full minute before digging into their backpacks.

Pi produced a handful of switches and approached the arch. The new switches were nearly identical. She snapped them into the gap, completing the circuit. A whiff of ozone entered the room.

"Is this really going to get us into the Tomb of Kings?" asked Pi, with a fist planted on one hip. "It doesn't look that impressive."

Aurie had a spiral notebook open in her hand, containing all the writings from her parents she'd collected. She addressed the arch, taking a deep breath before she launched into a series of quasi-Latin phrases.

As faez hit the ring, the earth groaned beneath her feet, nearly interrupting the spell. Electricity crackled at the edges of the runic switches, bringing an eerie luminosity. Beneath the illusion of the brick arch, the truth was revealed—etched hieroglyphics pulsed on sandstone with a frightful intensity. A shimmering field formed before the opening.

Pi's eyes were wide open. "Never mind what I said. That's really fucking impressive. Do you think that's the arch on the other side?"

"That's what Mom's notes say. Which means no one has seen those hieroglyphics for thousands of years. Until now."

"That's it? We can just walk into Egypt from here?" asked Pi.

"Almost. I mean we can, but I want to ask you something first, Pi, and don't just give me an answer, really think about it," said Aurie.

"If the question is, did I kiss anyone in Coterie, the answer is yes, and it was three boys and two girls," said Pi, then she made a face.

Aurie laughed despite herself. She was too glad to see her sister to be mad.

"I just want to make sure you know what you're getting into. I've read these books cover to cover, but you haven't. This is serious shit we're getting into. The pharaohs were gods of their time, wielding magic that we don't even really understand, even today. The Rod of Dominion is one of their most powerful artifacts. The kind of magic that protects it is stuff we might not even have defenses for. There's even a possibility that the curse was the reason for Mom and Dad's death. That it got them before they even stepped foot inside, that's how powerful it is."

"I don't even know why you're asking, Aurie. You know what my answer is," said Pi.

"I need to hear it from you," said Aurie, then held up her hand. "And not just a simple answer, I want to hear why. Or I'm not letting you come."

"Older sisters are such a pain in the ass," said Pi with a wry smile. "I want to come for the same reasons that you do. I want to complete Mom and Dad's work. I want to help people."

"What about the power? Isn't that why you joined Coterie? I need to understand your intentions," said Aurie.

"I didn't join Coterie for power, I mean I did, but not really. I joined to protect the people I love. Which means you, you big dumb idiot," said Pi. "Even if I cared nothing about the Rod, I'd go, just to make sure you came back out. The fact that we can help those kids at the hospital is a bonus. Plus, sticking it to the Cabal."

"Which technically, you're a part of," said Aurie.

"Not after this," said Pi. "Once we get the Rod, I'll give up Coterie. It's not a big deal. I passed the Trials once, I can do it again."

"What about the money?" asked Aurie.

"We'll figure it out. Haven't we always? Though I guess I should have saved Alton's alchemy set. We could have sold it for a pretty penny," said Pi.

"I'm sorry, Pi," said Aurie. "I know you worked hard this year."

Pi gave her that grin she did when she was planning

something. "I made some friends and learned some things. It's not all bad."

"Alright," said Aurie. "You can go. Let's get this started. I'd hate for your patron to show up now."

"It's not like you were really going to stop me," said Pi.

Aurie gave her sister a wink, but Pi was already moving.

"Race you there!" she said, then leapt.

Aurie stepped through the portal a moment later. The temporal membrane tickled as she passed through, then a punch of vertigo hit her in the stomach, depositing her on the other side. She had only a moment to orient herself before Pi started screaming.

33

Thousand-year-old dust puffed out from beneath Pi's boots the moment they impacted the stone. Her sister's hazy outline still moved through the temporal membrane like someone walking through a waterfall.

The air tasted stale, almost as if she was chewing through it. She coughed into the crook of her arm, the noise echoing into the ancient space.

Something skittered across the stone. Black. Shiny. The scarab leapt, its glistening wings fluttering momentarily before it landed on her leg.

She cried out as it bit her, and before she could reach down to knock it off, the scarab burrowed through her jeans and into her leg.

"Get it out! Get it out!" she screamed, horrified, clawing at the hole in her jeans.

Aurie stumbled into the tomb beside her. The scarab was digging through Pi's flesh, right to the bone. The pain brought tears to her eyes, but through it, she stayed aware enough to spot a second scarab before it could reach her sister.

Pi shot out a jet of flame to burn the scarab out of the air before it landed on Aurie. She crushed the beetle beneath her boot to be sure, before falling onto the stone, ripping at her jeans.

Aurie was frantic. "What is it? What's wrong? Did it get you?"

"Watch for beetles," said Pi, through sobs. She got her fingers into the hole in her jeans and tore them open. A red divot marked the area where the scarab had gone in, but there was no other sign. "Oh my god, this hurts."

"What's wrong? Tell me," said Aurie.

Pi pointed at her throbbing leg. "A beetle went in there."

The creature shifted against the bone, and Pi nearly passed out.

"Get the knife," she said.

Aurie pulled out a folding knife. The blade was barely two inches long.

"Give it to me," said Pi, pressing the edge against the skin once she had it in her hands.

"What are you doing? Are you sure?" asked Aurie.

After a series of short breaths, Pi prepared to dig the knife into her flesh. Then the pressure, the feeling of the beetle inside her leg, dissolved as if it'd been made of ice and melted at once.

The area around the red mark formed black lines, radiating outward, like the beetle had been made of ink and spilled into her skin.

"Oh shit," said Pi. "That can't be good."

Aurie cast a few spells over the leg. "No. Not good at all. That's a curse. A powerful one. I've never seen anything like it."

After tentatively climbing back to her feet, Pi said, "At least the pain's gone, though I ripped my favorite jeans."

The gallows humor wasn't appreciated by her sister. "Pi..."

"Hey, I'm the one who's cursed," said Pi, taking small mincing steps to test the wound.

"It almost got me too. That was quick thinking," said Aurie, poking at the dead scarab with the toe of her boot.

"Good thing we didn't both come through at the same time," she said. "Did you figure out what this curse does?"

Aurie's face did that thing where she looked like she'd just smelled a fart, which meant that she was lying.

"The truth, Aurie. I'm not ten anymore," Pi told her sister.

Aurie's lips scrunched up. "It's not good. I mean, you can already see that the black stuff is growing."

Pi poked at it with a finger, eliciting a grimace from her sister. "My skin feels hard here, like it's rotting or something."

"We need the Rod," said Aurie. "No second chances. We have to find this thing and fast."

"Let's go," she said.

The scarab curse ached and gave her a limp, but she could move, assuming she didn't have to do any sprinting.

A wisp went bobbing ahead, revealing a larger room filled with dozens of sarcophaguses. On the left wall, a painting depicted a pharaoh standing at the head of a vast field, a crook raised above his head. Men carried away bountiful grain in baskets. A line of infirm were lined up to see the pharaoh.

On the right side, a painting showed the pharaoh at the head of a huge army with a flail held above his head. Lightning shot down from the sky, driving his enemies before him, charring the nearest to dust.

A pile of bones and bronze armor at the opening to the room cracked into dust the moment Pi put a boot to them. She pulled her shirt over her mouth.

"I hope there aren't any mummies in there," said Pi.

"There won't be mummies in those. Probably old food and other stuff in preparation for the afterlife. The bones were guards they'd left in here," said Aurie.

"Bastards," said Pi, thinking about the poor souls stuffed in a tomb just because some idiot thought they would need them in the afterlife.

The next room glittered as the light from the wisp reflected off the jewelry piled on a stone table. Other tables had tin-glazed pottery depicting the pharaohs bestowing wheat upon the bowing peasants. Aurie grabbed her arm before Pi could move towards them.

"Don't touch," said Aurie. "We can't take anything out of here except for the Rod."

"I guess I'm going to have to earn my testing fee the hard way," said Pi, eyeing the jewelry. It had to be worth millions.

The black rot on her leg had moved past her knee. She ripped her jeans further upward to see how far it had spread. The flesh was growing harder, shiny and black.

The next hall had figures of guards painted onto the walls. More bones and bronze armor covered the floor.

"I bet those guards were supposed to attack us," said Pi.

"The magic faded with time. Let's hope the rest of the tombs have lost their protections too," said Aurie.

"Don't count on it. Those beetles were still alive," said Pi.

The lack of dust in the next hall gave them pause. Painted sarcophaguses were set in a circle, each one pointed out like flower petal. Gilded Canopic jars rested in shelves built into the walls.

"It looks like a museum diorama, except they have the colors a little wrong," said Pi. "Let's go, I can't wait all day."

Aurie grabbed her arm before she could move in. "Pi! Do I have to always look out for you?"

"I saved you from the beetles, didn't I?" said Pi, then noticed that Aurie was staring downward with a frown hooked to her lips. The floor had faint lines running through it like circuits in silicon.

"I didn't see it," said Pi absently.

"The earrings revealed them since they're magic. Normal torchlight would have failed to see them," said Aurie, cracking her knuckles just like she was about to perform a piano concerto. She coaxed her wisp over and whispered to it until it glowed brighter. When she was finished, a room covered in circuits and runes shimmered in the mage light.

"Shit," said Pi in admiration. "This is some serious mojo. Look at those designs on the far side. The circuits all connect to it."

Six prominent runes formed a circle: crossed feathers, the eye of Horus, the crook and flail, the jackal, and the lion. The many lines running through the floor, ceiling, and walls connected to the six runes. The intended magic of the runes was unknown, since it predated modern magic by a few thousand years.

"It's some sort of elaborate trap or puzzle. It could take hours to figure out," said Aurie.

"I don't think I have hours," said Pi.

The flesh around her knee and calf was as hard as black stone. She could barely flex her knee.

Aurie pulled out the notebook, muttering incoherently to herself. Pi examined the runes and lines as best as she could from outside the room.

She pulled a piece of bright green construction paper from her backpack and quickly folded it into an origami bird, a trick Orson had taught her in trade for help with his magic of materials studies.

With a bit of faez she breathed life into it, and sent it fluttering towards the runes on the other side. The bright green origami bird impacted with the top rune shaped like a feather.

A red glow raced out from the feather rune, zipping across the circuits until they contacted a sarcophagus. The painted stone lid ground open, and a jackal-headed warrior threw its leg over the edge, headed towards them.

"Pythia!"

"I'm trying to figure it out!" she exclaimed, backing down the hallway.

The jackal-headed warrior raised its spear as it marched forward. They each blasted it with magic, neither blows affecting it.

"It's made of stone," said Aurie.

They kept backing up. Aurie pulled a rope out of her backpack and whispered to it. The rope leapt out of her hand like a snake, slithering towards the stone warrior, who ignored it. The rope wrapped around the guardian's legs, cinching tighter until it teetered.

"With me," said Aurie, and together they blasted the jackal-headed warrior, knocking it onto its back. The impact broke the stone warrior in half, silencing its advance.

Aurie turned to Pi, a disgusted look on her face. "Can't you just wait for me? You're always charging into danger, and I have to save you."

Pi shrunk away from the words. "I'm the one who's cursed," she said quietly.

"I'm sorry, Pi. I'm just freaked out. I can't lose my little sister," said Aurie. "We learned something about the room, anyway."

They returned to the edge. The red glow had disappeared.

"Any ideas?" asked Aurie.

"I don't know, but I think I'm turning into one of those stone warriors," she said, poking her thigh. "On the other hand, I've never had muscles this tight. I bet I could win a competition or something."

Aurie was looking at her with tears in her eyes, bringing water to her own. "Oh, don't look at me like that, Aurie. We need to stay focused. We're going to beat this."

"That's what I'm supposed to be saying," said Aurie.

"When are you going to let me grow up? Or are you always going to try and be mom and dad?" asked Pi, internally cringing at the edge to her voice.

"Is that why you went to Coterie instead of Arcanium? To get away from me?" asked Aurie.

Feeling a little raw, Pi said, "Partially yes. I mean, it's not the main reason, but it certainly played a part."

It was Aurie's turn to recoil. Her arms retracted until she was hugging herself. Pi tried to think of a suitable apology, but the words wouldn't come. *Great, I'm going to turn into a piece of stone while my sister hates me for being ungrateful.*

Eventually, Aurie said in a low voice, "Let's figure this room out before something else happens."

It was clear the something else wasn't another triggering of the trap, but more truths between them. As Aurie put her nose back into the notebook, Pi reached a hand out to touch her sister, but shoved it in her pocket instead.

"I think I've got it," said Aurie after a few minutes. "These runes exist in other parts of the Valley of Kings on other tombs, mainly the primary wielders of the Rod of Dominion. My guess is they have to be touched in the chronological order that they ruled. A guess, but I'm not sure anything else makes sense."

"Shall I use the bird again?" asked Pi.

Aurie nodded reluctantly, which salted her wounds even more. With guidance from her sister, Pi flew the origami bird across the room and touched them in the order given: lion, eye of Horus, the jackal, crossed feathers, and crook and flail. At each one, silver light glistened through the circuits, until the final rune was pressed. Then a stone door formed in the wall where the runes were located, and split in two, revealing a room beyond.

"Way to go, Aurie," said Pi.

"Way to go, Mom and Dad," said Aurie. "We couldn't have gotten through this without their notes."

The size of the next room surprised Pi. It was about one hundred feet square. Each wall contained three stone arches that went into darkness. Stone urns sat between each exit.

After sending the wisps around the room to check for hidden traps, they went in themselves. Pi's leg was almost completely stone, forcing her to limp as if she had a cast on it. She figured she had an hour or two before she was a statue, and somehow she didn't think she'd be able to move anymore then.

They peered into the arches without going into them, but couldn't see anything beyond a few feet. Sandstone brick walls, mostly. They were debating sending a wisp inside one, when a flicker of movement at the entrance caught Pi's attention.

She turned, expecting an attacking scarab, or jackal-headed stone warrior, only to find a man in a shimmering shield instead.

It was her patron, Malden Anterist. He'd followed them into the portal, and they'd practically led him to the Rod. Pi felt like a giant idiot.

Aurie finally noticed Pi staring. "What are you looking...?"

She readied a spell, until Pi motioned for caution. Her patron hadn't moved, or spoken. He was watching them. Pi felt her life hang in the balance. There was no way they could battle him and win. But she couldn't let him take the Rod, especially when her life depended on it.

34

The man in the shimmering shield made Aurie twitchy. He'd been there the day her parents had died. Might have even caused it.

Had it been anyone other than Malden Anterist, the patron of Coterie, she would have sent torrents of rage magic after him, but even her anger wasn't that stupid.

"Reveal yourself, Malden. We know who you are. We know you were in our house the day our parents died," Aurie shouted, her voice cracking at the end.

The man in the shimmering shield took a few steps forward. Aurie eyed the archway, wondering if it were safe on the other side.

Then the shield dropped, revealing a younger man that Aurie didn't recognize, but she knew in an instant that it wasn't Malden Anterist.

"Professor Augustus?" asked Pi, the disbelief making her sister stumble on her words.

He adjusted his wire-rimmed glasses, looking like a nervous suitor preparing to ask someone's father for a date with his daughter.

"My apologies, Pythia," said the professor. "And greetings to you, Aurelia."

"Wait," said Pi, shaking her head. "You were the one I saw that day? I always thought I'd just remembered wrong."

Professor Augustus kneaded his hands together as if he were preparing bread.

"The runic switches," said Pi, jamming her finger in his direction. "You had us make them so you could get in here."

Other connections formed, and the words stumbled out of Aurie's lips as she made them. "That was why you were coming to visit my parents. You were the one who'd made the switches. But then you turned on them and killed them."

"No. No," said Augustus, holding his hands up, palms open. "I brought them the switches. Then the house exploded. I was saved, but not by my hand."

The truth hit her squarely in the chest, knocking her to her knees. She had killed her parents with her lack of control. She'd always held out hope that Pi had been right. Which she had been, just not in the way she'd wanted.

Pi tugged on her shoulder, forcing her to return to her feet. "Don't listen to him." Then to Augustus. "Why are you following us?"

The professor took a mincing step forward, just one. He glanced up, either unsure or to gauge their reaction.

"I was friends with your parents back then. Not close, but we knew each other in the Halls. We were on the same team during the second-year games. They asked me to make the switches for them. After their death, and my near immolation, I was curious why they needed them. Never really thought about it until last year, when Pythia started inquiring about a sponsor for Coterie. A surprise. But I knew you were the daughter of Kieran and Nahid right away," he said, taking another step.

"Then why didn't you say anything?" asked Pi.

"How could I explain that I knew your parents? Not after their tragic death," he said, with another lazy shuffle forward.

"Stop!" yelled Aurie, fists at her side. "Stop. Not another step. You still haven't explained why you're here, why you're following us."

"The same reason you are. The Rod of Dominion," he said, straightening. A whiff of ozone permeated the air. His voice turned harder, commanding. "You know, Pythia, I tried to warn you away from Coterie. It's not the place for you."

Pi took a step like she was going to charge the professor. "You were the one trying to kill me?"

"No," he said. "As I told you before, the likes of you and I are not welcome in Coterie. Sure, we got in on our ability, but they never truly accepted us. I was the best student that Coterie had ever had. I could do circles around the others, even with their trinkets and private tutors. But it didn't matter, they tormented me. Enchanted my clothes to disintegrate while I was out at parties, snuck potions into my drinks that gave me explosive gas, cursed me with tentacles that grew out of my back. Those were just the harmless pranks. If they didn't try to kill me at least once a week, I grew paranoid that they'd snuck something past my defenses."

"That's awful," said Pi. "You had it much worse than I."

The condescending laugh that came from Professor Augustus' lips was made to cut.

"Thanks to me," he said. "Do you think you survived the year because the morality of students has improved? No. You survived because I protected you from yourself."

"You were the one that kept sabotaging my work? I thought it was Alton," said Pi. "They were all against me?"

"All but that blonde twit you called a friend. Her grandfather would be ashamed of her," he said with a sneer.

"Yes. I sabotaged your work so they wouldn't hate you as much. And foiled the regular attempts on your life. I'll admit the enchanted spoon got past me. Quite ingenious of Orson. It nearly got you. I was quite pleased to see you pull out of it."

"Why?" asked Pi.

"Because of the Rod of Dominion," said Aurie, suddenly understanding everything. "He was hoping we'd find the tomb for him. Can I make a guess that it was you that put those books back into the Arcanium library rather than my mother?"

He quirked a grin. "Clever. Yes. I'd snuck them into the library so you would find them. I'd gotten everything I could from them, but could never figure out where the portal was. I hoped that you two would better understand your parents' notes. Which I was rewarded for, since I would have never known about the singing stone."

"That wasn't Malden who gave me the task," said Pi. "You sent me after the Rod so that I would learn about it."

He ran a hand through his hair, looking quite pleased with himself. "A bit of trickery, yes. You see, events like these are tied together somehow through the faez. Like a magical balancing scale. Your past would make it easier to find the truth about the Rod. Though I didn't think you'd summon a demon lord. *That* was a surprise. And you wouldn't believe what I had to give up so his succubus guardian would send you to me rather than him."

"*That* was you too?" asked Pi, stunned.

He knocked imaginary dust from his shoulder. "I told you that I ran circles around the rest of Coterie." Augustus removed his glasses and placed them in his coat pocket.

"Why then? Why all this? Why the Rod?" asked Aurie.

A flickering rage passed through the professor's gaze. "After all I did, after everything I accomplished, the people I killed for them, he made *me* the Master of Initiates. An insult.

They said I didn't have the right family, the right background. When I get the Rod, I will take control of Coterie, and the Cabal through it, and they won't care about their family heritage after that."

"So Patron Malden doesn't know anything about this? The Cabal isn't trying to find the Rod?" she asked, and when the professor nodded, she asked, "Then what are the Cabal trying to find with those gallium coins?"

Augustus smirked. "The entrance into Invictus' tower. Since they killed him thirteen years ago, they've been searching for a way to take his position as head patron. Without that power, they are limited by the charter of the Hundred Halls, bound by their own magic. The coins won't work. I tried to tell Malden that, but he's desperate. The Cabal is unhappy with him. After I get the Rod, he won't care much longer."

"So no one knows about the Rod but the three of us," said Aurie, thinking out loud.

"You've got the gist of it," said Professor Augustus.

When he'd first come into the room, he'd looked like a measly tweed-coat wearing professor who would blow away like a dandelion at the first stiff breeze. Now, he bristled with power, faez sparking at his edges.

Professor Augustus' expression softened for a moment. "I'm very sorry, for the both of you. I rather saw myself in you, Miss Pythia."

He struck faster than Aurie thought possible. He'd been carrying a spell, holding it back, then he unleashed it. She only had enough time to tackle her sister through an archway as the stone exploded around them.

They landed on the other side as the ceiling around the arch collapsed. Together, they crawled away as rocks landed on their backs and dust covered them. The avalanche was deafening.

When it was finished, Aurie and Pi were alive. Aurie coughed as dust filtered through the air.

"We're trapped," said Pi, rubbing her puffy eyes.

The darkness behind gave Aurie an itch between her shoulder blades. "I don't like this place."

"Neither do I."

Pi was sitting on her rear with her left leg sticking out stiffly. She ripped the rest of her pants away, revealing a shiny stone leg. The curse had traveled up beyond the curve of her thigh into her hip.

"I don't think I'll be doing much exploring," said Pi.

Then she pulled up her other pant leg. The curse had spread there. Pi had black spots all over her body, including one on her neck the size of a penny.

"That fucking asshole," said Aurie, pounding her fists on the ground with impotent rage. "He used us at every turn. All because I accidentally saved him. Why couldn't he have died with our parents?"

"Don't listen to him," said Pi. "He was lying. He's been lying the whole time. Think about it. If he said he'd killed them, we would have attacked. He was delaying so he could ready his spell. It was him the whole time."

"What do we do now?" asked Aurie.

"We get through that pile of rocks," said Pi.

Aurie nodded towards the black stone leg. "What about...?"

"You'll have to get the Rod and fix me," said Pi.

They stood up and examined the collapse together.

"Shit," said Pi. "Do you sense that?"

Aurie nodded. The professor had layered spells on the other side. Any attempt to magically move the rock would bring down more stone on the caster. He'd not only buried them, but made it impossible to escape.

After a moment of quiet contemplation, Pi said, "I know

how to get you out."

"*Us* out," said Aurie immediately.

"No," said Pi. "You'll have to get the Rod and come back for me. I won't be able to move much longer."

Aurie took a quivering breath. "Tell me."

"I'm going to lift the rocks, just enough that you can get through," said Pi.

"But won't that bring down more upon your head?" asked Aurie, then realized what she meant. The curse was turning her to stone, which would protect her from the worst of the collapse, unless of course it broke her.

"I can't let you do that, Pi," said Aurie. "You'll end up as a pile of rocks."

"Can't you let me be the hero just once? Let me save you, rather than the other way around," said Pi.

"But...but you're my little sister. I promised Mom and Dad that I would take care of you. I've screwed everything else up already. Can't I at least do that one thing right?" asked Aurie.

Tendrils of black stone were crawling up Pi's neck as she spoke. "Aurie, it doesn't matter what happened that day. Stop beating yourself up about it. You've been the best older sister you could be. I couldn't ask for anything else. But you're going to have to let me do this, this time. It's the only way."

Aurie bit her lower lip, hard, until it hurt enough that she could speak again. "Okay. Tell me what to do."

"You're going to let me turn to stone, like almost completely into a statue. I'll prepare my spell, and then like Augustus did, hold it until the last second. When I open a hole, you have to be quick. Use your truth magic, or something. Whatever, it doesn't matter. But you have to be fast. Faster than you've ever been."

"Does it hurt?" asked Aurie.

Pi frowned. "No, and that's what worries me most. It's sort of like being erased piece by piece. The feeling is worse the deeper it goes into me. I'm afraid that once I'm completely stone, all the way down to my guts and heart and brain, that even the Rod won't save me."

"Then let's do this," she said.

Aurie did as Pi had suggested, speaking softly to herself, convincing her limbs to move like lightning once the hole was opened. Pi made preparations of her own, casting her spell while she could still use her fingers. When she was ready, she nodded to Aurie, though it wasn't much of a nod, since her neck was black stone.

"We ready?" asked Aurie.

"Not yet," said Pi. "I want to wait until the last second for the maximum protection."

Aurie hugged her sister, but Pi couldn't return the favor, so she placed her head against Pi's forehead. They stared into each other's eyes.

"*Dooset daram,*" said Aurie.

A weak smile formed on Pi's lips as she fought the curse. "*Dooset daram.*"

"*Dooset daram,*" said Aurie, more emphatically.

"*Dooset daram,*" said Pi as her lips turned black.

Energy crackled between them, as if their sisterly bond was being transmitted through the magic. Static tickled Aurie's eyelashes as love burned in her heart.

"*Kheyli dooset daram, azeezam.* You're the best sister I could ever have," said Aurie. "Stay alive in there. I'll get you out, I promise."

The words barely whispered out of Pi's rigid mouth, but Aurie knew them just the same. "*Dooset daram,*" followed by a hard blink.

Faez crackled into existence as the spell thrust itself

beneath the rocks, forming a tunnel. As the hallway broke apart, Aurie threw herself into the hole, limbs churning.

She barely made it through before the secondary collapse took apart the remainder of the hallway, burying her sister beneath the stone.

Once Aurie was able to regain her feet, she placed her fingers against her lips, then placed her hand on the rocks.

"*Dooset daram.*"

35

With the fallen archway behind her, and Pi beneath the rocks, Aurie had no time to delay. There were ten other arches in the room, and she had no idea which one Augustus had gone into.

Focusing on him made her think about what they had spoken about. The silence screamed in her head: *You killed your parents*! It was a truth she'd fought since they'd died. Had it been her fault? She'd always thought that she'd never know, that it was a truth beyond the grave, and only when she followed them into the bleak would she learn.

Now she knew that Professor Augustus knew the truth. Her version of the facts wavered like a mirage on the hot desert. If she ran towards it, would it disappear or turn into an oasis? Could she even get him to tell her?

To track the professor, Aurie made a couple of gestures with fingers crooked and spoke a few words. Glowing mist formed at points of the room, revealing the areas that faez had been spent. As she'd guessed, the glow listed around one of the arches, showing where the professor had gone through, saving her from having to decipher the puzzle.

The next room glittered with gold, enough to make Fort Knox jealous. Granite pillars supported an enormous chamber. At the far end stood a massive statue of Osiris, the god of the dead. He had a pharaoh's head and mummy-wrapped legs, and in his grasp held two rods in an "X" across his chest: a crook and a flail.

Professor Augustus rocked on his heels, admiring the statue, whistling a tune. She thought he was just being flippant until she heard the spell amid the notes. The song coaxed dust and other small pieces of rock to bounce across the floor towards the statue, an explosion in reverse. The stones were like children running home to play, forming a series of steps that would help the professor reach the rods.

The demonstration made Aurie pause. She'd never seen someone with such exquisite control of their magic. He wasn't even using his fingers to help shape the spell.

The song came to an abrupt end. The professor spun around to face her with his hands behind his back.

"You've proved to be quite resourceful. I'm sure it would be quite a story to hear how you escaped the trap I laid on the passage," he said.

"You lie," spat Aurie. She'd planned on something more eloquent, but the words just didn't fit together.

He raised a petulant eyebrow. "Why would I lie about that? Certainly I would like to hear the tale. I am a connoisseur of magic."

"Not that," she said. "About my parents. You killed them."

The professor held his hands out as if the truth was somehow held there. His expression relayed his reluctant annoyance.

"I told the truth. Please do not mistake me," he said, seeming to say more with every shift of his eyebrows.

She squeezed her hands into fists. *Why am I wasting time*

on this when Pi is dying? But if she killed him—could she even kill him?—then she'd never know.

"I don't believe you," she said, feeling like a foolish young girl.

"I know you're mad. You have every right to be. I just tried to kill you. So why would I lie to you now? My suggestion for you would be to scurry out of here, take your sister if you can, and never let me see you again," he said.

"I need the Rod to save her," she said. "It's the only way to get rid of the curse."

He shook his head slowly as if what he had to say hurt him. "I'm sorry, but I'm afraid that can't happen. The Rod of Dominion was used by the pharaohs for two things: war and healing. The flail symbolizes war, and the crook, healing. You choose which one you plan to use, which makes the other useless. When I form the Rod using the flail from Osiris, it will give me the power to command people, to bring terrible lightning, to wage war like no one has ever seen before. But when I form the flail, the crook will become useless, and it cannot be reformed for another hundred years. Once I take the flail, I suggest that you not be standing in this room, though in the end, it may not matter."

He looked to the floor, as if he were thinking about something. Then magic flew from his fingers, a jet of fire to crisp her to bone. The white flame flew at her with a lion's head, roaring as it approached, giving her no time for a response.

She might have been immolated had she not been preparing her own spell. She'd noticed him constructing his spell during the speech, knowing that he had the ability to disguise it.

Complex spells were impossible, so he'd resorted to a higher level version of Five Elements. He'd thrown fire, while Aurie countered with water, a geyser formed from twisting water snakes. The two elements impacted in the middle, turning to steam.

The professor was her superior in the technical aspects of magic, but Aurie had raw power on her side. He didn't even try to switch elements. They battered each other, mist billowing from the conflict.

Rather than compete with her, he made changes to the patterns of the fire, deflecting water unspent, which made the fire more effective. She'd never considered it was possible, no one had ever done it before. It turned his flame into an impossibly hot drill, spinning through her water. The steam wall where the two magics slammed into each other started moving towards her.

Aurie panicked, releasing as much faez as she could muster, but it wasn't enough. He was overcoming her raw ability with subtle skill. She knew she had more to give, but it wouldn't come.

Why am I holding back?

Was she afraid to kill him? Afraid to lose the truth about what happened with her parents? Or was it something else: was she afraid to lose control? Was it guilt or fear?

Then again, she realized, *why does it even matter? They're dead. That's the only truth that's real.* If it'd been her, or Professor Augustus who had caused it, either way, they were dead and never coming back.

Acknowledging that, no matter how painful, released a weight from her shoulders that she hadn't realized was there. She felt like she could touch the ceiling. Was this what Professor Mali had wanted her to learn in the Verum Locus? Not the physical truth, but the underlying one?

The power flowing from her felt like a river was rushing right through her. It was exhilarating and frightening at the same time. Part of her reckoned that if she diverted the flow it would tear the room apart, her included.

By the time Aurie looked back up, she'd pushed the impact wall back towards the professor. She could barely see him through the mist, it'd filled the room.

But she could see when he took a step onto the stairs. Rather than fight back, he was going to make an attempt on the Rod. He'd realized she was eventually going to win, but not if he was able to grab the Rod of Dominion. There'd be nothing she could do against him once he had that in his hands, dooming her sister to a permanent death.

Aurie tried pushing harder, but the water magic was sputtering at the edges. She'd never fought this long with this much power. She tried twisting the elements, lacing in earth— she'd never done that before—and to her surprise, it worked. Only it wasn't working fast enough.

She needed another twenty seconds, twenty-five tops. Aurie knew she was going to win, eventually, but she'd run out of time. The professor reached towards the flail of Osiris. His fingertips brushed the thick handle. She felt her obliteration coming, like standing on a track before an oncoming train. His hand curled around the flail like a lover as his lips sneered with victory.

Something dark moved ponderously through the mist near the professor. A black arm reached out and grabbed his leg, yanking him away. It was Pi!

The professor's fingers bounced off the bottom of the flail. He flew backwards, his magic faltering. Aurie released the water magic as his fire went careening off the ceiling, charring gold plating to drip down like golden rain.

Aurie was running when Pi brought a stone fist down upon the professor's head. He was unconscious when Aurie pulled up short.

"Pi! You're alive!"

She was, but she wasn't. Her whole body was glistening black stone, even her eyes, which made her unnaturally creepy. Pi's lips moved but no sound came out. She motioned towards the statue of Osiris.

"I get it! No time!" exclaimed Aurie, racing up the steps.

She grabbed the crook without hesitation. When her fingers touched it, a spike of electricity went through her arm, nearly knocking her off the steps.

Aurie knew instinctively what to do, as if the Rod of Dominion gave her that knowledge. She pressed the curved end of the crook against the area of Pi's leg where the scarab had gone in. Power flooded from the Rod with the ease of simple intention. She felt, for a moment, a god.

Almost immediately, the skin turned translucent, revealing the beetle curled up against Pi's thigh bone. Aurie commanded it to get out, using the proper amount of profanity. The beetle burrowed back out and as it did, Pi's body turned back to flesh.

The scarab fanned its shimmering wings, and for a moment, she thought it was going to fly away, then it dove straight into Professor Augustus' midsection. The beetle dug into his belly before Pi or Aurie could stop it. The professor hardened into black stone before the sisters had taken another breath. The curse had been so powerful that even the crook hadn't dispelled it; it only removed it from her body long enough that it could find another host and finish what it had started.

As the mist faded, they threw themselves into each other's arms. Aurie still had the Rod of Dominion clutched in her fist.

"*Dooset daram,*" said Pi.

"I love you, too," said Aurie. "Especially for saving me at the end, a second time. But how did you do that? I thought you couldn't move anymore. You were practically a statue back there."

Pi's gaze glittered with happiness. "You don't have to be modest. You used your truth magic to give me strength."

"I did?" she asked.

"*Kheyli dooset daram, azeezam.* You told me to stay strong, then I felt the most wonderful warmth and love emanate from you, as if I was getting to feel your love, not just hear the words. It was bound up with faez, and when the hallway buried me, I just slowly worked my way out. It was your love that saved me," said Pi.

Professor Mali had told Aurie that truth was a powerful force. She'd never understood it until that moment.

"What do we do about him?" asked Pi.

"I don't think there's anything we can do," she said, knowing she was right by the magic of the Rod. "The curse was transferred to him. He's as good as dead."

"Do you think he killed our parents?" asked Pi.

"It doesn't matter. They're dead. If it was the professor, then he got the justice he deserved. If it was me, then I'm doing the right things to work on my control. That's all I can do."

"I can't believe we have the Rod of Dominion," said Pi, shaking her head.

"We're not going to have it for long," said Aurie, rubbing the overlapping pattern on the grip. Holding it was easy, but yet, she felt its weight, as if the magic of the Rod gave her the strength to hold it.

"We should keep it," asked Pi in wonder, entranced by the Rod. "How can we trust anyone else?"

Aurie twirled it in her hands, mesmerized by the balance. Part of her wanted to march out of the Undercity and start healing anyone she saw. She imagined the throng following her through the city like the Pied Piper as she healed the sick and infirm. She imagined herself climbing up a great pyramid.

"No," she muttered. "We need to give this to someone else."

The call was strong, but she had resisted.

"I know one person we can trust," Aurie said.

"Are you sure?" asked Pi, blinking hard as if she'd shaken off the Rod's snare.

"It's going to the hospital eventually, but we can't take it ourselves. It's too dangerous, and they won't let me in anyway. We need help to make sure it's guarded properly and that the wealthy donors like Camille Cardwell don't know about it."

Pi gave her a reassuring nod, but Aurie wasn't as confident, despite what she'd said. The only thing she did know was that the alternatives were worse.

36

A delivery guy in a red T-shirt balanced a stack of pizza boxes as he maneuvered through the main room in Freeport Games. A competitive card game tournament was in full swing. The occasional shouts of "Judge!" punctuated the cacophony.

Semyon Gray, the patron of Arcanium, looked quite out of place in his tweed jacket, silk vest, and tie as he surveyed the room with a keen eye. The participants of the tournament were too deep into their matches to give him much notice. Aurie waved him down from one of the side rooms.

"Miss Aurelia. Miss Pythia," he said, a little wide-eyed, as if the room he'd passed through had contained two-headed aliens rather than overly caffeinated gamers. "I received your urgent message. I assume this doesn't have to do with whatever ruckus is going on out there?"

"They're playing a card game...err...never mind, it doesn't matter," said Aurie. "This is about..."

Semyon held up his hand. He had long fingers. "If this is about your final test, I told you before, I can do nothing about it. Professor Mali's judgment is final."

Aurie had almost forgotten about the actual test. It seemed

like it'd been days ago, rather than earlier that morning.

"It's not about the test. C...can I ask you a question?"
She'd never felt so nervous in her life. "You knew my parents
and knew about the work they did."

Patron Semyon steepled his fingers. He made a noise of
agreement.

"What if I told you we found one of the artifacts they were
after?" asked Aurie.

His gaze immediately cast about the room. "I'd say you
were fools. Your parents were in terrible danger every time
they went on a mission, and they were brilliant wizards of
their respective fields. You are both initiates, barely a spark of
magical wisdom to your names."

Aurie cleared her throat as her patron's withering gaze fell
upon her.

"Theoretically, let's say we were successful, and let's say
the artifact was an item that could do a lot of people good, but
we didn't want it to fall in the wrong hands," she said.

"And who might be the wrong hands?" he asked dourly.

"Well, anyone really," she said, but when his expression
caught a twinge of disappointment, she added, "but specifically
the Cabal."

"The Cabal?" he asked with an exquisitely raised eyebrow.
"Are we believing urban legends now?"

Pi stepped forward. "The Cabal is real. I've met them.
Heard them talk about their plans."

Semyon frowned, the earlier disappointment returning in
full. He started stepping towards the door. "Girls. I'm afraid
I'm quite busy. I don't really have time for games."

Pi lunged into her jacket and threw Radoslav's rune on
the table. "Celesse D'Agastine made an offer to you to join
them, but you refused."

He took a step back towards them. A hint of ozone filled

the air. His power was subtle, but she had no doubt that he could take them both before they could even raise a finger. He snapped his fingers, and the sounds of the tournament outside disappeared, as if the small room had suddenly been transported to the moon.

"Out with it. All of it. As your patron and the person you came to for help, I want to hear it all, from the beginning, though it would be helpful if you stopped playing footsy with the truth and told me what it is you've acquired," he said. "And if you don't start speaking quickly, there will be consequences."

The threat was quite real, and Aurie had no illusions that they weren't in grave danger, despite her hopes that he was a generally good person. Even good people did terrible things when they were afraid.

"We have the Rod of Dominion," she said.

"Impossible," he said with a curt shake of his head. "It's widely considered the item with the most dangerous curse of the ancient world protecting it. No one has the slightest idea how to bypass it and many have died trying."

Aurie motioned to Pi, who opened the bench seat and pulled out the crook.

Semyon Gray stared at the artifact for a good twenty seconds. At first he seemed to be willing it not to exist, then his lip twitched as if he were allergic to it. As the realization dawned on him that they had actually retrieved the Rod, he snapped out of his stupor.

"You have it here? You *are* fools. While I've never been to this gaming shop, I'm well aware of this place," he said, with a particular emphasis on "place" that made her think of Hemistad. His expression broke into a softer, but disappointed countenance. "Still. You've done it and no harm has yet come, so we will continue. Please start from the beginning, the both of you. I want each of your stories, hold nothing back."

"Where do we start?" Pi asked, looking to her sister.

But Aurie knew the answer; it was the only way to truly explain to Semyon how they had acquired it.

"It began the day our parents died..."

After they explained that day, the sisters went over the events of the last year, starting with the summoning of the demon lord Pazuzu. Patron Semyon asked questions at various points, demanding details that neither of them thought important, but must have had some bearing on the larger conflict. It took them a few hours. Aurie tried to rush a few times, she wanted him to take the Rod to the hospital, but when she got frustrated, he admonished her for rashness.

"I appreciate your concern for this young lady, but if we are not careful, we will cause greater harm. I promise you that as soon as I'm satisfied you've not unleashed a plague on the city of biblical proportions, I will take the Rod to the Golden Willow and instruct them to heal this Emily first."

Satisfied, Aurie was able to continue. When they got to the portal, the tomb, and the battle with Professor Augustus, he seemed particularly interested in items in the various rooms.

When they were finished, and only then, did he ask to examine the Rod of Dominion. Whatever doubts he had before he touched it, they erased from his face once it was in his grip.

"Well, I'll be daft. This really is the Rod. I was certain that you had to be mistaken," he said, shaking his head. "No wonder they thought themselves gods with this in their hands. And to think, you just gave it to me."

A shock of cold went through Aurie's gut. She started to summon her faez, but Semyon winked, dispelling her fears.

"No worries. As tempting as it would be, I'd find being a modern pharaoh quite tiresome. There's a reason Arcanium is filled with libraries. I much prefer a good book to lording over others," he said.

"Will it be safe at Golden Willow?" she asked hopefully.

"Though it will be difficult, I will give the Rod a proper disguise, and tell them it's a lesser artifact. A few nondisclosure spells will ensure no rumors escape, though the hospital's reputation will grow with time. Don't worry. You've entrusted it to the right person. I will keep it safe."

Aurie let out a sigh of relief. She'd been worried that something would keep the Rod from being used.

Patron Semyon turned to leave, when Pi blurted out, "What about the Cabal? Aren't you going to do something about them?"

"You assume that I haven't been," he said. "Though my power is limited with Invictus no longer in this world. We are collectively poorer without him."

"Is there anything we can do to help?" asked Pi.

Semyon broke into an honest smile, something she would expect him to share with his mates, if he had any.

"You've done a lot already. Your parents would be proud. But the best thing you can do now is to finish your schooling," he said.

"What about—" asked Aurie, but Semyon held his hand up.

"I told you before, I can do nothing," he said. "I suggest you speak to her first."

"Can I tell her about any of this?" asked Aurie.

"No."

Aurie slumped onto the seat, dejected.

To Pi, Semyon asked, "What about you, young lady? What are your intentions with Coterie?"

"I'm resigning," she said. "As soon as I get back to the Obelisk."

Semyon turned to leave, when Pi spoke up again. "One more question."

"I feel like I could be here forever with 'just one more question.' Don't you want me to arrive at the Golden Willow posthaste?" he asked.

"It's quick. It's just you mentioned Hemistad earlier, like he was a problem. What or who is he? Should we be worried?" she asked.

Semyon thought for a moment before answering. "I'll leave it to him to explain, if he's ever inclined to, though under no circumstance should you ask him. But it's clear he's taken a shine to you two, and I can see why. Just be careful. No, wait. Just be yourselves. I'm not sure you know what careful is."

After he left, an emptiness consumed Aurie. It took a while for her to realize that she'd been pushing so hard for so long, that the lack of adrenaline actually bothered her.

"You feel it, too?" asked Pi.

"Yeah," she said. "What do we do now?"

"Go back to our Halls," said Pi.

"They won't be for long," said Aurie, and though she wanted to revel in self-pity, she couldn't allow herself. She'd decided months ago that it was worth saving Emily even if it meant getting kicked out.

She didn't go out right away. Leaving would somehow acknowledge the fate that she'd dealt herself. While she was standing in a side room at Freeport Games, she was still a member of Arcanium. Once she went back, reality would come rushing back in.

"Please make it until Semyon gets to you," said Aurie thinking about Emily before leaving the room. She envied the players at their tables, slinging cards and laughing at each other's stories. That was a life that was never meant for her.

37

The other students at Arcanium flooded from the initiate wing when Aurie walked onto the floor. Her ears buzzed. The sounds of running feet faded away as someone went to get Professor Mali, while a sea of stern looks twisted her gut. She'd never wanted to disappoint them, but here it was, unavoidable.

"Aurie!" came a bright voice from the back.

Deshawn maneuvered through the other initiates. He threw his arms around her in a hug. After a moment of shock, she hugged him back.

"I'm so glad you're safe." Then he turned around and pointed at her. "Aren't we glad she's safe?"

His bold declaration seemed to dispel the unsettled mood. Reluctantly a few people nodded, though in back, a flip of blonde hair storming out of the room announced Violet's feelings about her return.

Xi, Daniel, and the others crowded around Aurie. They looked a little hurt.

"I'm sorry. I really am. I had to go, right then, the test be damned," she said.

Xi quirked his lips. "Impressive spell. We all asleep like

snapping fingers. Maybe you can teach me sometime. Though next time, please warning first. I woke on Daniel's smelly butt."

The tension broke with nervous laughter. Aurie could have kissed Xi for it.

"I'd love to," she said, but remembered that her time in Arcanium was almost to an end. She didn't want to spoil the reunion, so she kept the thought to herself, not that they couldn't figure it out.

They tried to get what it was that was so important out of her, but Aurie shook them off, telling them it was a secret better left untold. Eventually, everyone but Deshawn returned to their rooms before the professor arrived.

"Thanks for saving me," she said. "I thought for a moment they were going to lynch me."

He raised an eyebrow at her comment. "Don't think I didn't consider it after you spelled me. But after I came to, and worked my anger off at the gym, I realized that it had to be important, or you wouldn't risk getting expelled from Arcanium for it. I mean, you're the best of us. I don't know what we're going to do if you're not here."

"Is she pissed?" she asked.

"Like Emperor Palpatine throwin' down his lightning on Vader kinda pissed. Her wheelchair practically levitated," he said.

Aurie pinched the bridge of her nose. "Great."

"But you've got a good story for her, right?" asked Deshawn. "I mean, if it was all that important, you should be able to explain it to her."

"I wish I could, but I can't," she said.

"Damn," he said, chewing his lip.

In a strange way, his disappointment cheered her up. This year at Arcanium had been the longest she'd been at any school since her parents had died. It was nice to finally make friends. Too bad they'd probably forget her after she was gone.

A glistening soap bubble burst nearby, releasing the professor's voice. "Aurelia Silverthorne. I need to see you in my office. Now."

Deshawn saluted before leaving. The walk to the professor's room felt both instantaneous and forever.

The walls were covered in pictures, framed medals, and other awards. Professor Mali had fought in wars around the globe. Seeing them always reminded Aurie how petty her problems were.

"Miss Aurelia. Do you understand the gravity of what you did this morning? In a court of law, that spell could be interpreted as an assault on their liberties. If you'd been on the street, any one of those students could press charges, and you would most certainly be prosecuted. But you are in Arcanium, for now, which gives you some level of protection. Which means you fall under our jurisdiction, specifically mine."

Aurie stiffened. Violet could have already called her mother, Camille, with plans to sue her once she was kicked out of Arcanium. Things were only getting worse.

"Do you have an explanation for your actions?" asked the professor.

A sudden overwhelming weight nearly drove Aurie to her knees. If she spoke, she'd violate Semyon's request, but if she didn't then she'd be kicked out of Arcanium. Aurie wasn't sure why he'd asked her to be silent about it. If Professor Mali was a trusted instructor, why couldn't she tell her?

"Professor Mali," began Aurie, "I...I'm afraid I cannot explain."

"So I'm to believe that you left the room of truth and assaulted the rest of your classmates *for no good reason*?" she asked.

"I have a reason, but I'm afraid I cannot tell you. I'm sorry.

I know this means I've broken your and the other students' trust," said Aurie.

Despite the reasons for it, and all she'd gone through, the disappointment in the professor's gaze nearly broke Aurie. All her life, even before her parents' death, she'd looked up to Arcanium, dreamed about being a member. So the professor held a special place in Aurie's heart. That visible disappointment was like a brand stamped into her chest.

"What then? Was it the room of truth that broke your will? Were you running scared, afraid to face the truth?" accused the professor.

"I wasn't running scared," said Aurie, clenching her hands to keep them from shaking.

"It certainly looked like that to me," said the professor.

"I left because..." She paused, realizing that she couldn't explain the part about her sister being in danger. But she could explain what she'd learned about her parents. "I left because I'd learned what I needed to learn."

Professor Mali went dangerously still. The back of Aurie's neck prickled for an unknown reason.

"Explain."

"For the last seven years, I've blamed myself for my parents' death. And not the kind of self-hate when something bad happens, like you deserved it for stealing a candy bar kind of thing. No, I *actually* might have caused my parents' death because I was a careless, arrogant kid. That's one version of what happened. In another version, I'm not the reason they died. It was something related to their choices, their lives. It had nothing to do with me.

"Each time I've gone into the room, I've had to relive that day. But the reality is that I've been reliving that day my whole life. I don't fall asleep at night, or have a meal, without considering that my actions caused the death of my parents, which not only impacted me, but my little sister. And I am truly sorry for that. I've always accepted the consequences for that day, but it's not fair that Pi had to suffer too. She'd done nothing wrong. She was this twinkle-in-her-eyes kid before, and now...now she's different.

"So I've been living this Schrödinger's Life. In one version, I'm a terrible kid who killed my parents. In the other, I'm just really unlucky. But I can't ever know the truth, because they're dead.

"Sometimes when I wake up in the morning, when my mind is groggy, and the sun's coming through the blinds just so, I sort of forget what happened. And I have this thought, as I'm curled up in bed, the blankets tucked under my chin. I'm not even sure I know how old I am, or what day it is in that moment. But what I do have, for a brief succulent moment, is the unwavering certainty that my parents are alive. That I'm not in a ratty old Section Eight apartment with water stains on the ceiling. But that I'm at home, in our brownstone, and Dad's cooking biscuits from scratch while Mom plays piano, some obscure song she learned when she was a kid growing up in Tehran, that sounds like rain on a city street.

"And then it hits me. Like I've been dunked in cold water and I can't come up for air. They're dead and I caused it."

Aurie caught her breath. She hadn't realized she'd been speaking for so long. She'd never said these things, to anybody, not even her sister. The professor sat so still she could have been a painting.

When Aurie didn't speak, the professor prompted, "Did you eventually learn the truth?"

"No," said Aurie. "Not about them. But I learned something more important, I think. They're dead. I *might* have caused it. I might not have. I will have to live with that for the rest of my life. But what matters more is not the truth, but how I react. My parents are dead, but since then I've done my best to raise my sister, to look out for her, to be there for her, as best as I could. Yeah, Pi's different now, but that's okay. She's still my sister and the most kickass sister you could ever want to have. And I've done my best to right those flaws in myself that led to that day. Regardless of my parents' death, I made a mistake that day. I accept that, and have tried to learn from it. I'm still learning. I know that I don't always have control of my magic. And I know that it's dangerous. I'm a powerful mage. Enough power that it scares me. I need to learn how to control it. I worry that if I don't, that more people will get hurt. So whether or not I was the cause of the explosion that day, I have a responsibility to make sure that doesn't happen to someone else. I have a responsibility to the people around me. To my sister, Pi.

"So yes, I learned the truth. I learned that what actually happens sometimes doesn't matter. That truth is a fiction that few get to understand. That our perceptions and hopes and fears cloud every action we take, every day, in every way. That in some ways, no one ever knows the truth, that truth is a mirage that blinds us, and that how you deal with the aftermath is really the only real version of truth," said Aurie, a wave of relief shuddering through her body as if a fever had just broken.

Professor Mali stared at her for a long time. Wheels turned behind those impenetrable, hard eyes.

Eventually, Aurie felt uncomfortable and moved to get up. "I understand that I'll be expelled for my behavior and for failing the class."

Without moving her mouth, Professor Mali said, "Sit down."

As if she'd been spelled there, Aurie welded her butt to the leather couch.

When the professor didn't speak, Aurie wasn't sure what to think until she saw a tear glisten at the corner of her eye.

"Aurelia," said the professor in a voice so soft it wouldn't have upset a butterfly. "Not only will you not be expelled, but you will pass with the highest marks in the class."

"W—what?" asked Aurie. "How can that be?"

"Because you learned the lesson of *Verum Locus* better than anyone could ever hope," she said, grabbing Aurie's hands and squeezing them tight. "Truth is a multifaceted thing. What I hope for most students is that they at least accept the possibility that they will never know and to get over the pain that it caused. But to turn that wavering mirage into a forceful plan of action and adhere to it despite the unpleasant consequences is sign of uncommon courage. You passed in ways that I cannot even describe."

"What about the assault?" Aurie asked hesitantly.

The professor soured. "There will be a punishment. But only for the sake of appearances. Given your actions to retrieve the Rod, I cannot truly punish you."

"Semyon told you?" asked Aurie, shocked.

"Semyon?" asked the professor with a tilted head. "Are we on a first-name basis now?"

"Patron Gray, I mean," said Aurie.

A soft smile that contradicted the hard lines around her mouth appeared on Mali's lips. "It's okay. I think you've earned it. Yes, he told me. It's my decision whether or not to pass you, but he wanted me to know the truth of your actions. The fact that you kept his trust meant a lot to me, and will to him when I tell him."

"So I get to stay in Arcanium?" asked Aurie.

"My dear, of course you get to stay. You have advanced understanding of truth, and exceptional access to faez. Though you are correct about your abilities and lack of control. It *is* a real worry. It would behoove us to ensure that you are properly trained. Not keeping you in Arcanium would be a danger to society."

"What will I do?" asked Aurie.

Professor Mali patted her hand as if she was a favorite aunt. "We'll save that for next year. For now, I'd like to hear more about the Tomb of Kings. Semyon only told me a little before he had to go."

"I...um...can I tell you later? I think Pi's going to need me after she gives up her place at Coterie, and then I really need to get to Golden Willow," she said.

The professor pulled her hands back into her lap. "You do that. But promise me a long visit before you go home for summer break."

"I will," Aurie said brightly.

"Before you go," said the professor.

"Yes?"

"Make sure you look properly admonished for your behavior. I have a reputation to maintain." She winked.

Aurie agreed, but there was no way it was actually going to happen. So she ran out of the hall before anyone could stop her, her boots barely touching the ground.

She'd made it. She was finally, truly a member of Arcanium. She'd never been happier in her life. The only thing holding her back from yips of joy was the thought that Pi would be hall-less and would have to go through the trials and the first year again.

38

The inside of the Obelisk was as cold as space. The warmth from the sun faded from Pi's arms as she hugged them against her chest.

Doubt. It lingered in the back of her mind. She knew she needed to leave Coterie, but would Patron Malden Anterist let her?

"Pi!" said Ashley in a girlish scream from the balcony. She ran down the carpeted steps, a look of supreme worry on her face. "Where have you been? The whole place has been mad with rumors."

"Nothing," said Pi. "Visiting my sister, I mean. What happened?"

"Professor Augustus is missing. Someone stole a bunch of runic switches from the storeroom. Alton Lockwood's in the hospital. Did you have anything to do with it?" asked Ashley.

"Why would I?" asked Pi.

"Not the other stuff," said Ashley. "But Alton. I was worried when you weren't around. Then I heard he was pretty messed up. I thought of you."

"Wasn't me," said Pi, trying to control her emotions. "He

never bothered me after the Smoke & Amber party."

Ashley threw her arms around Pi. "I'm so glad. I was worried sick. But now that I know you're safe, we can go celebrate surviving our first year! We made the cutoff!"

Pi had forgotten. She'd been so focused on the Rod of Dominion that she'd overlooked worrying about her finals.

"Wow," said Pi without any enthusiasm. "That's great."

Ashley held her at arm's length. "What's going on?"

"I'm leaving Coterie," said Pi.

"What? After all you've worked for?"

Pi bit her lower lip. "I can't stay here. It's not me. It's not you either, Ash. Quit with me. We can both retest next year."

"You know I can't do that. My grandfather won't pay for anywhere else, and I can't imagine doing my first year over, or those damn trials," said Ashley, in visible pain.

"I'm sorry, Ash. It was unfair of me to ask," she said.

"No. I'm glad you asked. I would have been mad if you hadn't. But you know I can't," she said.

Pi sighed. Choices were never easy. "I feel like I'm leaving you alone with a pack of wolves. We looked out for each other here. It's a cutthroat place. Who's going to watch your back?"

Ashley made a sassy Southern oh-no-you-didn't pose. "I've survived these people longer than you have. The guys just rate my looks on bangability and forget me. The other girls think I'm a ditz. They'll underestimate me. They always have."

Pi threw her arms around Ashley and squeezed like she would never see her again. Which was a possibility. Coterie discouraged fraternizing with other halls.

"Be good. Be safe. I'll see you on the other side," said Pi, then nervously added, "*Kheyli dooset daram, azeezam.*"

Ashley's smile widened. "Awww, that's beautiful. What does it mean?"

"I love you, dearest," said Pi.

They hugged again. "I love you too, Pythia Silverthorne. I'm glad I got to meet you, even if you're leaving me alone here." Ashley winked.

"I'd better go. I need to get this over with," she said.

The Coterie patron was in the grand study. He was in the Obelisk to attend the fifth-year graduations.

First years were not allowed in that area of the Obelisk, but Pi marched in, ignoring the offended stares she received. The patron was unmistakable in his shimmering shield, surrounded by fawning fifth years who were getting the opportunity to interact with him for the first time in their history at Coterie. Pi had a moment of pride that she'd met him twice already, until she remembered it'd really been Professor Augustus.

A fifth year in formal robes moved to stop her. "Hey, you can't—"

Pi clamped his lips shut with a cantrip, turning their well-manicured group to chaos. Before things got out of hand, the patron raised his hand, silencing their protests.

"I need to speak to you," she said.

A collective gasp permeated the study. Even though the shield shifted, creating perpetual motion, the man beneath it stilled to dangerous levels.

Doubt returned like a punch to the gut.

A shake of the hand and the attending fifth years shuffled out of the study. Heavy double doors thudded shut with all the gravity of a tomb.

The words tumbled out of her mouth. "I'm giving up my place in Coterie. I'm sorry I've wasted your time this year, but it's not for me. Thank you."

Pi held herself as if she were a piece of glass balanced at the edge of a cliff.

When the reply came, it was full of curiosity and command.

"Why?"

Pi could have said a lot of things, but she kept it simple. "My sister needs me."

"I see," he said, his tone meaning anything but.

She cleared her throat. "Is this a problem?"

The shield shifted. "While it's not unheard of that potential members of Coterie give up their spots, this would be the first time that a top student with multiple sponsorship offers has turned down my Hall."

"Multiple?" asked Pi, genuinely curious. She wished she hadn't heard this. Part of her wanted to stay. Her year in Coterie had been exhilarating and she'd learned so much. Pi worried that Arcanium, or one of the other halls, would be too stifling.

Beneath the shield, he steepled his fingers. "Not just multiple, but some of the most sought-after sponsorships. Which, given your family history, is quite impressive."

The last comment was a knife to her elation.

"My family history?" she asked with disdain.

"Please understand I offer no insult. I recognize my Hall has a hidebound view of breeding and grooming. It's a viewpoint I wish to change to something more meritocratic," he said. "Which is why I ask that you reconsider your choice. I don't think you understand what you're giving up. Your potential sponsors are the titans of industry, and world leaders in their rights. You're giving up an opportunity for power and influence. A seat at the table, so to say. If you give it up, you'll close the door for many like you."

She felt swayed by the offer of mentors, about getting an opportunity for power, until she really thought about what he'd said.

"Many like me?" she spat, not caring. "There's only one person like me, and that's me. If you can't recognize that, or understand it, then that's why Coterie is not my Hall. You say you want a meritocracy, that you'll ignore my *breeding* and *grooming,* but the fact that you even use those terms means you think in categories and boxes. That you only see me as a means to an end."

She realized she'd gone too far when she sensed his faez. Pi swallowed her rage, lest he punish her while he was still her patron.

"What if I don't release you from the link?" he asked, the implications like a fist around her heart. "No one would ever know. I could just tell your sister that you changed your mind. You've not yet seen even a hundredth of the mysteries of the Obelisk. They'd never see you again."

Her feet felt like they were sinking into the floor. "I doubt you would convince my sister, but you certainly wouldn't convince the man I work for."

He scoffed. "Radoslav? He's a small-time player who couldn't even hack it amongst his own kind. He'd sell you for a bauble if I asked."

Pi let a grin rise to her lips despite the quivering of her knees. "I don't mean him. I'm talking about Hemistad. My sister and I help him tend his Hunger."

For a moment, the shield winked as if his concentration had been broken. Pi didn't get a good impression of the man beneath the shield, the moment went by too quick, except that Hemistad's name had caused him concern.

"You know, Miss Silverthorne," he said tensely, "I now understand why you're giving up your place in Coterie. It's not because of your sister, or you don't like the way you were treated, it's because you've realized you're just not good enough. And that, and that alone, disqualifies you from being in the Coterie of Mages. There's a reason that Coterie is the most exclusive Hall in Invictus, that the heads of state and titans of industry come from here. It's because we're an organization of winners. And clearly you are not."

He made a gesture, severing the link. She gasped in agony, falling to her knees. It was like a giant icicle had been yanked from her soul, or a vat of dry ice had been dumped down her throat.

Before she could do anything else, he cast a second spell. Pi was certain he was going to kill her, until the rooms of the Obelisk flashed by in an instant and she tumbled onto the street, right outside the boundary of the Hall.

Pi rocked on her rear, basking in the sunlight, trying to get warm before she even tried to move. The cold had burned her from the inside, breath forming to mist before her lips.

Eventually, she climbed to her feet and began the long trudge back towards the twelfth ward, rubbing her arms. If she was lucky, maybe she could get her same apartment. It wasn't like there was a waiting list to get into that shithole.

Pi lamented not getting her stuff moved out before she went to the patron, but decided that surviving the encounter, especially after she'd insulted him, was probably as good as it was going to get.

When a black Lexus with tinted windows pulled up beside Pi, she started to summon her faez, but remembered she was patronless. She stopped.

The back window rolled down revealing the handsome dark face of the Arcanium patron.

"Pythia Silverthorne," he said with a nod.

"Yes?"

"Would you like a ride?"

Pi climbed inside. The backseat was brown leather with lacy seat coverings. A tea set steamed from a center table. The car moved without a driver, or at least without one that she could see.

"Tea? It might help soothe the nerves. A severed link can be rather soul chattering."

She held the cup between her hands, relishing the warmth. Each sip renewed her faith in the world, brought a little color back in.

"What are your plans now?" he asked. "In the Halls, of course."

"Spend the summer working at Freeport Games. Take the Merlins in the fall. Hope for the best," she said.

"And what halls will you put on your list?"

"Arcanium," she said. "I'd like to be reunited with my sister."

"Very good," he said. "We would love to have you."

"I guess I'll need to do well on my Merlins," she said.

"No," he said, confusing her. "I mean, we'd love to have you. Right now."

"You can do that?" she asked.

"You put us second on your list, we have a spot in Arcanium, so yes, I can bring you into Arcanium, today, if you'd like," he said.

She didn't know what to say. Then she did. "Yes. Double yes. Oh, thank you. I can't wait to be an initiate in the fall."

"Oh, you won't be an initiate," he said. "You've earned the right to be a second year. Professor Mali has volunteered to work with you this summer to get you caught up to the other students."

If it weren't for the tea set, and the fact that he was a powerful patron, she would have thrown her arms around him.

"Thank you, Patron Gray," she said. "Aurie is going to flip when she finds out."

"She'll get to 'flip' soon enough. I'm picking her up next and taking you both to Golden Willow," he said.

"But she's not allowed in?"

"I'll speak to the administration and get the restriction removed. I think that's only fair, right?"

A maelstrom of emotions roiled inside of her. It'd been a whirlwind last few days.

"Absolutely," she said. "How is Emily? Did they get the Rod to her in time?"

Semyon looked out the window while rubbing his fingers along the edge of the table. "I do not rightly know. When I left they were rushing her into the curse removal room. Even if it works, she might not survive."

For the sake of her sister, Pi hoped Emily pulled through. It'd been a difficult semester.

Semyon reached out to her.

"Now let's make you a member of Arcanium, as you should have been in the first place."

39

The Golden Willow Clinic for the Sick and Infirm glowed from within like a mage light. As the ER room doors whisked open, the shouts of desperate nurses and doctors shot into the cool evening air. Aurie rubbed her arms and stared at her feet.

Patron Gray had gone into the hospital to get the restriction removed. A big ball of worry had collected in her chest, making speech, or even thinking, difficult.

Pi squeezed her arm. The reddish-purple highlights in her sister's hair had faded.

"She's going to be okay," said Pi. "We got the Rod in time. You saved her."

Aurie looked at her sister's earnest face and realized that after all that had happened, she hadn't really talked to her sister since they'd been studying for their Merlins. Or at least about the important things.

"Do you remember when we were little and Mom would read to us in bed?" asked Aurie.

A wistful smile christened Pi's lips. "You always hogged the middle. I always felt like I was about to fall out of bed."

Aurie chuckled. "There was something magical about

hearing Mom read to us. My favorite was that one book where the little pig keeps getting into trouble. Mom would do that little piggy voice that sounded a little bit Irish. I'd lay my head on her arm, just breathing in her smell. It was like she was made of lilacs or something. And you'd lay your head on my arm, with your hand around my chest—"

Pi interjected, "Yeah, I was trying to hold on."

"Eventually Dad would wonder where we all went, and he'd find us and sit at the end of the bed, just gazing at us with his big green eyes. At that moment, I felt like the luckiest person in the whole world. That nothing, nothing, could ever touch that.

"Then Mom and Dad died, and I thought it was my fault. That I'd never deserved that feeling in the first place, because I'd been mean to you, or did something wrong. Or just been a bad person."

Pi grabbed her hands. "I never blamed you."

Aurie shook her head. "No, just listen. I blamed me. I thought I'd caused it. So I made sure that I did the best for you. But that's the thing. I wasn't doing it for you. I was doing it because I felt guilty. Which is the worst kind of selfishness. Mom and Dad's death had affected you too, but I never asked how you were doing, I never asked what you wanted to do, hell, I didn't even believe you when you told me about the guy in the street. Worst of all, I haven't let you be yourself. I've been trying to control you this whole time, using my guilt as the justification, which only drove you to Coterie. I see that now. Mom and Dad loved us unconditionally. They gave of themselves, read to us, cared for us, listened to us. But I did none of those things for you. I did them for me. I see that now. I'm sorry."

By the time Aurie looked up, tears were flowing down Pi's face. She wiped her nose with her sleeve, then punched Aurie in the arm, hard.

"You *were* selfish. Always trying to control me, fixing my hair the way you thought Mom liked it best, or yelling at me when I did anything wrong, even if it was just not looking both ways before I crossed the street. You tried to make me into some perfect ideal because Mom and Dad died. You used that as the worst kind of guilt trip, and I hated you for it for a long time," said Pi, sniffling.

Then Pi jabbed her finger into Aurie's chest. "But don't you *ever* think for one second that I didn't love you, and didn't appreciate everything you'd done. I mean, it's only natural that I was going to rebel, and without Mom and Dad there, you had to be the poor sucker that had to take the brunt."

Aurie blotted away the tears with her palm.

"Why couldn't we have said this at the beginning of the year before the Merlins? It would have saved us a lot of trouble," said Aurie, sighing.

"I still would have tried to get in Coterie," said Pi with a raised eyebrow. "I'm serious when I said that I didn't do it to get away from you. I really thought it would help protect me, protect us better."

"Yeah," said Aurie, slowly coming to that conclusion. "You're right. But don't get any ideas that I'm still not going to try and be your big sister."

"As long as you don't forget that I'm better than you at magic," said Pi, then she stuck out her tongue.

"We're in the same hall now, so we'll see about that," said Aurie.

A ghostly version of Semyon Gray stepped out of the air.

"I spoke to the administration. You are free to enter," he said. "But you'll have to find another way home. I have other business to attend to in another part of the city."

After he left, Aurie could barely convince her feet to move

forward.

"Aurie," said Pi from beside her. "We should go in. Waiting out here isn't going to change anything. Whatever has happened, has happened. You did your best."

Aurie's reply was lost to a racket of noise from the alleyway next to the hospital. Drawn by the ruckus, the sisters went to investigate.

An orderly was throwing long metal rods with wires attached to them into a dumpster. It took Aurie about three blinks to realize it was the scaffolding they used to keep Emily from floating away.

"No!" Aurie screamed, and went running towards the doors, blowing past security before they could even get up from their chairs.

She dodged around gurneys and carts full of dinner trays, sneakers squeaking at each footfall. The line for the elevator made her veer into the stairwell.

By the time she reached the Children's Floor for the Irrevocably Cursed, Magically Ailing, and Supernatural Virology, Aurie was out of breath. Shouts rose up from the bottom of the stairwell, combined with Pi trying to explain to security who she was, but Aurie didn't care.

She ran straight to room 438. There was no sign that said "WARNING. No perfumes, magical ointments, or any alchemy reagents within thirty feet." A faded square with four empty screw holes was still on the wall.

The special bed, the scaffolding, all of Emily's stuffed animals, and the wind dancer figurine were gone as if she'd never been there. A standard-issue medical bed with remote control tilt sat in its place.

It was too soon for Emily to have been discharged if she'd been healed. There was only one explanation. One Aurie didn't even want to contemplate.

But she had to know for certain. She kept the knot in her chest from unraveling until she knew for sure.

An orderly she didn't recognize was mopping the nearby hall. Aurie hurried over and tugged on his sleeve. The kid pulled his headphones off.

"Yeah?"

"Room 438. Where's the girl who was in there?" she asked desperately.

He shrugged. "438? Room's empty? I think she died or something. Happens all the time here."

Boom. One massive heartbeat in her ears. Then she could hear nothing. Just a faint buzzing as the world pulled away from her.

Emily. She was too late. Too late to save Elegant Emily, who liked to make up stories about having superhero powers, and actually liked the hospital food, and always kept a brave face when they were taking blood samples.

There might have been angry shouts behind her. Security had finally caught up, followed by Pi. The commotion drew the floor nurses, and somewhere in there, she thought she heard Dr. Fairlight's name. But none of it really registered.

Not until a security guard yanked on her arm, followed by the nurses shouting something at them. It wasn't until Dr. Fairlight put her face right up in front of Aurie's that she actually become aware.

"Aurie. Aurie," said Dr. Fairlight, shaking her.

"I was too late, Dr. Fairlight. I was too late," said Aurie.

The doctor wrinkled her face, then glanced down the hall as she started to comprehend.

"Oh no. Aurie, no. It's not too late. It's not too late. Emily's alive," she said.

"But I saw her scaffolding in the trash, and her room's empty?" asked Aurie.

A relieved smile broke across Dr. Fairlight's face, bunching the wrinkles around her mouth. "She's responded spectacularly well to a special treatment. A mysterious benefactor donated a minor artifact to the hospital. It saved her life. She was really down to the hours."

"Where is she?" asked Aurie, not capable of believing it until she saw Emily.

"With her doing so well, they moved her to the observation floor. They'll discharge her by the weekend if she shows no signs of relapse," said Dr. Fairlight.

The security guards left once they realized she was allowed back into Golden Willow. Dr. Fairlight led Aurie to the lower floor. She felt like she was made of glass and could break into a million pieces at the slightest touch.

When they reached the observation floor, Dr. Fairlight led her to an older well-dressed couple standing in the hallway, which confused Aurie, since she thought she was going straight to Emily's room.

"Mr. and Mrs. Calloway. This is the girl I was telling you about, Aurelia Silverthorne," said Dr. Fairlight.

The Calloways latched onto her as if she were their savior, patting her back and squeezing her arms.

"Oh thank you, Aurelia. Thank you for saving our daughter," said Mrs. Calloway. "Can I give you a hug?"

Aurie was stunned. She didn't think anyone would know about the Rod. "Sure. But I didn't do anything."

Dr. Fairlight chuckled. "Our Aurelia is very modest. If it weren't for your lichwood tea, Emily would have never survived long enough to make it to the final cure."

Relief that the secret hadn't been exposed left Aurie feeling a little wobbly. Far too much had happened in a short time.

"With your permission, I'd like to see Emily. It's why I came," said Aurie.

The Calloways moved out of her way. Mr. Calloway put his hand on her shoulder like they were old friends.

"Dr. Fairlight told me about your situation. If it's alright, we'd like to pay your tuition in the Hundred Halls. It's the least we can do," he said.

Aurie choked. "But that's a lot of money."

He smiled, and Aurie realized how perfect his teeth were, how fine a cut his suit was, and how many gold rings he wore. For all she knew, he was a CEO or major executive.

"Just say yes," he said.

"Yes!" she said, sharing an incredulous look with Pi. Only having to pay for one tuition would be huge. Together they could earn Pi's without killing themselves with extra jobs during the summer.

The Calloways pushed her towards the open door. "Now go see Emily. She's been asking about you."

Emily was on the bed, reading a book called *Uprooted*. She was still bird-thin. Her aerated bones would probably never truly recover, but she could actually grow up now. Just like she and Pi had after their tragedy.

"Awesome Aurie," said Emily, eyes big and round, glistening with emotion.

"Elegant Emily," said Aurie.

"I'm so glad you got to come back," said Emily. "I missed you."

"I missed you too," said Aurie.

Emily set the book down on her lap. "You know, I'm not going to be a wind dancer now."

"You can be whatever you want to be," said Aurie.

Emily squeezed her eyes shut, her lips tightening as she held tears back. "Thank you, Aurie. Thank you for saving me."

Aurie moved to the bed and put her arms around Emily.

Some signal must have been passed, because the Calloways, her sister, and Dr. Fairlight came in. They crowded around her. The press of people gave her the feeling of lying in bed with her parents and Pi, listening to the story about the mischievous piglet. In that moment, she felt so warm and content that she thought she might be the center of the universe.

With nothing holding her back, the tears flowed freely down her face as she laugh-cried. The others joined in until it was one big sobbing mess. Even a few nurses from the floor peeked in, and once they saw the pile of people, they couldn't help but smile and let a few tears fall.

After a time, which seemed like forever and a blink of an eye, it passed. They stayed for an hour chatting. Aurie got caught up on everything that had happened. And Emily pestered her for details about her first year in the Hundred Halls.

Before Dr. Fairlight left, she offered Aurie a summer internship, which of course, she accepted. When it was finally time to leave, due to the end of visiting hours, the Calloways gave Aurie another round of hugs. They gave Pi hugs too, just because she was Aurie's sister.

When they were standing outside, Aurie didn't want to leave.

"Come on, sis. I need to get some bedsheets before I move into Arcanium. Ashley's going to retrieve my stuff for me once the coast is clear. You can come back and visit Emily again later."

"It's not that," said Aurie, looking at the endless glass walls of the hospital. "I mean, it is, but it isn't. I was just thinking about Mom and Dad."

"Hard not to," said Pi.

Aurie grabbed her sister's hand and entwining their fingers. They started walking away.

"They'd be proud of us. They really would," said Aurie.

"Mostly," said Pi.

"Mostly?" she asked with a raised eyebrow.

"I mean, there *was* a demon summoning," said Pi.

Aurie chuckled. "That's true."

"And we put a pretty fucked up curse on someone's nutsack," said Pi, as if mentally checking things off a list.

"Yeah, that too. But otherwise, pretty proud," said Aurie.

"And you let me rent my soul to a city fae," Pi said with a grin, clearly taunting.

"Let you? Ha! That was totally on you," said Aurie.

"Don't forget we nearly blew up a subway bathroom," said Pi.

They walked for a while in silence. Pi punched her sister in the arm. "You know what?"

"What?" asked Aurie, suddenly curious.

"I get the top bunk," said Pi.

"Who said we're rooming together?"

"The patron," said Pi.

"I'll play you Five Elements for it when we get back," said Aurie.

"Deal."

"You know what else?"

"What?"

"*Dooset daram.*"

"*Dooset daram.*"

§ § §

Continue the action with book two of
The Hundred Halls

WEB
OF
LIES

November 2016

Also by Thomas K. Carpenter

ALEXANDRIAN SAGA
Fires of Alexandria
Heirs of Alexandria
Legacy of Alexandria
Warmachines of Alexandria
Empire of Alexandria
Voyage of Alexandria
Goddess of Alexandria

THE DIGITAL SEA TRILOGY
The Digital Sea
The Godhead Machine
Neochrome Aurora

GAMERS TRILOGY
GAMERS
FRAGS
CODERS

THE DASHKOVA MEMOIRS
Revolutionary Magic
A Cauldron of Secrets
Birds of Prophecy
The Franklin Deception
Nightfell Games
The Queen of Dreams
Dragons of Siberia
Shadows of an Empire

THE HUNDRED HALLS
Trials of Magic
Web of Lies
Alchemy of Souls
Gathering of Shadows
City of Sorcery

ABOUT THE AUTHOR

Thomas K. Carpenter resides near St. Louis with his wife Rachel and their two children. When he's not busy writing his next book, he's playing soccer in the yard with his kids or getting beat by his wife at cards. He keeps a regular blog at www.thomaskcarpenter.com and you can follow him on twitter @thomaskcarpente. If you want to learn when his next novel will be hitting the shelves and get free stories and occasional other goodies, please sign up for his mailing list by going to: http://tinyurl.com/thomaskcarpenter. Your email address will never be shared and you can unsubscribe at any time.

CPSIA information can be obtained
at www.ICGtesting.com
Printed in the USA
LVHW01s2124080518
576448LV00001B/24/P

9 781539 067962